KILTED IN COLORADO

Loveday Ferries

Loveday Ferries

To G and Alex, my best guys.

CONTENTS

CHAPTER 1

Tuesday, August 21

Angus MacBangus parked his aging pickup truck in front of a three-story house in northeast Colorado Springs. He scanned the area for signs of his boss. Traffic had been light on his way across town, so it did not surprise Angus that he had arrived early to the job site. Seeing no signs of Jack or his truck, Angus drove to a neighborhood park a few blocks away, where he had eaten his lunch the past couple of days.

He turned off his truck and spent a few minutes admiring the natural beauty of Colorado. To the east, the sun was rising over the plains, leaving the sky streaked with pink and orange hues. To the west, the Rocky Mountains towered like the wall of an ancient city. A full moon was setting over Pikes Peak, and from this part of town he could just glimpse Garden of the Gods in the foreground. As a boy growing up in the Scottish Highlands, Angus had enjoyed the outdoors, but Colorado Springs took it to a new level. He was grateful every day that he had settled here.

Despite the early hour, the temperature was already rising to the mid-60s, and Angus sat basking in the sunlight like a cat. He took a sip of his coffee and let his mind wander. Lately he'd felt restless and had been reflecting a lot about both his past and his future. Angus was quite satisfied with the life that he had made in Colorado, but he also wondered if he had settled and become complacent. He had a stable job, good friends, and a purpose in life, but Angus still debated if his life would be any different if he met his father.

In a very tangential way, Angus had come to Colorado as part of the search for his father. Growing up, Angus's mother told him that his father was an American serviceman, who had been on holiday in Scotland. At the end of two weeks, he had returned to the United States, leaving his address and promising to write. By the time Angus's mother Heather had discovered that she was pregnant and been able to contact the man, he claimed he had married his high school sweetheart and there was nothing he could do. The tale seemed quite improbable, and Heather was vague about some details. However, Angus had always believed his mother's story to be largely true. He suspected she wasn't creative enough to have constructed such an elaborate and convoluted story.

Left to raise her son without his father, Heather took to drinking and relied on her mother and sisters to help raise Angus. When he was 15, Heather had died in a car crash. After the funeral, Angus's favorite Aunty Ivy went through Heather's belongings with him. They found a letter from Private Sylvester Thompson with a return address in Fort Stewart, GA postmarked 1981 and a single snapshot with "Si – 1981" written on the back. Angus knew nothing more about his father.

When Angus finished high school, he moved to Edinburgh to work with his Uncle Rory as an apprentice bricklayer. While Angus excelled at his job and enjoyed living with his aunt and uncle, within a few months, he felt listless and unhappy. After his miserable childhood, he knew he should be thankful for what he had, but the one thing that had kept him going through all those turbulent years was the idea that he would grow up, leave Scotland, and find his biological father. In his cheery, early fantasies, Angus pictured meeting his father as a pilot in the Air Force who would invite him to move in with the rest of his family some place beautiful and sunny, like California. However, particularly after his mother's death, Angus's expectations became more realistic. He wanted to meet his father and get the measure of him as a man. The only flight of fantasy he still harbored was the desire to leave the awful name MacBangus behind and ask his father if he could take his surname.

It didn't take long for his Aunt Ivy to figure out what was troubling him, and together they spent months researching ways for Angus to get to America to search for his father. Their problems were chiefly that Angus had little money and no way to prove that his father was an American. His aunt discovered that if Angus joined the American military and served for a certain number of years, he could become an American citizen. As soon as he could arrange the paperwork, Private MacBangus was off to America and basic training.

With the enthusiasm and naivety of the 18-year-old he was, Angus assumed that once he arrived in America, he would track down his father in a matter of weeks. He underestimated the time his military commitment would consume, but more importantly, he discovered he did not know how to search for his father. The bulk of his experience with solving mysteries came from reading cheap detective novels. Angus also didn't anticipate how much he would thrive on the order and discipline that the military gave him. He did as he was told and embraced the life of an infantryman. In his small amount of free time, he contacted the historian for each unit that had been stationed in Fort Stewart in the early 80s searching for whatever information they had about Private Thompson, but the work was slow and fruitless. After 1981, Private Thompson seemed to disappear and had not joined any veteran's organizations.

In his second year in the Army, September 11th happened. Angus's unit shipped out to Afghanistan, and he spent the better part of the next decade deployed to one combat zone or another. It was during his last deployment that he had met his current boss, Jack Evans. Jack was due to retire when their unit rotated back to the States and had an idea to start a handyman business. At first, he called Angus for an odd job here and there, but when Angus had to decide whether to reenlist in the Army, Jack offered him a full-time job.

Angus proudly wore a US Army uniform for 12 years, but he was weary of going to war zones and getting shot at. He had applied and been granted US citizenship at the earliest opportunity, his original reason for joining the armed forces, and the constant cycle of deployments had all but put a stop to his search for his father. However, by that point in his life, Angus had become his own person, independent of his family. He liked to work with his hands and spend time outdoors, so it wasn't a hard decision to transition to civilian life.

Growing up in poverty, Angus had few clothes to choose from. During his time in the Army, his commanders had dictated his uniform. When Angus had out processed from the military, he was rather at a loss of what to wear day to day. He had rarely shopped for clothing, having purchased any civilian clothes from the post exchange with little thought. While Jack wore an assortment of old clothes on the job, he purchased several sets of coveralls for Angus as a kind of signing bonus. Angus took impeccable care of his coveralls and wore them every day. After years of a high and tight haircut, he let his coarse dirty blonde hair grow out a bit. In his spare time, he took up weight training to fill out his tall, skinny physique with mixed success. And for his "off duty" wardrobe, he acquired many kilts. He had a formal kilt in the US Army tartan and a variety of sport and tactical kilts for whatever mood struck him. Unless he was working, Angus completely shunned the idea of trousers.

Today Angus wore his oldest set of brown coveralls that already had paint splatters and a ratty pair of boots. He and Jack were converting the basement of a house into an apartment for the owner's daughter. When he had started 10 days ago, Angus had felt a flicker of dread, a little voice in the back of his head telling him he should stay away from this house and these people. Normally, Angus would have told Jack about his intuition right away, but this was a big job. They had already added a kitchenette and hung drywall over the concrete walls, besides painting a couple of rooms in the main part of the house. Today they were scheduled to paint the entire basement apartment, and the next day other contractors would put in the carpets. After that, Angus and Jack's wife, Maggie, planned to inspect the job and do any necessary touch ups.

Throughout the entire project, Angus worked warily and tried to put his finger on the exact cause of his worries. He often experienced flashes of insight into situations, either a bad feeling or a sense of comfort and well-being. While his Highland relatives would have called his experience "second sight," Angus believed there was a rational explanation for most things in life, including his uncanny instincts. Whatever their source, Angus followed his gut feelings, and this practice had come in handy in the past.

Every day Angus went to work, his feelings of apprehension grew, but with nothing concrete to present to Jack and Maggie, he had soldiered on. Mrs. Peterson, the owner's wife, had been pleasant and not overbearing throughout the repairs. The longest conversation that Angus recalled with her had occurred about a week into the job. After noting how much work the renovations were turning out to be, Mrs. Peterson had launched into a convoluted justification for the expense. "Ever since she was little, Karen's loved to be outside doing physical things – soccer, skiing, running club, lacrosse – and I just can't imagine her stuck in an apartment or townhouse," she had stated. Angus, himself the owner of a townhouse, had pointed out that there were townhouse communities near both of Colorado Springs's megagyms, which would have given Karen many opportunities for individual and group sports and activities. "Call me old fashioned, but I don't feel like townhouses are very safe. Lots of people coming and going," Mrs. Peterson had said. "No, it's better for Karen to be home with us, and these improvements will increase the resale value of our house." At that point, Angus had just nodded his head and let Mrs. Peterson prattle on for a few more minutes. He remembered what Jack had told him. "The client isn't always right, but unless it's a safety hazard, don't sew doubts in their mind."

While Angus didn't like Mrs. Peterson's self-serving justifications, he reminded himself that it wasn't his job to question the motives of clients. People undertook home improvements for a variety of reasons. Mrs. Peterson might have had another reason for wanting her daughter close. That wasn't any of his business.

When Mrs. Peterson had asked them to paint the dining room and office on the first floor of the house, Angus had balked at the idea of prolonging the job but had given in when Maggie had insisted. Yesterday when he had almost been done in the dining room, Mrs. Peterson has asked him when he would be finished, as her husband was due in half an hour. Angus felt the band of muscles around his head and every other muscle in his body tighten and had the overwhelming thought that he should leave the house. The sensation was so intense that he could only finish his work by using breathing and relaxation techniques that he has learned at the veterans counseling center. As soon as he was in his truck that afternoon, Angus had phoned Maggie, asking if she could move things around in the schedule so that they could finish the job as soon as possible. After some back and forth, Maggie arranged for Jack to help him with today's painting.

A rapping on his window disturbed Angus's thoughts. He turned and saw Jack standing next to his truck.

"Were you away with the fairies?" Jack asked, grinning. He had a full beard and mustache, which had once been brown but were shot through with grey, and a shaved head, which he covered with a boonie hat.

"Nah. Just enjoying the view and having a think." Angus started up his truck and looked at the dashboard clock, realizing that he has been sitting here for 20 minutes and they were now late.

"I was kind of hoping they were giving you further intel."

Jack turned back towards his own truck, which was parked behind them. "I mean, is it like that time you knew the guy would try to stiff us on the bill?"

"No, I don't think it's that," Angus said. He rarely minded talking with Jack, but right now all he wanted was to finish this job and never have to see the Petersons or their house again.

"Well, they haven't asked us to cut any corners." Jack worked through the list of factors that could signal trouble with a job. "Wife hasn't gotten handsy, has she?"

"Nothing like that." Angus blushed. Middle-aged women took a shine to him. Some of them wanted to mother him, while others entertained more carnal fantasies. Mrs. Peterson had been professional, greeting him every morning and leaving him alone. "It's just a feeling that there is evil in the house. It's not like I have visions or the little people appear to me as portents."

"Well, usually your feelings are more specific." Jack scratched his beard, a habit he engaged in when he felt irritated or nervous.

"And sometimes they are general, and this one tells me not to be in that house." Angus was frustrated as well. "This isn't the first time I have had a strong feeling about a situation, and it won't be the last."

Angus's mind flashed back to a day eight years ago in Iraq. He and Jack had become good friends, and one night he had awakened with a feeling of deep foreboding. Soldiers went out on convoys regularly, so the next morning he has tracked down Jack at breakfast and asked about his assignment for that day. When Jack had said that he was scheduled to go outside their perimeter, Angus had told him to be extra vigilant. Jack had thanked him and not thinking much of it at the time, he had gone out as always. A few miles from the compound, Jack's Humvee had hit an IED. The vehicle had rolled over, and Jack had suffered a concussion and a severely broken leg.

While recovering in Germany, Jack remembered Angus's warning and contacted him. Angus had told no one about his abilities, because he didn't want people to think he was superstitious. Also, before Jack's accident, Angus's feelings had always been about trivial matters. He might know, for example, that a friend would not come to a party or that someone that he had just met was a person of good character, but these insights were hardly worth mentioning. On the face of it, Jack's Humvee hitting an IED wasn't outside the realm of possibility. After all, he was driving through a war zone. In the end, Jack didn't care how Angus had known what he had known. He was just happy to be alive, and the incident had solidified their friendship.

"Hey, Angus," Jack called his friend back to reality. "None of the patented MacBangus stare. We've got a job to do."

"Sorry, Jack." Angus brushed off the memory. "Maybe I'm more spooked that I realized."

"Look, brother, let's just get in there and get this done," Jack said. As he walked back to his truck, his limp was barely noticeable. Over his shoulder, he added, "Maggie got last minute tickets to a concert in Denver tonight, and she wants to spend most of the day up there."

By the time Angus and Jack made it back to the Peterson house, it was almost 8:30, so it did not surprise Angus when Mrs. Peterson met them outside. She was a woman in her late 40s or early 50s whose hair was expertly cut with many layers and highlighted in shades of blonde. Despite the thickening of her waist from age, Mrs. Peterson had made an effort to apply light make up and dress in a simple but flattering blouse and trousers, which she embellished with a chunky necklace and several large rings.

Before Angus could apologize, Mrs. Peterson cut him off. "I just wanted to let you know Gary has a horrible headache and would appreciate it if you two didn't play any music or make a lot of noise."

"No problem," Jack said as he unloaded supplies from his truck. "We'll do our best to not disturb him."

"Thank you so much." Mrs. Peterson gave a nervous smile. "He thinks it's the paint fumes, but there's nothing for it. You have to paint the basement."

"We'll do what we can." Angus was eager to end this small talk and get to work.

The basement was a walk out, so Mrs. Peterson led them around and let them. "Just send me a text when you finish." Then she took the stairs to the main body of the house.

"She's a bit on edge, but Maggie always says that when men don't feel well, they are super crabby." Jack started applying painter's tape to door and window frames. "Have you ever met the husband?"

"Never," Angus said, putting down drop clothes. "She was almost as nervous yesterday, and he wasn't even home yet. That's why I broke down and called Maggie."

"When's the daughter supposed to come home?" Jack continued around the room. "Maybe Mom isn't excited about having her move back home."

Angus pried the lid off a paint can and tried to remember. "I think she is due back on Saturday. Mrs. Peterson was very firm that we need to inspect and do touch ups Thursday in case we find something big."

"That's a bit of a tight timeline, but there's nothing she can do about it," Jack said as he put in his ear buds and got to work.

The two men painted for about 90 minutes in silence, each in their own world. Jack listened to a podcast about surprising scientific phenomena, while Angus jammed to 90s grunge music on his phone. When they finished up the first coat, Angus produced a thermos of coffee and some homemade shortbread cookies and offered them to Jack.

"These are amazing," Jack said between bites. "Where did you get them?"

"I baked them with Lily and her son Jaiden on Sunday." Angus finished up his coffee and rinsing and replacing the thermos cap. "I've never quite got the hang of baking at 6,600 feet above sea level, but Lily makes it seem easy."

"So, things are going well with Lily then?" Jack asked.

A loud crash from upstairs cut Angus off before he could reply.

"We'd better make sure she's ok." Jack brushed crumbs off his shirt and headed for the stairs.

Angus followed. As they entered the main floor of the house, a man, who they assumed was Mr. Peterson, was coming down from upstairs. He was a short, round man wearing silk pajamas and house slippers. He was balding, and what remained of his black hair was greasy and disheveled.

"What the hell was that?" Mr. Peterson yelled at his wife. He didn't seem to notice Angus and Jack.

"I'm sorry to disturb you, dear." Mrs. Peterson had gone quite pale, and Angus was afraid that she might faint. "I was moving the china back to the cabinet, and a platter slipped out of my hands and fell onto the floor." Her voice was barely above a whisper.

"You stupid bitch!" Mr. Peterson's voice boomed. His face was red, and a vein was pulsing in his forehead. "That was my grandmother's serving platter."

Angus stepped forward. "Now, then," he said quietly. "Accidents happen and there are places on the internet that specialize in replacing china and crystal. I can have Maggie send you some websites." This sort of thing happened frequently during home renovations and moves.

Mr. Peterson turned towards Angus and Jack. "What are

you two even doing up here?" he asked in an imperious tone. "I am paying you to renovate the basement not interfere with private family matters." Taking a ragged breath, he gestured towards the door to the basement with his arm. "Go back downstairs immediately and finish your job!"

"Certainly, sir." Jack's voice could barely conceal his anger and frustration. "We just wanted to make sure no one was hurt." He turned towards the stairs, motioning for Angus to come with him.

As they made preparations for the second coat of paint, the conversation upstairs continued, although they could only hear Mr. Peterson's side of it.

"I don't care if it was an accident! You need to be more careful. If you didn't scuff the paint on the walls, we wouldn't have had to pay to paint the room or move the china and cabinet out!"

A pause

"I'll remind you that this whole silly scheme was your idea. For the amount I'm spending, we could have paid to rent Karen an apartment for a year."

When Mr. Peterson's tirade appeared to be over, Jack turned to Angus. "Well, I'm rather glad that we've wrapped up 'Angus MacBangus and the Case of the Broken Serving Platter.' Now that we've had our disaster, we can finish this job and get paid."

"I have a feeling we aren't quite done yet." Angus looked toward the stairs. "Leave out your earbuds and look busy."

Both men raised their rollers and began to paint. Just when Jack was about to give up and restart his program, they heard someone stomping down the stairs. Mr. Peterson was wheezing.

"Something we can do for you, sir?" Jack turned towards Mr. Peterson and let his roller rest in the paint tray.

"I was going to come down here and ask you to deduct 15 minutes from your bill to account for the time you came upstairs," Mr. Peterson began. He sneezed, and Angus wondered if the poor man had a headache from the paint or seasonal allergies. Mr. Peterson blew his nose on a monogrammed handkerchief. "Then I remembered you were late today and went up to check the time on my security cameras." He sneezed again.

Jack seized the opportunity to speak. "We don't start charging our clients until we arrive at the job site, Mr. Peterson." He got out his phone. "I texted my wife Maggie at 8:28 to say we were here and ready to begin work. Does that agree with your cameras?"

"It does," Mr. Peterson admitted. He suddenly looked tired. "But what was the other fellow's truck doing here earlier?"

Angus didn't feel that he had to explain anything to this bully of a man, so he said nothing.

"Angus still has that Army idea that being on time is being late." Jack wondered if why he was justifying their actions to this man. "He usually beats me to the job."

"Then why did he sit across from my house for five minutes and then pull away?" Mr. Peterson fidgeted with his handkerchief.

Angus just wanted to get back to work and wondered if next Mr. Peterson would tell them to dock their time by another 15 minutes for this stupid conversation. "I don't get paid until Jack gets here, so I drove to the park and watched the sunrise."

"Watched the sunrise indeed! You're an odd duck," Mr. Peterson sneered. "Don't forget to subtract 15 minutes from today and tell your wife that I will check my recordings from previous days to make sure you are logging your time honestly."

As soon as the door to the main floor was closed and they heard footsteps upstairs, Jack shook his head. "I'm sorry, Angus. He's an asshole."

Angus poured some more paint on his tray. "I really don't like him. He's a bully, and now I feel like he is going to try to make trouble about paying us, even though it seems like he has the money."

Jack unlocked his phone. "I'll text Maggie and let her know, but she'll take care of him. We bill in blocks of an hour, so he actually won't be able to nickel and dime us on time."

Angus smiled. "Thank God for Maggie. I'd rather auger a toilet than deal with billing."

"Agreed." Jack sent the message and put away his phone. "Now, let's finish up and get out of here before anything else happens."

After another hour and a half, Jack and Angus finished the second coat and went their separate ways. Angus had planned to have lunch at the park, but all the drama of the morning had him running behind. He settled for eating his sandwich on the way to his next appointment.

The afternoon played out like many others. Angus went to fix a running toilet and ended up putting new guts in it. Then he was off to connect a washing machine and dryer for a military family, who had just moved into a house. While he was at it, he reversed the door on the dryer and did a couple of other minor jobs. Angus ended his day by replacing a garbage disposal. It was a disgusting job, but still better than trying to get clients to pay. Besides, his last job was near East Public Library, so he dropped by to visit his girlfriend Lily at work.

Angus entered the library and walked all the way to the back. An assortment of tables, chairs, and sofas faced a wall of windows, which gave a panoramic view of Pikes Peak. Outside the windows was a covered patio that was also equipped with seating. Angus picked an open seat inside and waited. He felt self-conscious in his coveralls and wondered if he should have grabbed a magazine on his way in.

"Good afternoon, sir. How can I help you?" A voice whispered. Angus turned and saw Lily Rodgers. She was a tall, curvy woman with curly black hair and brown eyes. Today she was wearing a navy-blue dress and flat shoes.

"Well, I need some information about places to take an intelligent lady in Colorado Springs." Angus always pretended to be a patron in need of help or advice.

"You're a big goof." Lily laughed. "Let's step out on the patio for a minute."

Angus got up and walked to the nearest door. Despite an awning, the patio was quite warm.

"I don't suppose there's a chance you can come with me to trivia tonight?" Angus asked. Lily didn't come with him often, but he always invited her.

"I can't." Lily sighed. "Mom and Dad are having dinner with friends, and I don't want to leave Jaiden at home by himself late at night. Best-case scenario, he will eat everything in the kitchen and order a pizza." When Lily's husband had been killed in a training accident with the Army, she and her son Jaiden had moved in with her parents. They had been living with them for five years, and the arrangement suited everyone well.

"Can't blame a growing boy for eating." Angus remembered how he had eaten his family out of house and home when he was Jaiden's age.

"I have Thursday off," Lily offered. "Didn't you say that you might be free? We could go for a hike."

"I'd like that." Angus hated to make plans and then break them. "Maggie blocked off the entire day for last minute touch ups on a big job, but the husband is being difficult."

"Is it that job?" Lily's voice dropped. Angus talked little about work, but Lily had dragged the story of the Peterson house out of him. She and Angus had only been seeing each other for six months, but she could tell that recently he had been on edge.

Angus nodded and Lily said, "Well, let's play it by ear. If we can't get together on Thursday, at least come to dinner on Sunday. Mutti is making rouladen." Lily's father had met her mother while he was stationed in Germany, and they had married a few weeks before the Army had transferred him back to the States. Despite having lived in the United States for 40 years, Mrs. Saunders cooked like she was still in her native land.

"Is that the dish where she wraps beef around a pickle?" Angus asked. He had grown up with simple food and was a bit suspicious of new things.

"It is, and you seemed to like it last time." Lily looked back into the library. "I'd better get back to work."

"See you soon." Angus headed home while Lily returned to the Reference Desk.

CHAPTER 2

Wednesday, August 22

The next morning, Angus and Jack started on a new project, a rehab of a rental property that the tenants had trashed. When Angus arrived, Jack had already ripped out part of the flooring and trim and carried it out to a giant dumpster sitting in the driveway.

"Sorry to be late," Angus said after they had exchanged greetings. "Trivia went late last night, and I slept through my alarm."

Angus spent every Tuesday evening at Macduff's Bar taking part in their Trivia Night. As its name implied, Macduff's was Colorado Springs's Scottish bar, which was what had initially drawn Angus to the place. However, despite not being much of a drinker, he returned for their excellent food and to spend time with a few of his countrymen who were regulars. His trivia team comprised several Scottish expatriates and a couple of retired military service members.

"Since this is the first time in six years, I'll let it slide," Jack said. Angus had been quite anxious about the Peterson job, and Jack wondered if maybe he'd drank a bit more than usual the night before. "Everything's ok though, right?"

"Ach. Mostly. The issue was my neighbor Hank."

"The old guy who lives in your complex with his dog?" Jack knew that Angus's routine was to buy Hank a corned beef sandwich from the kitchen at Macduff's and bring it by the older man's apartment on his way home.

Angus chose his words carefully. "I was later than usual, so Hank was pretty drunk by the time I dropped by. When he gets like that, he wants to talk about the old times, his wife, Vietnam. I stayed way too late."

"Poor old guy. It's good of you to help him out."

Angus felt sorry for Hank and his dog Murphey, a Jack Russell terrier - chihuahua mix. Hank had lost his wife almost a year ago and had sold his house. He had considered a retirement home, but they wouldn't let him keep Murphey, so Hank's son had convinced him to buy a townhouse in the same complex as Angus. The townhouse community wasn't a good fit, and Hank seemed listless and isolated.

Both men were silent for a minute. Then Angus shifted his attention to mess in front of him. "So, all the flooring and the trim needs to go?" The carpet Jack was working on was stained in several places and smelled strongly of animal urine.

"Yup. We're pulling the carpet and the pad and painting the subfloor with something to seal all this in." Jack knelt down and pulled back a corner of the carpet and cringed. "Yuck."

Angus picked up a piece of molding that Jack had already removed. Based on the tooth marks present, he guessed a dog had gnawed on it. "What sort of people do this to a house?"

"People that keep us in business," Jack said. A good portion of their jobs were helping landlords fix up a property at the end of a lease. Usually it was a few small repairs, but every once in a while, it was a substantial job. "The landlord told me it was a short-term lease, and they only had one dog. I honestly don't know how they did all this damage."

"Some people are just slobs." Angus grimaced in disgust. He was a fastidious housekeeper, and while he didn't hold everyone to his high standard, this was unacceptable. "And some people just have no decency."

The two men worked for about 20 minutes before Jack's

cell phone rang. By the ringtone, both men knew it was Maggie. Jack wiped his hands on his shirt and answered the phone. "Hey, what's up?" he asked, followed by a pause and then. "Did they say what it's about?" He and Maggie talked for another minute, and then Jack hung up.

"Maggie says a couple of police detectives are heading our way." Jack's face was grave. "She says they were very vague about it."

"OK." Angus wasn't sure what to say. Peterson had been annoyed with them, but that was hardly a police manner. He wondered if someone who had been at Macduff's had been in an accident.

Jack looked around, seeming uncertain what they should do until the police arrived. "Did anything out of the ordinary happen to you yesterday?"

Angus replayed the previous day. "Not really. I mean, Mrs. Peterson broke the platter, and trivia went late, but that just happens sometimes."

"About the same for me. Let's just answer their questions and get back to work."

About 15 minutes later, the doorbell rang. Both men went to the door, and Jack opened it. Two plainclothes officers stood outside. The shorter of the two was a woman in her mid-40s wearing a fashionable blue pantsuit, and the other officer, who stood perhaps 6'2", wore a cheap suit that had probably come off the rack at a big and tall store.

The officer introduced herself as Detective Tiffany Green and her companion of Detective Dan Harrington. Jack let them in, but with no furniture in the house, they ended up standing in the entryway.

Detective Green took out a pocket notebook. "I'm here to speak to Jack Evans and Angus." She paused and looked down at the page again. "MacBanger? I'm sorry, I assume Mr. Peterson misremembered you name."

"MacBangus," Angus corrected. This was not the first time someone has messed up his name. He waited stoically to see if the detective would make a joke about it.

"Thank you, sir," Detective Green coughed, and Angus couldn't tell if she was stifling a laugh or just trying to get past the awkwardness. "Would you mind talking outside? It's a bit ripe in here."

"Certainly," Jack said. "There are some benches on the back deck."

Jack led the group through the house to a patio. When everyone sat down, Detective Harrington took out a tablet computer, and Detective Green flipped through her notebook. She turned towards Jack. "Mr. Evans, were you and Mr. MacBangus working at the Peterson residence at 1495 Complacence Lane yesterday?"

"Yes, we were." Jack tugged his beard and wondered what kind of trouble Peterson was making.

"And what was the nature of the job?" Detective Green flipped to a new page in her notebook and wrote something down.

"We painted the basement."

"Did you have occasion to be in any part of the house besides the basement?" Green scribbled more notes. Meanwhile, her partner was absorbed with tasks on his tablet.

"We were taking a break when we heard a crash upstairs and went to the kitchen to make sure no one was hurt," Jack said.

The detective asked Jack for further details and then about the rest of his day. Jack told the detective of his trip to Denver and his late return to the Springs after the concert. Then Detective Green turned to Angus. "And you, sir, can you describe your movements yesterday?"

Angus recounted his afternoon and evening as precisely as he could. He ended by mentioning his conversation with Hank.

"And what time did you leave your neighbor's townhouse?" Detective Green asked.

"I'd say it was maybe 12:30 or 1." Angus shrugged. "I didn't really look at the time."

The detective jotted something down. "Do you think your neighbor could pin the time down more precisely?"

"Probably not." Angus blushed. "He was pretty drunk by the time I left."

The detective paused. She seemed deep in thought. Jack took advantage of the break. "So, what is this about, anyway?"

"Someone broke into Mr. Peterson's house last night," Detective Green said. This time she didn't refer to her notebook. "A laptop computer and a tray of valuable watches were stolen from his office." She let her statement hang in the air. "Mr. Mac-Bangus, I believe you painted Mr. Petersons' office the day before yesterday."

"I did," Angus confirmed. His mouth felt dry. While the Petersons had moved most of the furniture before he painted, he remembered that Mr. Peterson's desk had been too heavy, so he and Mrs. Peterson had put a drop cloth over it.

"And when you were painting the office, did you see a laptop and some watches?"

"Not that I recall," Angus said. Then he added, "We ask clients to remove as many items as possible from a room when we are painting it. Mrs. Peterson had already moved most of the items from the office by the time I arrived."

Detective Green considered this. Then she paged through her notebook. "Did Mrs. Peterson show you the office prior to the day you painted it? If so, did you see a computer?"

Angus took a minute to think. He had briefly walked through both rooms to confirm Maggie's estimate about the amount of paint and labor required, but he had primarily been looking at the walls. "I looked at both the office and dining room last Friday," Angus finally said. "I believe there was a computer on the desk, but I don't remember any watches. Why did he have watches in his office? Shouldn't they have been in his bedroom or a safe or something?"

Detective Green closed her notebook and put it on the patio's wooden railing. Angus wondered if she was done with her questioning or simply used the act of paging through the book to buy herself time between questions. "Mr. Peterson normally stored the watches elsewhere, but he had put them in the office, because he intended to take them to a jeweler to have them valued. He thinks he got them out of the safe on Sunday night, but he hasn't been feeling well, so he can't be certain."

"That seems rather dumb," Jack commented. "If I was having strangers working in my house, I wouldn't leave something so valuable lying around. Especially in a room that I knew the workman would be alone in."

"I don't disagree," Detective Green said. "People do foolish things all the time. Mr. Peterson claims he forgot about the painting appointment. He also says that he planned to take the watches to the jeweler on Monday, but a meeting ran long and he wasn't able to make it before they closed."

Angus knew that something was fishy in this story. Well, actually lots of things. He wondered if Detective Green found the whole situation as contrived as he did. "Then why didn't he just go on Tuesday instead?"

Detective Green smiled. Mr. Peterson had described this MacBangus fellow as a crude, idiotic buffoon, but he was making some excellent points. "Mr. Peterson claims he wasn't in a hurry to get the watches valued, so when he woke up with a migraine on Tuesday, he put the errand off until today." Detective Harrington gave her sideways glance as if to reminder her not to share details.

"That's all well and good." The frustration in Jack's voice was palpable. "But how does he know the watches were stolen last night? If Angus didn't see them on Monday, someone could have stolen them on Sunday night."

"Mr. Peterson says that he felt better after dinner on Tuesday night and spent an hour in his office catching up on emails," Detective Green stated. "He claims he saw them in their tray on his desk when he went up to bed at 8:30 PM but that the watches were gone when he went to pick them up at 7 AM this morning."

Angus looked at the sun's movement across the sky. He wondered when this interview would be over. They had already lost at least a half an hour's work.

Detective Green took out her notebook again and opened it to the notes that she had taken during their interviews. "You both say that you left the property around 11:30 AM. Can you be any more precise?"

Jack checked his phone. "I sent a text to my wife and to Mrs. Peterson at 11:34 AM saying we had finished the work and were leaving the property. Why does that matter?"

Green took the question in stride. "While you were working at the Peterson's, did you see or hear anything else unusual besides the plate breaking?"

Both men shook their heads. "We were both wearing ear buds while we painted," Jack said. "Why?"

Detective Green nodded as she processed this information. "Well, a funny thing happened. Around 11 AM, someone smeared black grease over the lenses of the cameras at the Peterson's house. The first camera that was vandalized was the one that covered the entrance to the basement."

"It wasn't us," Angus huffed. "We were working. Besides, the camera would have captured us coming out the door, wouldn't it?"

"How did you know about the placement of that camera?" Green asked. "Do you make it a habit to case houses you are working on?" Evans and MacBangus had done a pretty good job acting like honest tradesmen up to this point, but they might just be smooth operators.

Jack's face turned red. "That would be terrible for business, Detective." His voice was barely controlled. "As it happens, Mr. Peterson made a big deal about the cameras when he came down to tell us to mind our own business after his wife broke the serving platter. He said he would review his recordings to make sure he wasn't being overcharged for labor, so on the way out, we saw that camera and waved at it."

"And you didn't notice the grease?" Detective Green asked. When she had looked at the cameras earlier this morning, she hadn't noticed it until she had inspected them close up, but she wanted to see what the two men would say.

"I didn't," Angus said, "but it wasn't a big thing. I quickly looked around until I found it and then pointed it out to Jack. We just sort of glanced at it, gave it a wave, and carried our supplies out to the trucks."

"You don't seem to notice much, Mr. MacBangus." Detective Harrington spoke for the first time. "Look, Mr. Peterson treated you poorly. Maybe you two thought you'd play a little joke on him and mess up his cameras. And then maybe when you'd been drinking awhile, Mr. MacBangus, you remembered the computer and expensive watches just sitting in his office ripe for the picking. You'd been in the house before and realized that the basement door wasn't alarmed. So, you snuck in and made off with them." He smiled as if pleased with his scenario.

Detective Green gave Harrington a warning glance. MacBangus had given a believable explanation for why he hadn't known about the watches. However, he had a shaky alibi, and she thought it would be productive to push him, but sometimes

Harrington pushed things too hard.

"That's preposterous!" Jack interjected. "Angus is not a thief, and my wife would have insured that we were fairly paid for our work." He spent a minute explaining Maggie's plans to get Mr. Peterson to make good on his contract.

"You're awful quiet, MacBangus," Detective Harrington jeered. "Did I get too close to the truth? The only thing I don't understand is why you couldn't come up with a better alibi. Couldn't you find a gal at the bar to say she'd come home with you? With a name like MacBangus, I expect you are quite the ladies' man."

Angus looked down at his hands. He knew Detective Harrington was doing everything he could to get a rise out of him. Making fun of his name had almost pushed him over the edge. "I'm an honest man," he said quietly. "I had nothing to do with sabotaging the cameras or breaking into the Peterson house."

Detective Harrington took a breath to prepare for a fresh tirade, but Detective Green held up her hand. "That's enough, Dan." If these men hadn't robbed the Petersons, they were valuable witnesses, and she couldn't risk alienating them.

To Angus and Jack, she said, "Here's the problem, Mr. MacBangus. You don't have a reliable alibi. Plus, you have a motive and a knowledge of property." She paged through her notebook. "Finally, Mr. Peterson claims you were loitering outside the property yesterday morning. My next step will be to get a search warrant for you house and truck." She had enough evidence to justify a warrant, but Green already suspected that she would find nothing suspicious in Angus's house.

Without even thinking, Angus said, "You don't need to do that. Look where you like."

Jack turned to Angus. "Don't be stupid. She might never get a warrant."

Angus looked at Jack and then at the investigating officers.

"I didn't do it, and I have nothing to hide. I just want to get this over with."

"Thank you, Mr. MacBangus. I appreciate your cooperation." Detective Green closed her notebook again and put it in her pocket. She retrieved her cell phone.

After making a few phone calls, Detectives Green and Harrington walked out front with Angus and spent 15 minutes going through every nook and cranny of his truck. It helped that Angus kept his truck interior clean and his tools well organized, but it took a while to search the locking toolbox in the back of his truck. Once they were satisfied that the items weren't in his vehicle, Green and Harrington followed Angus and Jack to Angus's house, where the process was repeated with the help of additional officers. As the police worked, Jack and Angus sat on the front step of Angus's townhouse. While people walked past, no one approached the men.

"I hope this won't cause trouble with your neighbors." Jack tugged his beard. "I know you've done a lot of work to make your house nice."

Angus considered this and looked around. "They would have searched eventually. At least it's during the day, and most people are at work."

"Good point, but you know that Maggie and I would never think that you would steal from a client, even a bastard like Peterson."

"I know, and I appreciate it." Angus picked at an invisible speck of dust on his coveralls.

At that moment, Detective Green came out. She was holding a tarnished pocket watch. "Mr. MacBangus, can you tell please tell me where you got this watch?"

Angus took the watch from her and examined it. "It was my grandfather's." He pressed the stem to open up the case. "His initials and his wedding date are engraved right here." He handed the watch back to Detective Green.

"Thank you." She examined the watch further. "Would you accompany me inside, please?" She led Angus up to the second story of the townhouse and into the second bedroom, which served as his office.

"I assume you can tell me when and from whom you purchased this computer." Green pointed to an aging laptop sitting on Angus's desk.

"I believe I bought it from an online retailer about three years ago," Angus said. "I could probably go to my account and find the receipt."

"That won't be necessary," Detective Green said. "It's a different model than the one that was stolen."

"Then why ask?" Angus raised his voice. He was tired and just wanted everyone out of his house. "Did you want to make sure I hadn't stolen this as well?"

"It's just procedure," Green said. Actually, it wasn't. She had just wanted to gauge Angus's response. While his patience was wearing thin, he had reasonable answers to all her questions. "We're almost done here. I was the one who searched this room, and I noticed you have a lot of pictures and documents. What are you researching?"

"May I?" Angus gestured to his desk.

"Certainly."

Angus took a box from a shelf next to his desk and noticed with relief that while it had obviously been opened and searched, the officer had replaced the contents neatly. He confirmed that the picture of his father and his letter were still in the box, and then showed the photo to Detective Green. "This is my father, Sylvester Thompson. He was an American soldier who briefly knew my mother when he visited Scotland. I became interested in genealogy when I started looking for him, and since then I have started to trace my mother's side of the family as well."

Detective Green smiled. "Before I was married, my maiden name was Forgie, which is part of Clan Fergus. We have a beautiful tartan with lots of red and blue. Have you discovered what clan the MacBangus family comes from and do you know what the tartan looks like?"

"With a name like MacBangus, I picture less of a tartan and more of a picnic blanket stained with violent splashes of color like a Jackson Pollock painting." Detective Harrington had appeared in the doorway at some point.

"Don't be crude, Dan." Detective Green spoke firmly. "I think we're done here." To Angus, she said, "Thank you for your time, sir, and if you think of anything else that might help our investigation, please contact me." She handed Angus a business card and motioned for Harrington to follow her down the stairs.

Angus put his father's photo away and then took a few minutes to look through his office. Detective Green had been thorough, but she had been kind. He walked over to his bedroom and had little doubt who had searched it. The contents of his drawers were scattered on the floor, and his mattress had not been properly replaced on his platform bed.

Jack came up the stairs and whistled at the sight of the mess. "They gave this place a pretty thorough going over."

"I've seen worse," Angus said. "Remember when we did that estimate on a rental property before the cleaning crew came through?"

"The place that had a mushroom growing in the fridge the size of your head?" Jack chuckled.

Angus laughed as well. "Yeah, that one. They've got this room beat by a mile." He walked over to the mattress and shifted it back into place and started remaking the bed.

"Don't do that now," Jack said from the doorway. "You've had a rough morning. That can wait until later."

Angus looked up from the bed. "So, what is the plan? Are we going back to that demo job?" He looked around the room and walked over to the corner where he had a 3-bin clothes hamper and started putting the dirty clothes back in their correct bins.

"Brother, have you looked at the time?" Jack said. "It's after 1. We're going to get some lunch. After that, we'll just see."

Angus hadn't looked at the clock in a while, but he wasn't even remotely hungry. At the moment, he wanted everything back to normal, and that started with making this room look somewhat decent. "What about the job?" Angus moved towards the dresser. "Is Maggie mad?"

As Angus started picking up clean clothes and putting them away, Jack smiled. "Maggie isn't mad at you, but she's been on the phone all morning, and she's mad as hell." Jack picked up an overturned chair. "A friend of mine is going to come help me with the demo tomorrow, and as for Mr. Peterson, Maggie has plans for him."

"Hopefully plans that do not involve a shovel and quick-lime." Angus laughed. As he got more distance from the morning, he realized how weary he was. Everything seemed funnier than it should be.

"Nothing like that," Jack said. "I'll let her tell you. Maggie thinks you should stay with us tonight, but let's eat first."

"Give me five minutes." Angus did a final bit of straightening and then went to the bathroom to wash his hands.

When he got downstairs, Jack was sitting on his sofa. "Where do you want to go?" Jack asked. "My treat."

Angus thought for a minute. He still wasn't hungry, so if he was going to force himself to eat, he might as well eat something he knew he liked. "Let's go to Macduff's. I feel like something fried and/or smothered in brown gravy."

"Good man." Jack stood up. "Your truck or mine?"

◆ ◆ ◆

Macduff's Bar and Grill tried very hard to be a "Scottish Bar," but in reality, it was more of a "British Isles Bar." The interior was furnished in dark woods and featured prints of hunting dogs and people in tartans, which was a solid start. The menu was an eclectic mix. Offerings included traditional British favorites such as Cornish Pasties, Fish and Chips, and Bangers and Mash and dishes named after famous Scots that stretched the imagination a bit, chiefly the Mary Queen of Scots Rueben and Robert the Bruce's French Dip Sandwich. The two most popular beers on tap, Guinness and Harp, were Irish. However, Macduff's made up for its lack of accuracy with a friendly atmosphere, a variety of activities such as trivia nights and pay-per-view events, and good cooking. Even though Angus had a self-imposed a one drink limit, he still appreciated a place that reminded him of home and allowed him to meet up with other expatriates.

By the time Angus and Jack walked in, the lunch crowd had left. William "Scotty" Jenkins was alone wiping down the bar while drinking a pint of a dark beer. Scotty was the owner of Macduff's and spent most of his days behind the bar. His wife Pearl ran the kitchen. The couple had been in the restaurant business their whole lives, and several years ago when a DNA test had revealed that Scotty's maternal grandfather was Scottish, he'd travelled to Scotland and come back to Colorado Springs with the idea to open a Scottish Bar. Thanks to Pearl's excellent cooking and Scotty's expert marketing, the place kept them busy and made a modest profit.

Scotty was an African American man with vivid green eyes, a gift from his Scottish grandfather or so he said, although he had no color photos of the man. He wore a tartan print kilt and a white dress shirt. Despite working behind the bar all day, the ensemble was immaculate.

"Angus MacBangus and Jack Evans." Scotty greeted the pair as they came in and sat at the bar. "I've never seen you two as day drinkers, but with the day you must be having, it's a good excuse to start. What can I pour you?"

"A Black and Tan." Jack picked up a menu that he had memorized.

"And for you, Angus?" Scotty asked. With his deep voice and greying hair, Scotty filled the role of surrogate father for many young men.

"Oh, I don't know. Maybe I'll just stick to water," Angus muttered. He looked over at a chalkboard that announced the day's specials. "Does Pearl have any Cornish Pasties left?"

"More than likely, but as soon as I get your drinks, I'll go back and check." Scotty layered Jack's Black and Tan into a pint glass. "I had some beat cops in here a couple of hours ago asking after you. Are you in trouble, Angus?"

"It's a long story." Jack accepted the drink from Scotty. "But we've got it cleared up."

"Well, storytelling is thirsty work." Scotty grabbed another pint glass. "I think you need a lager and lemonade, Angus, on the house."

After years of dealing with his mother's alcoholism, Angus wasn't much of a drinker, but he liked to be social, so he had taken to drinking lager and lemonade. Scotty always made his first one with lager and then switched to lemon-lime soda and lemonade if he had another. Scotty made the drink and handed it to Angus.

"Thanks, man," Angus said and took a long drink.

"You welcome. I'll just go back and see what Pearl has left. Jack, do you want pasties as well?"

"I'd prefer fish and chips," Jack said, "but I don't want to be too much trouble."

"No trouble at all." Scotty headed back to the kitchen.

He returned 20 minutes later with a plate of three Cornish Pasties and a large bowl of brown gravy for Angus. Pearl followed with an equally generous portion of golden fish and chips for Jack. "Same again?" she asked everyone.

When they all nodded, Pearl replaced their drinks except Angus, for whom she poured a lemonade. Then she helped herself to a small whiskey and asked, "So, what's the story?"

Angus hesitated, not wanting to relive the entire morning. Jack gave him a look and then launched into the story between bites of fried fish and crispy chips. Scotty and Pearl listened as they sipped their drinks, while Angus felt his attention wane as the fatigue of a rough day caught up with him.

"It sounds like this guy is a piece of work," Pearl said when Jack paused and took a long pull from his beer. "I'm sure there's a long list of people who he pissed off. Why concentrate on Angus? He's not exactly 'Hard MacHard of the Clan MacHard.'"

Everyone laughed, and Angus looked up from his plate for the first time in several minutes.

"Pearl was just saying that while you can take care of yourself, you're a nice guy at heart." Scotty brought Angus up to speed on their conversation and threw in a free complement. "But she makes a good point. Why focus on Angus?"

"It's like the detective said," Angus answered. "I had motive, means, and opportunity. I was an obvious suspect. If they hadn't questioned me, they wouldn't have been doing their job well."

"That's a fair point." Scotty looked down at his empty glass as if considering another and then put it down on a coaster. "But I'm sure you aren't the only person whose worked in that house recently. Why not any of the other contractors?"

"Probably because he was the last person in the house." Jack had finished his meal and pushed away his plate. "The plumber and the electrician finished up last week. They would know the house setup, but they wouldn't have been around when Peterson left the watches sitting around."

"And they're good guys." Angus used a spoon to get the last bit of pasty filling off his plate. "We work with them all the time, and I just can't see them as thieves. They make enough from their work."

"Peterson leaving those watches just sitting there in his first-floor office, that seems pretty careless," Pearl said. Her whiskey was long gone, and she was swirling the ice cubes around the glass. "How do we know that some random person didn't walk past, see them, and come back later to take them?"

"You're forgetting the cameras, woman," Scotty rebuked her. "How would some random person on the street know about where the cameras were enough to vandalize them?"

"Good point." Pearl paused for a minute and wrinkled her brow. "You know, it wouldn't be just tradespeople who knew the house's set-up. What about close friends and business associates?"

"Ok, I buy that, but what's the motive? I don't go around casing people's houses at parties." Jack finished his beer and pointed to his empty glass. "Can I get one more?"

"Sure." Pearl poured another black and tan. "I imagine if Peterson is as nasty of a man as you all describe, that he's one of those guys who brags and shows off all his nice things to guests. Maybe one of his friends needs some cash, or one of his co-workers is in the same position."

Angus held up his glass, and Pearl refilled it. "I suppose that's plausible," he said, "but how would they know the watches were going to be in his office? It seems unlikely."

Scotty has been quiet for a moment, but suddenly there was a twinkle in his eye. "It would just take one offhand remark, and an observant person might figure it out. You wouldn't believe the little tidbits I pick up working the bar." He bussed the empty glasses and plates into a plastic tub. "Maybe he said something to his secretary about having to leave early to go to the jeweler, or maybe she overheard him talking to his insurance agent. People don't always get pieces valued to sell them. Sometimes they need the paperwork for insurance. If someone overheard something, they might have asked him about it casually, and he might have given them all the information that they needed to know."

"Seems a stretch to me," Pearl argued back. "But now that you mention insurance, maybe it's a scam. He takes the watches out of the safe, intending to get them valued and sell them, and then Angus annoys him, and he pretends to be robbed and set Angus up as the patsy. His insurance pays, Angus gets put through the ringer, and he still has the watches stashed somewhere."

"Why stop there?" Jack asked. "Maybe he got rid of the watches months ago, sold them privately or lost them gambling, and then after he told us about the cameras, he had the idea to pretend to be robbed and point the finger at Angus."

"That really seems convoluted." Scotty wiped down the bar counter. "You all have been watching too many of those murder mysteries."

"But this isn't a murder mystery." Jack pointed out. "It's just a property crime. That's pretty common in the Springs. Chances are the police won't spend much more time on it. They'll give Peterson a report, and Peterson will give it to his insurance agent."

He turned to Angus. "You've been pretty quiet. Do you have any ideas or feelings about the matter?"

Angus thought for a moment. While Mr. Peterson appeared to be a bully and blowhard, he had been more moved by Mrs. Peterson's fear and nervousness. "I agree with Jack. Mr. Peterson setting up a false insurance claim is a stretch, but Mrs.

Peterson seemed very edgy on Monday. Maybe she damaged one of the watches when she moved them out of the office and was afraid of her husband's reaction, so she covered the whole thing up by having them go missing, but she forgot about the security cameras until Mr. Peterson went down and yelled at us. When he went up to bed, she could have sabotaged the cameras and waited until the evening to take the watches to some place safe."

Pearl laughed, "Oh, Angus, that takes the cake! What are the chances?"

"Speaking of chances and statistics," Jack said. "I keep going back to thinking that this is just a simple theft. There's probably a person or crew working the neighborhood. They go through during the day and mess with the security cameras and then come back at night and rob the houses. The simplest answer is usually the best." He took out his phone and unlocked it.

"Rob a house at night with people in it!" Scotty took his turn to laugh. "That's not a good bet in Colorado Springs. More than likely, you would get yourself shot."

Angus looked at the time. "In the end, it doesn't matter to me if they find Peterson's stuff or not. My part in the story is over." To Jack he said. "So, are we going to put in a couple hours on that demo job or what?"

"Dude, I've had three beers." Jack yawned. "I'm heading home, and so should you. Maggie says dinner is at 6, and she expects you there. Go home and pack a bag, and I'll get a ride home." He opened up a rideshare app.

"Ok." Angus had little interest in staying with Jack and Maggie, but he also didn't want to spend the night in his house. He got out his wallet and looked at Scotty. "How much to settle up?"

Pearl spoke first. "Don't worry about it. I'm sorry that you had so much trouble, but this is the most interesting thing I've been a part of in a while."

"Yes, much more interesting that all the work you should have been doing in the kitchen," Scotty joked picking up everyone's glasses.

"You don't always get to keep all the fun stories to yourself," Pearl teased. She and Scotty had the natural banter of a couple who had been married forever.

"Thanks, you two," Angus said. He gave a nod to Jack and headed for the restroom.

Five minutes later, Angus was sitting in his truck in the parking lot of Macduff's. Jack had just gotten into an SUV headed back to his house, and Angus was alone for the first time in hours. He had only had maybe eight ounces of beer with a large meal, but the cumulative stress of the day was catching up with him. He was tired but his mind was racing, and he wondered if maybe he should call for a ride himself. Angus had a brief argument with himself and then started up his truck. He wasn't drunk or impaired - just ready to go home.

Angus turned onto the main street and headed back to his townhouse near Academy and Maizeland Roads. Traffic was pretty light, so he drove towards Interstate 25. Just after he changed lanes, he heard a police siren and saw a sedan with a flashing light on the roof. Could this day get any worse? Angus signaled and pulled over to the side of the road.

The car pulled up behind him, and Detective Harrington got out. Angus had been wondering what he'd done to get pulled over, but he realized that this situation probably had little to do with his driving. Angus rolled down the window.

"License, registration, and proof of insurance please," Detective Harrington said when he had approached the vehicle.

"Certainly." Angus retrieved the documents from the glove compartment.

"Thanks." Detective Harrington took the documents back to his car and spent some time on his computer.

Angus tried to wait patiently. Detective Harrington was wearing the same cheap suit Angus had seen him in a couple hours ago. Angus wondered what the detective had been doing for the last two hours. He pictured him sitting in the car a block from Macduff's while he and Jack had lunch. This guy was either very thorough or a world class dick or maybe both.

When Detective Harrington returned, he handed Angus his documents. "Have you been drinking, sir?"

Angus considered the best way to response. He fought the urge to be terse and just say yes. Instead, he replied, "I had a beer with my lunch and then stuck to soft drinks."

"Really?" Detective Harrington cocked his eyebrow. "Would you be willing to take a field sobriety test?"

"Sure." Angus knew that field sobriety tests were open to interpretation, and he had concerns about whether Detective Harrington was on the level, so he added. "I'd like to ask for a breathalyzer test as well."

"Have it your way then," the detective said in frustration. He looked at the traffic whizzing past them. "I'll call for a patrol car. They'll have a breathalyzer."

Harrington walked back to his car and made a call on his radio. Angus sat and waited in silence for a police cruiser to show up. He wanted to turn on his radio and listen to music, but he realized he needed to do everything possible to make a good impression. Three minutes later a patrol car pulled up behind the detective's car, and a uniformed police officer got out. Detective Harrington joined the other officer, and then two of them proceeded to Angus's truck.

"Would you please exit your vehicle, sir, and stand on the side of the road in front of it," the second officer said.

Angus complied. The uniformed officer, whose nametag read Morales, led Angus through a series of activities. Then she produced a breathalyzer device and had him blow into it. After she checked the reading, she asked him to do it a second time. She showed the result to Detective Harrington.

"Sorry I wasted your time, Morales." The Detective shook his head in disbelief. "I was certain I saw him weaving in his lane."

"I'm sure you did, sir." The uniformed officer struggled to keep the ring of sarcasm out of her voice. "Better safe than sorry," she added and went back to her car.

As soon as she'd left, Detective Harrington turned to Angus. "I'm sorry to have wasted your time as well." His tone had changed from abrasive to apologetic. "But you went to a bar for a couple of hours!"

"Aye." Angus still felt the need to be cautious around this mercurial man. "That I did, but my ma was an alcoholic, and I don't imbibe in strong drink."

Detective Harrington nodded trying to take this information in. Morales's patrol car drove by. "You are too good to be true. Don't tell me, let me guess. Do you rescue puppies in your spare time?" There was a trace of irony in his voice.

"Nope." Angus looked Harrington up and down. The man's posture and the neatness of his haircut made Angus wonder if he had also been in the military. "However, every Thursday, I volunteer at a helpline for veterans in crisis, and sometimes I help lead support group meetings for veterans."

The detective relaxed. "You served in the military? But you're Scottish."

Angus smiled. The ice was finally broken. "Yeah, but my dad was an American, so I joined the U.S. military and served for 12 years. What about you?"

"I did eight years," Harrington said. "I joined right after 9-11, but after a while I lost my taste for it." He turned sober. "When my marriage broke up, I got out and become a cop."

Angus waited a minute to see if the officer would say more. "That's a pretty common story. Long deployments leave people unable to cope with the home front. Relationships suffer, and it's no one's fault."

Harrington looked Angus in the eye and extended his hand. "I really am sorry that I rode you so hard. I just get carried away sometimes."

Angus shook Harrington's hand. "I get it. We all struggle from time to time, and I was a pretty obvious suspect."

"Almost too obvious," Harrington said softly, almost to himself.

Angus pulled out his wallet, extracted a business card, and handed it to Detective Harrington. "Look, if you ever need to talk or something, these are good people. They offer a variety of options from groups to a helpline to a service that helps people find individual therapists."

"Thanks." Detective Harrington looked at the card. "Can I get in touch with you through them?"

"Wouldn't that be a conflict of interest?" asked Angus.

"Probably, but if I had any additional questions for you about the Petersons?"

"I'll put my cell on the back." Angus took the card back and wrote down his number.

When he was finished, he got back in his truck. Detective Harrington drove away first, and Angus took a minute before he got back on the road. Then he looked at his phone and realized how late it was getting.

Traffic had picked up in the time Angus had been pulled over, and it took him longer than usual to get back to his town-house. He threw a change of clothes and a book in a bag and then spent 15 minutes tidying up his bedroom from the search. After realizing Lily had the day off tomorrow, he dug out his hiking daypack and a couple water bottles, just in case. Angus put everything in the truck and walked over to Hank's townhouse.

Murphey didn't run to the door barking, so Angus figured that he and his owner were out on one of their many walks. Despite his age and his drinking problem, Hank was a remarkably fit man. He even took Murphey hiking in Palmer Parker. Angus had felt obligated to check on Hank, but he was also relieved. The last thing he wanted to do after his day was to listen to some variation off Hank's rant that he and Murphey were "discarded old bastards, the both of us." More than once he had suggested that Hank might enjoy one of the groups for older veterans that he know about, but Hank had resisted. He spent most of his time alone with Murphey.

Angus went back to his townhouse and scrawled a note to Hank saying he would be gone for a day or two and taped the note to Hank's door. He knew he could just send Hank a text, but that wasn't Hank's style.

After fighting through rush hour traffic, Angus made it to Jack and Maggie's house in northeast Colorado Springs. The couple lived in a neighborhood that had been built in the early 1990s and somehow didn't have an HOA, so Angus parked on the street and knocked on the front door.

"Angus, so good to see you," Maggie said as she opened the door. She was a tall woman in her late 30s with a big smile and thick, wavy blonde hair. She wore a short-sleeved blouse and capris. "Come on in."

"Thanks." Angus sat down in the entry way and removed his shoes and then followed Maggie to the first-floor guest room.

"Now just take your time and get settled in," Maggie instructed. "I made spaghetti bolognaise, but there's no rush."

When she left, Angus set his bag down on the bed and opened it. He put his book on the bedside table and his toiletries on the dresser. There was a bathroom on the first floor, but it wasn't ensuite, so he decided not to leave anything in there. He thought about putting his clothes in the drawers, but decided against it. Instead, he placed his bag and his daypack on the floor of the closet.

Angus looked at a vintage travel alarm clock that was on the bedside table and saw that it was 5:45. He knew he should go out to the dining room, but he was hesitant. He sat down on the bed for a minute and despite the warmth of the day, he felt a chill. Part of him wanted to crawl under the covers and not come out until the next day, while part of him realized his obligation to be a polite guest.

He heard a knock on his door and said, "Come in."

"You looked knackered." Jack stood in the doorway.

"I am," Angus admitted. "Dinner smells delicious. I'll be out in a minute." He made to stand up.

Jack put up his hand. "Don't worry about it." He looked out the door and then at Angus. "Maggie knows we had a late lunch, but dinner was already in the works. You can get cleaned up and join us after dinner for a drink."

"Maggie really won't mind?" Angus asked as he sat back down.

"Not a bit," Jack said. "In fact, I think she could use a break. Neveah and Natalie are going to a movie with friends tonight." The girls were Maggie's 15- and 16-year-old daughters from a previous marriage. They were short and dark-haired like Maggie's ex-husband but had their mother's outgoing and bubbly personality. Sometimes both girls and their mother were a bit much for even the biggest extroverts.

"Sounds good."

Jack left, and Angus got cleaned up. A hot shower did little to warm him up, and in the back of his mind, Angus wondered if he might be suffering from delayed shock. Not one for pajamas, Angus took a soft t-shirt and a tactical cargo kilt from his bag. The kilt was made of a khaki-colored material and was longer than a standard kilt. Angus had owned this particular kilt forever, so it was soft and well broken in. He had picked it, because all its pockets were handy when he went hiking. It was just a fringe benefit that it also served the role of comfy, casual bottoms for him. After running a brush through his hair and putting on a pair of sandals, Angus felt ready to face Jack and Maggie and went out to the kitchen and informal dining room area.

Maggie was loading the dishwasher as Angus came in. "You look a little better. What can I get you?"

"Aunty Ivy always said that a cup of hot tea with lots of sugar would cure most anything that ails you," Angus said. "Do you still keep the tea bags in the same place?"

"Yup. Help yourself. The kettle is in that cabinet over there." She pointed.

Maggie had one of those "by the cup" hot drink makers, but she knew Angus took a more traditional view of brewing tea. He had grown up with cheap tea bags, and she kept a supply just for him. Maggie closed the dishwasher and brought out the sugar bowl and filled a small jug with milk.

Angus filled the kettle and put it on the stovetop to heat. He found a cup and placed a tea bag in it. While he waited for the kettle to sing, Maggie wiped down the counters. Jack took a couple of beers from the fridge, opened them up, and poured them into pint glasses for himself and Maggie. The three of them continued with mundane domestic tasks until Angus had a cup of tea in his hands and could sit down on a chair in front of the gas fireplace in the adjacent sitting room.

"So, what's the status of the Peterson job?" he asked Maggie and then took of sip of his tea. Angus wished they would turn the fireplace on, but it seemed silly to ask.

Maggie followed Angus's gaze and flipped the switch on

the fireplace. Little blue flames came to life and danced. She sat down on a sofa next to Jack and took a sip of her beer. "Well, Peterson's wife called around noon and said they were cancelling the rest of the job." She stretched her legs out and rested them on an ottoman. "And Mrs. Peterson said that her husband refuses to pay for the work and will sue us. More like we'll be suing him, but whatever."

"Do you think it will come to that?" Jack let Maggie take care of the money side of the business, but this was a big job, and he didn't fancy waiting to get paid until after a long legal battle.

"Probably not," Maggie said. "Look the job was almost done, and we can prove it. All the inspections with the city happened last week. Peterson is in a huff right now, but next week I'll send him the bill, and we'll just see. More than likely, he'll pay it when we threaten to sue him."

"But what about the touch ups?" Angus hated to leave a job unfinished.

Maggie waved her hand dismissively. "It's usually just putting a few outlet covers back and touching up some paint. If they don't want to pay up, they can do it themselves." She giggled to herself. "Ok, I was naughty. When they said they wouldn't pay, I called a few of our fellow contractors and told them about it. I don't think the Petersons will find anyone to do any work on their house until they pay in full and apologize."

"That was kind of mean," Angus commented.

"Turnabout is fair play." Maggie's cheeks were flushed. "I'm sure we aren't the first people who have had trouble with the Petersons, and I don't want the people we know to have to deal with that kind of drama."

"I suppose." Angus preferred not to escalate situations, but Maggie was the one with the head for business. "How did Mrs. Peterson sound when she called you?"

"Agitated. Worried. Anxious," Maggie recalled. "I had the

feeling that Mr. Peterson was standing next to her telling her what to say. Why?"

"Just a feeling I had." Angus was sure that his feeling of foreboding about the job had been a reaction to Mrs. Peterson's state of mind. "I don't know why I still care about that poor woman."

"Poor woman, my eye," Maggie said. "If he's so insufferable, she should leave him."

The remark hung in the air. Maggie had a fiery temper at times, and neither Angus nor Jack were in a mood for a fight.

"What took you so long to get here, Angus?" Jack changed the subject. He had finished his beer and placed his glass on an end table.

Angus described his second encounter with Detective Harrington and ended by saying that he hoped the man would get some help.

"This is why I love you, Angus," Maggie said. "Even on your worst day, you treat people with compassion. That man doesn't know how lucky he is. You could sue him for harassment."

"Aye, probably, but what good would it do?" Angus had finished his tea, and although it was only 7, he was weary of dealing with people. "I'll say good night, if you don't mind."

"Not at all," Jack said. "And take tomorrow off and spend it with Lily. You deserve it."

"Will do." Angus rinsed his tea cup and put it in the dishwasher before going to the guest room.

Angus brushed his teeth and crawled into bed. He picked up the mystery novel on the bedside table. Angus loved British murder mysteries. Even though most of them were written about rich people with a lifestyle that was unfamiliar to him, he couldn't put them down. This novel took place at a country house party. A bunch of guests and their servants had come for a weekend of hunting, and the lord of the manor was shot during the first twenty pages. As the plot thickened, guests and one servant were pushed down the stairs, strangled, and poisoned in turn. Angus got the sneaking suspicion that he had read this novel before but couldn't remember who did it or why. The bodies were stacking up like cordwood, and Angus was glad that this was fiction. Who had it in them to kill six people?

The barking of Maggie's dog Baxter startled Angus out of his thoughts. He realized he had been reading for three hours. The caffeine and the sugar in the tea must have kept him up. Baxter stopped barking, and Angus assumed that Neveah and Natalie were home safe.

Angus waited for the girls to get upstairs and then popped off to the bathroom before settling himself into bed and turning off the bedside lamp. He couldn't shake the feeling of being simultaneously exhausted and spun up. Sleep didn't come quickly and when it did, it was filled with strange dreams. Angus was the lord of the manor, which came with the advantage of a snazzy smoking jacket, but instead of being shot, he was accused of embezzling money from the church steeple fund. The vicar jumped from the bell tower in an apparent suicide. The hounds of Hell wouldn't stop barking, or maybe that was Baxter again.

CHAPTER 3

Thursday, August 23

Angus woke with a start. He was disoriented and did not know what time of day it was. His phone was dead, and Angus realized he must have forgotten to plug it in last night. He looked over to where his window should be and saw unfamiliar black-out drapes. It was only then he remembered he was at Maggie and Jack's.

Sounds of conversation drifted from other parts of the house. As Angus shook off the fog of sleep, he recognized Lily and Maggie's voices. He also smelled pancakes, and his stomach rumbled, reminding him he had skipped dinner last night.

Angus got up and snapped on his kilt. He found his sandals and ventured into the kitchen where Lily and Maggie were chatting over coffee.

"Well, good morning, sleepyhead. I thought you'd never wake up," Lily teased. She poured a cup of coffee and handed it to Angus.

"Thanks." Angus looked up at the kitchen clock. It was only 7:30. Why did it feel like he had slept in late?

Maggie was making pancakes on a portable griddle. "I was just filling Lily in on everything that's happened in the last day or two." She transferred half a dozen pancakes to a serving platter. "I figured you were pretty tired of repeating the story."

Angus sipped his coffee and eyed the pancakes. "That I am. I'm ready to move on."

"So that means you are still up for a hike?" Lily asked. While Maggie set the table, she took a platter of bacon out of the oven where it had been staying warm and then took a bowl of cut mixed fruit out of the refrigerator.

"Definitely, but I don't understand. Why are you here this morning?"

Lily smiled. Even dressed in an old T-shirt, zip off hiking pants, and trail runners, she was radiant. "Maggie got in touch with me yesterday afternoon. She figured you had a lot on your plate, but she wanted to make sure that you had something to do today to take your mind off things."

"That was kind of you, Maggie, thanks." Angus sat down with the ladies at a small table in the kitchen.

Everyone tucked into breakfast and ate in relative silence for a few minutes. When they were finished, Maggie cleared the table. "Why don't you get ready for your hike," she said to Lily and Angus. "There's sunscreen in the guest bathroom and extra bottled water in the fridge in the garage if you need it."

"Thanks." Lily retrieved a day pack from the entryway. To Angus, she said, "I packed us a picnic lunch, so all you need to bring is water."

"Sounds good." Angus motioned for Lily to follow him to the guest room, where he found his own pack. He checked the contents and verified that he had rain gear, sunscreen, and energy bars. "Did you have a particular hike in mind?"

"I found a gorgeous path around the outside of Garden of the Gods a couple years ago." Lily took out her phone and consulted it. "The weather is supposed to be rather mild today. Fancy five or six miles?"

"Sounds just about perfect." Angus picked up his own phone that was dead and wished that it had a little charge. He enjoyed taking pictures with it.

Lily noticed his predicament and pulled out a supplemental battery pack and cord out of her bag. "I think this is compatible, or you could plug it in while we drive there."

"Thanks." Angus noticed Lily had also brought a digital SLR camera. "I take it there will be some magnificent vistas."

"We'll start on the eastern ridge of the park." Lily pulled out a tube of cream sunscreen. "It has the best views in my opinion. After that, the serious hiking begins."

The two of them took a few minutes to apply sunscreen and fill their water bottles. Then they thanked Maggie and headed out the door. Angus grabbed the charger from his truck and got into Lily's hybrid sedan. One thing that he liked about Lily was that he didn't always have to plan activities. She was an experienced hiker who had her own ideas about the best places to go.

Thirty minutes later the pair squeezed into the last parking spot in the South Garden Lot of Garden of the Gods. Even though it was a Thursday in early August, the park was packed with tourists and Colorado natives alike enjoying the site's natural beauty and plentiful hiking trails. Fins of orange and white sandstone stuck out of the ground like the armored plates on a stegosaur's back with Pikes Peak and the rest of the Rocky Mountains towering behind them to the west.

Like many people, Angus had frequently gone to an area of the park called the Central Garden. That part of the park featured ample parking and a paved path that allowed visitors to walk amongst the rocks. Families with children in strollers might encounter tourists riding electric scooters or middle-aged people walking their dogs. The Central Garden had even been made wheel chair accessible. At ground level there were many gorgeous photo ops, including a rock formation resembling a heart that couples posed in front of, and to top it off the trail wound around several famous rock formations like the Kissing Camels and North Gateway Rock.

However, Lily's plans for the day did not involve the Central Garden. As Angus took their packs out of the backseat, she removed a map from her pocket and unfolded it. "There are multiple overlooks in this part of the park." She pointed to them on the map. "But I find the best views are from the Niobrara Trail along this ridge."

Angus glanced at the map and then decided not to worry about it. "Lead the way."

Lily donned her pack and locked the car. She led Angus out of the parking lot along a trail that climbed upwards. "Once I was hiking here, and I came over this ridge and saw 20 hot air balloons," she said offhand.

"Aye, that must have been beautiful." Angus wasn't in the mood to talk, but he appreciated Lily's attempts at conversation.

Before they reached the overlook at the top of the ridge, Lily turned down a trail that led into a valley. She negotiated several trail junctures, and eventually she took a path that headed upwards towards of crest of light-colored sedimentary rock. She and Angus had said very little since they had started their hike. While Lily was curious about Angus's troubles over the last few days, she could also sense his reluctance to revisit his stressful experience. Or perhaps he was tired and too winded to say much.

Following the trail, they meandered through a series of switchbacks. From time to time, Angus stopped and took in the view. When they reached the summit of the trail, it split into a northbound and a southbound path that followed the ridge. However, what had initially looked like a single slap of rock actually contained distinct layers of sediment.

Angus and Lily stopped in a small, flat area where the trails met. "I've never quite had this perspective on the park," Angus said. "It's gorgeous."

"Isn't it?" Lily grabbed her water bottle and took a long drink.

"How did you know about this?" Angus also took the opportunity to hydrate. "Did you just pick it out on the map one day and come here?"

"It was completely by chance. My mom and I went hiking with a friend from her church and her dog Sadie. The dog gets anxious around crowds of people, so her owner knows a lot of infrequently travelled trails."

"The path less travelled has advantages," Angus quipped.

"It's one of the best places for pictures along the trail. Shall we take a couple?" Lily removed the lens cap from her camera and took some landscape shots.

"Sure." Angus got out his somewhat charged phone.

The couple took turns snapping pictures of each other and were about to take a selfie together, when an elderly hiker came along. She had been hiking at a brisk pace but stopped when she came upon the couple. "Would you like me to take a picture of you together?" she asked.

"Yes, thanks." Angus handed her his phone. While he had expected to have to explain how to the use the camera to the woman, she was quite adept at it and took several pictures from a variety of vantages.

"Now do one silly one," she suggested, and Angus and Lily complied.

When the woman returned his phone, she leaned in and asked lecherously, "So, young man, I just have to ask. What are you wearing under your kilt?"

Angus, who at this point was used to little old ladies fawning over him, said with a straight face, "Socks, Ma'am, and shoes of course."

"My, my," the hiker smiled without even a blush. To Lily she said, "He's got moxie. I'd keep him." Then she set off down the trail they had just come from.

Lily stifled a laugh. Angus put his phone away and looked

down the two trails. "Which way are we headed?"

"South." Lily couldn't stop giggling. "How many times a week do you get that question?"

"Too often." Angus smiled for a second. He enjoyed wearing a kilt but could have done without the attention.

Angus and Lily resumed their hike. From time to time, they stopped to take a few pictures, but they still walked in silence. Lily debated what to say to Angus. He was a decent guy who never complained, so she figured if he wasn't talking, he was trying not to act grumpy and ruin the hike. Unfortunately, his silence was ruining the hike.

They travelled a variety of paths in the southern part of the park and eventually crossed Garden Lane. At this point, the trail moved steeply upward to a formation called the Siamese Twins. The two almost identical pillars of rock stood side by side at the top of a hill, which contained several large flat rocks that were convenient to sit on and eat lunch. After taking a few pictures of Pikes Peak through a keyhole shaped opening near the base of the twin rocks, Lily took off her pack and spread an old sheet on an unoccupied rock.

"It's a little early, but I thought we'd stop here." She began taking food items out of her pack.

"It's as good of place as any," Angus said. They had only walked about three miles, but he found he was hungry again.

Lily had fit quite a large picnic in her pack. She had a liter of a fizzy lemonade drink, several large roast beef sandwiches, a couple of apples, and thick slices of a fruit bread slathered with butter. Angus sat down and helped himself to a sandwich.

"This is quite good," Angus said between bites of food. He picked up the fruit bread. The dough was brown and sweet, and pieces of dried currants, blueberries, and golden raisins were mixed into it. "What the heck is this?"

Lily smiled. "It's called Bara Brith. Mom wanted to try her

hand at Scottish cooking, but I think it is actually Welsh."

Angus took another bite. "It's delicious, but it's not like anything my mom or aunts every baked." He continued to eat the bread and stare at the view.

After a few minutes, Lily couldn't wait any longer. "Angus, you haven't said much all day. Are you still upset about being accused of theft?"

Angus took a minute to consider his response. "Not really," he finally said. "I knew I was innocent, and after a while, so did they."

"Then what have you been thinking about all morning?" Lily had never seen Angus brood before and wondered if this was the moment when everything in their relationship would change and all his flaws would come to the surface.

Angus looked off into the distance. "This and that. Growing up in Scotland, doing a lot of hiking, wondering where I came from and where I'm going. The usual existential crap."

Lily was surprised. She knew bits and pieces of Angus's story, but he had never made a big thing of it. "Is Colorado a lot like Scotland?" she asked.

"The Highlands of Scotland aren't much like this. They are greener, and the climbing is a lot more difficult, more dangerous." Angus looked at Pikes Peak as he remembered. "The closest thing to it is Palmer Park, and it's different in lots of ways."

Lily hiked avidly and had gone to Palmer Park numerous times, but after getting lost multiple times, it wasn't her favorite place. "I can't imagine the hikes being any more challenging than Palmer Park," she said, her food forgotten. "It always seemed like every time I turned around, I was at the edge of a cliff and did not know where the trail continued."

"Aye," Angus sipped his water. "At least there are trails in Palmer Park. When I was a kid, I spent a lot of time exploring hills and cliffs where there weren't really trails. It was mighty dangerous and pretty stupid, but there it is."

"But you had your pals with you, right?" Lily asked. Angus hadn't ever talked about childhood friends, but Lily assumed Angus had hung around with some other kids.

"Not really. I spent a lot of time by myself. It's one thing I enjoy about Palmer Park. You can hike for a long time, sometimes even an hour, without seeing anyone. It's where I go when I want to be by myself."

"Is that what you wanted today, some solitude?" Lily wondering if she was imposing on Angus.

"Nah." Angus gave her a smile. "I didn't want to be alone with my thoughts, but I'm glad you let me have some space."

"Huh?" Lily didn't quite understand.

"Growing up, I spent so much time alone wanting to be with other people." Angus tried to clarify. "We were poor, and I was a kid with a funny name. I got picked on a lot and didn't have many friends."

"That's rotten." Lily felt uncomfortable. She had always naturally made friends and couldn't imagine Angus's pain.

"But then I joined the Army, and suddenly I had lots of friends and acquaintances. I enjoyed it a lot, but there were times I missed the solitude."

Lily nodded. She didn't get what Angus was saying, but now that he was talking, she was going to let him.

"But as for yesterday." Angus looked Lily in the eye for the first time that day. "That police detective making fun of my name got under my skin." He paused. "I know that it's just a technique, good cop-bad cop, to put a person under stress and see if they will let something slip, but it hit a sore spot."

"Because everyone always made fun of your name?" Lily asked. The sun went behind a cloud, and she suddenly felt a little cold. She shivered.

"Yes, but something more." Angus reached over to his pack. He pulled out a flannel shirt and handed it to Lily. "A man gets to middle age, and one day he starts taking stock of his life. After years of not thinking about it, I have spent a lot of time lately wondering about where I come from and what it means for me."

Lily accepted the shirt and wrapped it around her shoulders. "You mean you want to look for you dad again?"

"Aye," Angus replied. "I came to America to find my father, and somehow I lost focus along the way. I wonder if it is time to get back on track." As if to reinforce his resolve, Angus cleaned up the packaging from their lunch and put it in a plastic bag that he kept in his pack for trash.

"But in the meantime, you seem to have made a good life for yourself." Lily heard some crickets and wondered if that meant that a storm was on the way, despite the forecast.

"I have," Angus said. "It's a life that I could have never predicted when I left Scotland, but it turned out nicely. This seems like at a watershed moment. Before I can move on and start my own family, I feel like I need to know more about mine."

Lily wondered if she should read any meaning into Angus's comments about a family, but decided not to worry about it. They hadn't talked about being serious, and she wasn't sure that she was ready to settle down again either.

"Well, there are worse responses to a midlife crisis than to hire a private detective to find your dad." Lily drank the last of the sparkling lemonade from the bottle and replaced the cap. "You could, for example, buy a motorcycle or a sports car."

Angus laughed, "I always wanted a motorbike, but Aunty Ivy said they were too dangerous." Angus took the plastic bottle, put it in the trash bag, and tied the bag shut. "But it feels like cheating to hire a private detective. I've always felt that I had to be the one to find my father, that the process was just as important as the result."

"Well, do it the hard way then." Lily folded up the sheet. "I was going to offer to help. After all, I am a reference librarian."

"I didn't say that I had to do it all myself." Angus stuffed the trash bag in his pack. "Just that I don't want to hand the whole task off to a third party."

"Fair enough." Lily wanted to continue the conversation, but ominous clouds were rolling in. "Shall we stay on this trail?"

"Alright." Angus zipped up his pack and stood up. "How much longer do you want to hike?"

At that moment, they heard a rumble of thunder. Lily stood up to put on her pack, but then thinking better of it, she removed an oversized plastic zipper bag from a pocket, sealed her camera inside it, and put it the whole thing in her pack. Then she slung her pack on her back and looked down the trail. "I had planned to go around the northern tip of the Central Garden on the Palmer Trail, but now I wonder if we shouldn't cut through the Central Garden and get back to my car."

"I'm not afraid of getting wet, but I didn't get this far in life by taking too many chances. Let's take the most direct way back."

Lily led the way. After a few minutes, she asked, "So why is it so important for you to find your father? At this point, you are your own man. What will finding him do besides satisfy your curiosity, which is a completely valid reason to look for him?"

Angus looking out at the trail in front of them. "Well, I guess you have a point there, but it comes back to my name. I don't like it, and one thing I always wanted was to take my dad's last name."

They heard another rumble of thunder from the west and turned just in time to see a bolt of lightning hit Pikes Peak. Both hikers quickened their pace.

"But you know your dad's last name," Lily said. "It's Thompson, isn't it? Why don't you just change it now?"

"I guess I could." A droplet of rain hit Angus's face, and he wondered if he should get out his rain gear. "But I want to meet him first, maybe ask his permission. Also, what if he's a jerk? At that point, I might as well pick a random name and go with it."

"Maybe you could just take your wife's last name," Lily suggested. "Save yourself the trouble."

"Maybe," Angus said. Angus Rogers just didn't have a ring to it, in his opinion. A gust of wind followed by a volley of huge raindrops saved him from further comments. The trail quickly turned to mud.

"Shit," snapped Lily. "My raincoat is in the bottom of my bag."

Angus took off his pack and placed it on a rock. After a quick dig through it, he produced two plastic unisex rain ponchos. Putting them on while it was downpouring wasn't a straightforward task, but they managed.

"What a date this is turning out to be," Lily said. "If I remember right, we can get back to the road soon. Maybe we should just follow it back to the parking lot."

"Sounds good to me."

They soon found Garden Drive and followed it to Juniper Way Loop. The rain continued to lash down for another 10 minutes. Then as quickly as it had started, it stopped, and the sun came out. By then Angus and Lily were soaked through to the skin and their shoes were caked with mud and squelching with every step.

"Ach. I just want a shower and a hot drink," Angus said, as they trudged along the road toward Lily's car.

"Me too," Lily agreed. "Mutti won't be happy if we track a

bunch of mud inside."

"We'll go to my place. It's still a mess from the search, but if you are interested, I can show you the few pieces of information I have about my dad." Angus stopped and took off the poncho and helped Lily out of hers. By the time they reached Lily's car, much of the water in their clothes had evaporated, but their shoes were still a mess.

When Lily unlocked the car, Angus put his pack in the backseat and then spread the ponchos out along the floor. He took off his shoes and laid them on the layer of plastic. "Can you drive barefoot?"

"I think I have some sandals in the trunk." Lily dug them out.

Twenty minutes later, they pulled into the parking space behind Angus's townhouse.

"I don't even know where to start," Lily said as Angus unlocked his back door.

It was then Angus remembered his house was still a mess from yesterday's search. He hesitated at the door. "I'm sorry. I didn't take time to put everything right last night."

"Oh, Angus, Maggie told me all about it. It's a drag, but it's not your fault." Lily entered the townhouse, took off her sandals, and left them by the back door.

Angus gazed over his kitchen. A few of the cabinet doors were still open, and their contents had been disturbed, but the first floor wasn't nearly as affected as his bedroom had been. He was glad that he'd spent 15 minutes taming the worst of the chaos.

Lily was waiting for him, so he said, "Just head upstairs and jump in the shower. There's a robe on the back of the bathroom door that you can use if you like. Or I can set out a T-shirt and the pajama pants that Aunty Ivy left on the bed for you. Whatever you prefer."

"I'll take both and see what fits best," she said.

After Lily went into the bathroom, Angus searched through the drawers in the guest bedroom for anything that might fit her. Then he went downstairs.

When Lily came down 20 minutes later, the contents of their packs had been laid out to dry and their shoes had been scrubbed and left out on the small patch of concrete that served as Angus's front porch. Angus was barefoot in his kitchen, heating a pan of what appeared to be hot milk.

"I thought I would make hot chocolate from scratch." He poured the mixture into two cups on the counter. "I found a bottle of brandy in the cabinet above the fridge if you'd like to doctor yours."

Lily walked over and accepted the cup. She tasted Angus's concoction and was pleased with the result. "It delicious, thanks."

"I'll just go up and get in the shower then." Angus took his cup with him. As he walked over to his fireplace, he picked up a remote. Angus had converted it to gas when he'd moved in. "I know it's not frigid outside, but would you like me to turn this on?"

"Please." Lily took a seat on the couch and watched the little tongues of blue flame lick the fake log and sipped her drink. She heard water running upstairs and let her eyes wander around the room. Angus had furnished his townhouse simply. Over the years, he had purchased a sofa, a recliner, and a couple of comfy chairs, all in different neutral colors. On the walls, Angus had put up framed photos of nature scenes that he had taken on his travels. There was no television set, although a bookshelf held a variety of paperback novels.

The room was warm but not stuffy, and Lily felt sleepy. Not wanting to nod off, she picked up a library book that was sitting on an end table near her. Even before she read the blurb on the dust jacket, she knew it was a mystery novel. Angus was gaga for them.

Lily thought about getting her phone from the kitchen table and posting a photo of their hike on social media, but she also didn't feel like getting off the couch, so she started reading the novel. Days before the village's annual flower show, a British detective inspector was called out to investigate vandalism of a local woman's garden. Lily giggled at the thought that anyone would have time to investigate such a petty crime, but she assumed the murders would soon begin.

"That one has quite a body count," Angus said as he walked down the stairs in a fresh kilt and T-shirt. "By the time it is done the per capita murder rate of that charming hamlet is on par with Chicago."

Lily laughed. "I'm sorry, but this is unrealistic. No one would actually kill someone over first prize in a local contest."

Angus walked over to the table and looked at the objects that he had set out to dry. "Aye, you're right in the idea that no one goes on a killing spree about just roses or something trivial like that, well no one in their right mind." He picked up Lily's phone and brought it over to her. "But the one thing that I think these books get right is that people's motivations are complex and that small things add up. You never know what the straw that breaks the camel's back will be."

Lily accepted her phone and considered Angus's point for a moment. "Maybe. I don't understand why you are fascinated with this genre though. What about Westerns or those books with the adventurer who has the neat cars?"

"I read a lot of adventure stories when I was a kid," Angus admitted, sitting down. "But I got started on mysteries because I thought it would give me ideas about how to find my dad." He looked down at his hands. "It's kind of stupid, but I work hard all day, and I like the escape that these books provide."

"Fair enough." Lily put the book back down on the end table.

"So, I have something that I'd like to show you. Let me go get it." Angus went upstairs and returned with two boxes that had once held hiking boots. Both appeared to be labelled. He put the boxes on the coffee table in front of them and opened the first one, taking out a picture and a letter. "This is the only picture that I have of my dad that's not a unit photo." Angus handed it to Lily.

Lily took a moment to examine the snapshot. It was a 3 by 5-inch color photo that showed a man and a young woman in front of a small waterfall. The man was casually but neatly dressed and seemed to have a blonde crewcut. The woman looked quite young and thin, almost more of a girl, and was wearing a simple print dress. Although the overall quality of both the picture and the print weren't great, Lily had to remind herself that in the film era decent photos were much harder to come by. Lily turned the photo over and read the name and date.

"I assume the woman in the picture is your mom," Lily said after a few moments. She was glad that Angus was opening up to her, but she wasn't sure what to say.

"Yeah." Angus took the letter from its envelope. "Her name was Heather. She was 16 when that picture was taken."

"That's young." Lily instantly regretted the words. "Sorry."

Angus nodded. "It's alright. She was a bit young to be keeping company with an American soldier, but she and I both grew up in a small town, and I think she saw my dad as a way out."

Angus's candor surprised Lily. "Why do you think that?" she asked.

Angus opened up the letter and smoothed the pages. "While I go check on the laundry, you can read this. The tone of it speaks volumes." He handed Lily the letter and headed to the utility room near the back of the townhouse.

Lily looked at the letter in her hands. It consisted of two pages which might have been a sheet of typing paper folded over and torn in half. The writer had printed his message with a blue pen. His handwriting was neither sloppy nor neat, and the signature was unreadable. Lily skimmed the letter, and the gist was clear. Private Thompson was sorry to hear that Heather was pregnant, but he had looked on their time together as a casual affair. As soon as he had returned to America, he had married his high school sweetheart, and he felt he could not provide any support, financial or otherwise, to Heather. Lily noted that Thompson neither acknowledged nor denied being Angus's father. The letter seemed apologetic but firm.

"I can see how you drew your conclusions," Lily said as Angus reemerged and sat down.

"It's a pretty common scenario," Angus acknowledged. "I try not to judge either of them too harshly. They were both young."

Lily felt the need to tread lightly, so she changed the subject. "That seems like a pretty distinctive waterfall. Any idea where it was taken or by whom?"

Angus took back the photo and examined it. He already knew the answer to one of the questions, but he wanted to confirm it in his mind's eye. "The waterfall doesn't have a name. It's about a mile or two east of my grandparents' house at a popular picnicking spot." He turned the photo over in his hands a couple of times absentmindedly. "One of my mom's friends probably took this photo. Aunt Ivy seems to remember that Mom had a friend who was a real shutterbug."

Over the years, Angus had stopped referring to the town where he was born by its actual name. When he was in the Army, people would ask him where he was from, and most of the time Angus sensed they couldn't have found Scotland on a map of Europe, let alone have a clue where his village of 500 people was. It was like his friend Chad Larson said, "I'm from Oconomowoc,

WI, a town that even people from Wisconsin can't locate." Instead, Angus had used phrases like "my grandparents' village" or "it's an hour north of Edinburg." People would nod and then the conversation would move on, usually to asking what Angus wore under his kilt or if he liked haggis.

Lily folded the letter and returned it to Angus. "Sylvester Thompson isn't that common of a name. What have you been able to find out about him?"

Angus returned the letter to its envelope. "I know that Private Sylvester Thompson was stationed at Fort Stewart, GA in 1981, but apparently he was an unremarkable fellow." He withdrew a photocopy of a large group photo from the box and pointed to a head in the third row. "There he is with his unit in the spring of 1981. He wasn't in the unit photo the next spring, and no one seems to remember where he transferred." Angus paused. "Part of the problem could be that by the time I was asking questions, it was almost 20 years later."

Lily watched Angus put everything back in the box. "That makes sense. The Army must keep track of where it sends soldiers though."

Angus nodded. "They do, but where those records are and who has access to them? That's something I don't know how to find out."

"Maybe you should just hire a private detective." Lily was sure that if she contacted several colleagues that she could track down Angus's dad, but she knew that wouldn't satisfy him. Neither would a private detective, but maybe if Angus hired the investigator himself, it would be enough involvement for him.

"Maybe." Angus stared at the box as if in thought.

"So, what's in the other box?" Lily asked.

"Pictures of my family, some that my Aunt Ivy brought over the last time she visited me in the States." Angus opened the box. He flipped through the loose photos until he found the one he wanted. "This is my grandfather Angus MacBangus on his wedding day."

Lily looked at the picture. It was a black and white studio portrait showing a bride and groom and their two attendants. Except for the bride's dress, everyone else's clothes looked worn but clean and well pressed. At least everyone was smiling, although it was hard to make out on the groom's face because of a large burn scar.

"It was the late 1940s, and there was still rationing, so they made due." Angus pointed to the bride and the best man in turn, he said, "That's my grandmother Mabel, and her brother John."

Lily tried to see a resemblance between the siblings without success. "Who is the maid of honor?"

"No idea. Probably a friend of Mabel's."

"Tell me about your grandfather. He looks like a fellow with a few interesting stories. Are there lots of MacBanguses in Scotland?"

"There aren't." Angus set the photo aside. "In fact, my grandfather is a bit of a mystery man, but not in the same way as my dad."

"What do you mean?" Lily asked. Angus's fixation with his origins became more understandable.

"Well, my grandmother's maiden name was Wilson. She grew up on the same farm I did, and she had five older brothers." Angus found a family group photo. "This was taken on my great grandparents 25th wedding anniversary."

"That must have been quite an occasion." Lily looked at the black-and-white photo that was still in the special cardboard sleeve from the photographer.

"I'm sure it was. Unfortunately, a couple of years later all five brothers went off to fight in WWII, and four of them were killed."

"That's horrible." Lily remembered that one of her great uncles had been killed in WWII. It all seemed so pointless.

"Aye," Angus said. "Mabel kept the farm going the best that she could, and when her brother John came home, he brought a fellow soldier home with him to help."

"Your grandpa Angus?" Lily saw where this was going.

"Indeed." Angus picked up his grandparents' wedding photo and pointed to his grandfather's scar. "He'd been injured by flying shrapnel and was apparently a city boy at heart, but he was a hard worker and learned quickly. After a few months, he was pretty much indispensable on the farm."

"Was it a love match with your gran or just a practicality?" Lily asked.

"A little of both," Angus said. "There weren't a lot of young men around after the war, and most of them wanted to live in the city. From what I remember of my gran, I wouldn't say she was unhappy."

"So why did you say your grandfather was a mystery?" Lily asked. "It seems like a pretty straightforward story."

"It would be, except that when it came time for the wedding, he didn't have anyone to invite. Now this is all coming second hand from my Aunty Ivy who got it from my gran, but Grandpa Angus said he had no family left. When he was in his cups, he'd sometimes talk about his mother in Glasgow, but she was dead by the end of the war. In any event, my gran said that he received no letters in the entire time they were married Of course, that could have been because he struggled to read and write."

When Angus paused, Lily tried to take it all in. "That seems unusual for the time."

"Gran got the impression he hadn't gone to school much,

63

that he had spent his youth working odd jobs," Angus said. "Or it could have been that he wasn't good at school and quit to go to work."

"That's quite possible," Lily said. Then she asked. "By the way, what does 'in his cups' mean?"

"When he had a lot to drink," Angus clarified, "Which wasn't often. Angus was a usually a temperate man."

"Another rather uncharacteristic feature," Lily said. "Did Ivy ever get any more backstory?"

"Not a lot." Angus shook his head. "John never was the same after the war, and he took to drink. He was killed in an accident with a tractor a couple years after my gran got married. Maybe that's why my grandfather didn't like to have alcohol in the house, or it could just be a coincidence."

"It's hard to know. Are you planning to do research on your grandfather as well, when you have the time?"

"Nah, I leave that all to my Aunt Ivy. She's retired now, and she seems to enjoy it."

"With a name like MacBangus, you would think it would be easy to track down relatives," Lily said.

"You would think so, but Ivy can't find a single MacBangus in Glasgow or anywhere."

"Maybe it got misspelled somewhere along the line." Lily knew that the spelling of many names changed over time, but she couldn't figure out how to get MacBangus from any surname she was familiar with.

"Maybe." Angus considered this idea but decided not to worry about it. "One mystery at a time." He put away the photos and took the boxes upstairs.

CHAPTER 4

Monday, November 5

Angus tried to put his three days of drama behind him and to go back to his usual routine. Tuesdays he went to Trivia Night at Macduff's. Thursday nights he worked an eight-hour shift at the Veterans Support Helpline. Saturdays he got up early, cleaned his townhouse, and shopped for his weekly groceries. Sundays he spent all or part of the day with Lily and Jaiden. The other days weren't as predictable, but Angus felt like he had a good balance of work, relationships, and volunteer work.

After Maggie sued him, Mr. Peterson paid his bill in full plus court costs. Maggie had heard through the grapevine that he had paid a friend of a friend to do all the touch up work in his basement. She laughed when her source told her the person botched it and another contractor had to be hired to redo the repairs.

Detectives Green and Harrington didn't find Mr. Peterson's watches or computer. They listed all the serial numbers in a database of stolen property and gave him a police report for his insurance company, who promptly paid out the claim. The entire process took less than a month during which they investigated many other burglaries, some with similar modus operandi and some that were completely different.

Detective Harrington put the card that Angus had given him in his wallet and forgot about it for a couple of weeks. Then he got a call from an old Army buddy to inform him that a mutual friend had been killed in a helicopter crash in Afghanistan.

The next three days were a bit of a blur that ended with Dan waking up on his bathroom floor in a pool of vomit. Once he was semi-functional, Dan retrieved Angus's card and called the main number. He'd started to attend weekly meetings and had even run into Angus once or twice at the Veterans Center.

In early November, just when he had recovered from investigating Halloween related shenanigans, Detective Harrington received the following cryptic message on his voicemail. "If you want to clear a bunch of cases, look at where Angus Mac-Bangus has been working lately."

Dan went through the motions of following up on the tip, even though he was pretty sure it was bogus. A quick trace revealed that the call had come from a prepaid cell phone. No surprise there. Dan realized he was going to need to bring in Jack and Angus again, and he was not looking forward to it. When he met with Detective Green to inform her, he found she agreed with him.

"I just don't see those two as criminal masterminds, and I think this will be a waste of time." Green had been going over the previous month's statistics when Harrington had found her. "But with the number of open cases on our books, we have to investigate any lead."

Harrington shifted in his chair. "Look, maybe I should stay out of this. I run into MacBangus from time to time at veteran's events."

Green looked up at Harrington. He'd been through a rough patch a couple of months back and taken a week off, but lately his explosive anger had been a lot more controlled. "You didn't mention knowing him when we first questioned him."

Harrington began to sweat. He'd been very vague with Green about pulling over MacBangus. She had also given him the impression that she preferred not to know.

"When I followed up with him, he mentioned he counselled veterans and gave me some information. I checked out one of their groups, and I've run into him once or twice."

Green raised an eyebrow. "I don't see a big problem with that," she said. "Besides, let's keep this simple at first. I'll call Jack's wife and ask her for a list of addresses where they have worked in the last three months. We'll see if there is any overlap with robberies in the same time period. Chances are it won't go any further than that."

"Sounds good." Harrington hoped Green's prediction was correct.

Wednesday, November 7

"So, I'm guessing by that look on your face that you're not happy with what you found." Detective Green had just come into the office and found Detective Harrington staring at an anno-tated map and calendar, which he had put up on a white board in their squad room.

"Not in the slightest, although I should be," Dan said. De-tective Green had asked him to brief her this morning, and he had come in early to review the details. "I'll get us some coffee, and then I can take you through it."

Detective Green considered looking for the zipper in the back of her colleague's head to confirm that aliens had switched him out. While Harrington treated her with respect, he rarely did nice things like get them coffee. Something must have jarred him.

"I'll get the coffee." Green offered. "Give me five minutes. I need to check my email and phone messages." She walked over to her desk and got to work.

A little while later, she and Harrington were sitting in front of the white board sipping coffee so bitter and burnt that no amount of cream and sugar could cover up the taste. Green often wondered how anyone could mess up coffee this much.

"The tip panned out then?" Green saw 10 dots on the map and 10 dates on the calendar.

"Beyond my wildest dreams." Harrington's voice was full of irony. "I had come around to the idea that MacBangus was a good guy. I mean he just seems so squeaky clean, but the evidence is compelling."

"Well, you know what I always say about people who appear too good to be true." Green put down her cup and took a small notebook from the pocket of her blazer.

"That they usually are," Harrington said. Generally, they dealt with scumbags, but Green had a point. Most fine, upstanding citizens had a secret or peccadillo, and while they were seldom criminal and usually financial infidelity or just regular old infidelity, it was rare to find someone without something that they'd rather keep out of the public eye.

"Exactly." Green flipped open the notebook and took out a pen. "Why don't you fill me in."

Dan stood up and walked over the whiteboard. He took a marker out of the tray and removed the cap. "In the last seven weeks, 10 properties that MacBangus has worked at have been burglarized." He used the marker to gesture at the map.

"What about Jack Evans? Was he at any of the properties?"

Harrington looked at his notes on a yellow legal pad. "Jack worked with Angus on two of the jobs, but Angus is the common denominator. All the burglaries happened at places that he worked. No robberies happened at locations where only Jack worked."

"How do you know that?" Green asked. "Did Maggie give you that information?" The Evanses had been very cooperative, but Detective Green wondered if they might be throwing Angus under the bus.

Harrington took out an invoice from a sheaf of papers

and handed it to Green. He pointed near the bottom of the paper. "Maggie always notes which person is at which job on the invoice. I asked if it was about payroll, and she says that part of it, but the other half is that people sometimes call months later with issues, and it helps to know who did the repair."

"That Maggie is a smart cookie." Green observed. "What else do the robberies have in common besides Angus working at the property?"

"The robberies never occurred on Tuesday or Thursday nights." Harrington showed some dates on the calendar. "We already know that Angus attends a Trivia Night on Tuesday, and I know he volunteers at the Veterans Support Center on Thursday nights."

"Convenient," Green said. "Ten robberies in seven weeks, so that a robbery or two each week. What's the most common day?"

"That's a little problematic to nail down," Harrington said. "The robberies all occurred when the residents weren't at home. The ones that happened on Monday and Wednesday nights were noticed immediately, but four of the robberies occurred while the residents were out of town for the weekend. They could have happened any time between Friday and Sunday nights."

Green made some notes, and Harrington waited on her. "As I recall, the Petersons were home on the evening that their house was robbed, but all the subsequent burglaries occurred when the houses were empty. I don't like it when things don't fit a pattern."

Harrington considered this. "Well, maybe it was because Angus knew Peterson intended to take the watches to the jeweler, and he had to act fast. He couldn't wait for them to both leave the house."

"Make sense, but still it's bold, especially if it was his first robbery. Wait, was it the first robbery?"

"From what I can tell." Harrington popped the cap back on the marker and nervously clicked it on and off. "We started by asking Maggie for their jobs from the last three months, but when I found several burglaries, I asked her for records back until the beginning of the year. No robberies of Jack and Maggie's clients occurred before the Peterson robbery on August 21. All the robberies have happened since then. However, Angus hadn't been to some of the properties that were robbed in almost six months."

Green took a large sip of her coffee. It was too early in the morning. "I think I get that, but can you give me an example?"

Harrington scanned his yellow legal pad. "On March 22, Angus fixed the drain on a bathtub at 9152 Nevermind Drive. Sometime over the weekend of October 12th to the 14th, some-one broke into the house and stole some jewelry and a tablet computer."

Green laughed at the unusual street name - only in Color-ado Springs. "Seven months is quite a long time to wait to rob a house. It's long enough that I almost wonder if it's related."

"I would agree if there weren't this." Harrington took out a folder with a police report. "In this particular case, the house had two security cameras, which were disabled late Friday morning with black grease."

"Like at the Peterson's house," Green said. "I'm guessing several people knew they were going out of town."

"Yeah." Harrington consulted his notes. "They were going to Vegas for their anniversary. The wife planned the trip four months in advance. They got a friend to come and feed the cat, and the husband announced their trip on social media."

"Practically asking to be robbed." Green tisked. "Did the Evans or MacBangus know the residents socially, by chance?"

"Nope, but as you pointed out, the residents made some

bad choices."

"Well, it looks like we'll need to bring MacBangus in again," Green said. "What else do I need to know?"

"Except for the Peterson burglary, the robberies have a lot in common." Harrington took the cap off the dry erase marker and wrote each item. "First, none happened on Tuesday or Thursday nights. Second, the residents weren't at home when the property was robbed. Third, only small items were taken like watches, jewelry, cash, tablet or laptop computers, never more than could fit in a small bag. Fourth, most of the properties didn't have cameras, but if they did, the burglars avoided them or disabled them with black grease."

"And none of the items have showed up in local pawn shops?" Green asked as she copied the list into her notebook.

"Nope, gone without a trace. Lots of jewelry though, so maybe there's a fence involved."

"I just don't see MacBangus knowing a fence," Green said. "That doesn't seem to be the crowd he runs with."

Harrington pondered this for a moment. "Maybe an old friend from the military. Most people land on their feet, but not everyone."

"Seems like a stretch to me," Green said. "Bring him in. Hopefully he and Jack will have a decent alibi for one or more of the robberies."

Harrington called Maggie and tracked down Angus and Jack with her help. All three of them agreed to meet Green and Harrington at the station to be interviewed. The detectives began by questioning Maggie, who provided herself and Jack alibis for two of the weekend robberies. The couple enjoyed travelling, sometimes by using last-minute deals. It didn't mean that they weren't colluding with Angus, but it reinforced Green's instinct that this might all just be a bizarre coincidence or a setup.

When the officers left their interview with Maggie, they went to down the hall to the room that Angus was being kept in.

"He's just been sitting there reading his book for the last 45 minutes." A uniformed officer informed Green and Harrington. "He's been fidgeting a bit, but generally he's been pretty chill."

Green thanked the uniformed officer and turned to Harrington. "How do you want to play this? You know him better than I do."

"Straight," Harrington said. "I think we'll get more if we just lay it all out." He glanced into the interview room through a one-way mirror. "Besides, does a criminal mastermind bring a book called 'Death of an Honest Man' to a police station with him?"

Green looked at the cover of MacBangus's paperback and did a double take. She couldn't suppress a giggle. "I've got one better. A friend of mine once took 'Death of a Dentist' from the same series with her to a dental cleaning. It was just the book she had with her; she didn't even think of it."

"What happened?"

"Well, the hygienist thought it was hilarious, but the dentist got nervous. Thankfully, she didn't have any cavities." Green smiled. "Although her next visit, she was scheduled with another member of the practice."

Harrington chuckled as well and after composing himself, he opened the door to the interview room for Green.

Angus looked up from his book and, seeing the pair, marked his page. "Good afternoon."

"Good afternoon, Mr. MacBangus," Detective Green said. "We have a couple of dates we'd like to ask you about."

Over the next ten minutes, Detective Green went through the dates of several robberies, and each time Angus's answer about his whereabouts was that he was probably at home. "I'm a creature of habit," he said.

Maybe that's the problem thought Green. She flipped her notebook to a new page. "Let's try this then, Angus. Tell me any time in the last few months when you've broken your routine. Have you gone out of town or called in sick? Anything."

Angus thought for a minute. "I took Lily and Jaiden camping at Eleven Mile State Park on the second weekend of September. Jaiden turned 12, and his mom bought him a kayak. I rented one, and we spent a lot of time out on the water."

Green glanced at the notes on Harrington's legal pad. There had been a burglary the Wednesday before and the Monday after that weekend. "When exactly did you leave and return?"

"I left early Friday morning," Angus recalled. "We had reserved one of the primitive camping sites, and I had arranged for a boat to transport our gear out there at noon. After that, I stayed and set up camp, and Lily brought Jaiden as soon as he finished school for the day." Angus paused. "They left Sunday morning around 9, but the boat to pick up our gear wasn't scheduled to meet me until noon, so I stayed and waited for it. I got home around 4 or 5. I stopped for a meal on the way."

Harrington frowned. "Did you work the next day?"

"I wasn't scheduled to." Angus changed his tone. "I wanted a day to recover, but Jack went out to fix a dripping faucet and ended up redoing most of a bathroom. Maggie needed me to pick up some routine jobs."

"So, did you work a full day?" Green asked.

"Maggie called me about noon. I got to the first job at maybe 1:30 and worked until maybe 9. That's a little late for me, but we had jobs that needed to get done."

Harrington recalled the circumstances of the Monday robbery. A single woman had gone up to Denver for some sort of event and had met an old friend for dinner. One thing had led to another, and she had stayed the night with him. She'd only intended to be gone from noon Monday until maybe 10 or 11, but she had actually been away until midday the next day. It would have required Angus to act on the fly, but he could have robbed the property. "Can you tell us the exact time you finished with work?" Harrington asked, remembering that Maggie asked Jack and Angus to text her to clock in and out.

Angus took out his phone and scrolled through his messages. It took a while. "I texted Maggie when I left the job site at 8:30. Maybe I got home around 9."

"Can anyone confirm that?" Harrington asked. "Your neighbor, Hank, perhaps."

"Nope," Angus said. "I was exhausted. I had a sandwich and went to bed."

Green had written something in her notebook, but now Harrington saw she was doodling. "Can you think of any other unusual events in the last couple of months?" she asked. "Maybe something a bit more spontaneous than a camping trip."

Angus considered this for a minute. He spent some time looking at his phone. "Wednesday, October 17. My girlfriend Lily called me around 11 PM. She and Jaiden had been throwing up since after dinner, and she wanted to go to the ER for some anti-nausea drugs. Her dad doesn't like to drive at night, but Jaiden had thrown up nine times in an hour, and she figured he wouldn't stop."

Harrington consulted his notes. As he had mentioned to Green earlier, there had been a robbery sometime over the weekend of the 12th through 14th of October and then another on Saturday, October 20. The robbery on the 20th had been unusual in that it had happened during the day while the family had been at a Cub Scout day camp. Sadly, Angus had what sounded like a really credible alibi, but not for any of the robberies that they suspected him of.

"So, I drove over to her house and picked them up," Angus continued. "The emergency room was super busy. It always seems to be."

"And how long were you there?" Harrington asked.

"Hours, I mean hours," Angus said. "They gave Lily and Jaiden some medicine when they triaged them. Having people barfing in the waiting room isn't good for business, but then we sat there a long time waiting on this and that. For good measure, they tested the two of them for the flu, and they both had it. In the end, the doctor sent them home with an antiviral and a bunch of meds. I dropped them off at maybe 5 AM."

"Did you take the day off?" Green asked.

Harrington didn't know where she was going with this, but he played along.

"Not exactly," Angus continued. "I had texted Maggie the night before, and we kept in touch. After I got home, I caught a few hours of sleep and did a couple of jobs in the afternoon. But I was still pretty tired, so I asked someone to cover my shift at the Veterans Center."

"Did you get the flu as well?" Green asked.

Angus shifted in his chair. "Yeah, I did. I felt really run down on Friday afternoon, so I texted Maggie to get Jack to cover my last job, and stopped by an Urgent Care on the way home. They confirmed I had the flu, gave me a bunch of medicine and sent me home."

"And how many days did you spend at home in bed?"

"I felt pretty rotten. I spent all of Saturday in bed, and then Sunday Lily brought some soup over to me."

"And you never left your townhouse on Saturday?"

"No. I could hardly leave my bed let along walked downstairs, get in the truck, and drive somewhere."

"Would you excuse up for a moment, please?" Detective Green motioned for Harrington to follow her into the hall. She closed the door. "He didn't rob anyone that Saturday, and as I recall Jack and Maggie got last minute tickets for a German food festival in Denver and were gone from 9 AM to 11 PM. We'll need to confirm details like times from their toll transponder and that Angus went to the Urgent Care, but as far as I am concerned, this puts them in the clear."

Harrington nodded. "You're saying that having the flu is enough of an alibi for you? I'm sorry, I don't think MacBangus did it either, but it's shaky."

Green sighed. "Look, last winter my entire family got the flu. I am a tough gal, but even with antivirals, I was down for two days minimum." She paused. "He still could have done it, but wouldn't you think if you felt like death that you would postpone the robbery you had planned for another day?"

"Yeah. I probably would." Harrington looked at his notes for the list of stolen items. "Nothing was time sensitive. A tablet computer, gaming system, several rings, and maybe $50 in cash."

"A decent haul, but not worth getting out of bed if you felt like shit, and bold. You'd have to be pretty desperate to rob someone in broad daylight while not at 100 percent."

"Unless one of them has secret debts or a drug problem, I don't see these three as being that desperate." Harrington observed. "Still, it's a lot of coincidences. I think we need to dig a little deeper."

Green hesitated. "You're right. We have to rely on facts, not our instincts." She looked back at MacBangus in the interview room. He had returned to his book. "I'll ask them if we can search their residences again, while you work on their finances."

"Will do." Harrington doubted that Angus and the

Evanses would agree to a search, but it never hurt to ask. It would save time asking a judge for a warrant. Then he added, "They might also have a place where they store equipment for the business. Make sure that gets searched as well."

◆ ◆ ◆

While Harrington went off to his tasks, Green went back into the interview room with Angus. Once again, he agreed to a search of his vehicle and house although he looked worried. Next Green went to talk to Jack and Maggie, whom she found not nearly as cooperative.

"I have nothing to hide," Jack said firmly, "but if you want to look at my house and storage shed, get a warrant. This is ludicrous."

"If you and Angus didn't rob those people, who do you think did?" Green asked. "Have you pissed someone off?"

Maggie was defensive but calm. "We've had several dissatisfied clients, but who doesn't? A lot of times we've been able to work with them to address their concerns, and once or twice, I have called another company who's in our line of work and asked them to make changes for clients at our expense." She looked Green in the eye. "We fix toilets and paint walls. At the very worst, our clients will leave us a bad online review or maybe report us to the Better Business Bureau."

Green continued to question Jack and Maggie for a few more minutes but learned nothing more of consequence, so she went with the team that was preparing to search Angus's townhouse. While Angus sat out front, Green and two uniformed officers searched every nook and cranny of the residence including the crawlspace, which Angus helpfully showed them. As they were wrapping things up, one of the uniformed officers came back from the carport.

"Ma'am," he said. "I've just remembered. This fellow's

neighbor has security cameras. Do you think they would be of any help?"

Green raised her eyebrows. "Security cameras?"

"They had a problem with kids breaking into cars a couple years back, and some residents installed cameras in their carports and by their front doors, helped us catch some teenagers a couple of months ago."

Green motioned for the officer to follow her and found Angus on the front stoop. "Angus, do you know which of your neighbors has cameras?" she asked.

Angus's townhouse was the second in a block of four units. A sidewalk ran along all the front doors of the townhouses, and each residence had a covered parking space, which could be reached by the back door. The sidewalk led from the main road that ran through the center of the townhouse community to a fence that separated the property from a steep sandstone bluff.

Angus scanned the front of the building. "I think Nick Swartz installed one last year." He pointed to the unit on the end, beyond which you could see the sheer rock wall. "But I think he only has a camera on the carport. I don't see how that helps."

Green considered this. "Well, it could tell us that your vehicle didn't move on the evenings of certain robberies."

"Aye." Angus realized he still could have gone out the front door and used a different vehicle, but he decided not to mention it. "Maybe Nick is working from home today."

The group walked down to Nick's door and rang the bell. After a minute, a middle-aged man wearing a dark colored polo shirt and tactical cargo pants came to the door. "Angus, Officer Miller," he said as he stared at the people on his doorstep. "Is everything all right?"

After Officer Miller introduced Detective Green, she filled Mr. Swartz in on the situation. "It would be very helpful for us to see your footage for the dates in question," she concluded. "Although I imagine you don't keep footage for very long."

"I'll see what I can do." Nick motioned for them to come in. "I keep 30 days of videos backed up in the cloud." Nick excused himself and went upstairs to get a laptop, which he placed on the kitchen table. He went to a website and logged into an account. "What date do you want me to pull up?"

"Saturday, October 20th." Green knew the date without having to consult her notebook.

Nick tapped a few keys and brought up a video showing the carport that all four residents shared. He started the video at midnight when there were four vehicles parked and fast forwarded through the day. Vehicles came and went, but Angus's truck didn't move.

Green nodded. "Can we go back and see when Angus arrived home?" she asked.

Nick returned to midnight and then rewound the recording. At 5:42 PM, Angus pulled his truck into his spot. He exited the vehicle carrying a brown paper bag and a lunch sack. Nick paused the recording.

"That's all the medicine they gave me at the Urgent Care." Angus pointed to the bag.

"Can we look at Sunday as well?" Green asked. Angus hadn't taken his truck out, but she wanted to verify some other details.

Nick obliged and soon everyone saw Lily coming from off camera, heading toward Angus's back door holding a plastic container.

"What about the front entrances?" Green asked.

Nick furrowed his brow. "I have one installed, but it's been on the fritz since we had that storm in early August." He confessed. "I've been working from home more lately, so I haven't bothered to get it fixed."

Green felt bile rise into her stomach. As unlikely as it was that a flu-riddled Angus had gotten out of bed, walked out his front door, and hitched a ride with an unknown accomplice, reasonable doubt still existed. It would be nice for him to have a cast-iron alibi.

"What about that guy who has the camera pointed at the visitor parking next to here? Does that pick up the end of your walkway?" Officer Miller remembered reviewing footage from that angle on his previous visit to the complex. The teenagers from the last spree of robberies had been dumb enough to park in the visitor lot.

"Maybe," Nick said. "Those are Jimmy Kim's cameras. Want me to find out?"

"Yes," Green replied.

While Nick made a couple of phone calls, Angus thought about his experiences with Jimmy Kim. When he had first moved to the townhouse community, Angus had attended a few HOA meetings, but he had been turned off pretty quickly. The first meeting he had attended had been in the aftermath of a string of cars being broken into and some of the community's mail boxes being vandalized. Jimmy had proposed that the HOA install security cameras throughout the complex, and since he owned a security company, he had put together a bid. The cost wasn't outrageous, but the HOA had encountered problems with using residents for contracts, and then a few residents had brought up privacy concerns. In the end, Jimmy had told every-one he would give them a discounted rate to have cameras installed on their property and left it at that. Angus hadn't realized that Jimmy lived in the building across the road from him.

Nick interrupted Angus's thoughts. "Jimmy will be home from work in a couple of minutes and can show you the footage you need."

While they waited, Nick brought up footage for two other robbery dates, each showing Angus at home for most of the time. The only thing that Angus brought home the previous weekend in October had been groceries in sacks from several local markets. When Mr. Kim arrived, his videos showed similar results. Angus had not exited his apartment from the evening of Friday, October 19, until the morning of Monday, October 21. Similarly, Angus had brought no suspicious items into his house during the weekend of the previous robbery.

"Well, thank you, gentlemen," Detective Green said. "That clears some things up."

She walked Angus back to his front door. "If you want a piece of free advice, I'd vary your routine a bit more. I doubt there's a conspiracy to frame you for these robberies, but it's just a good practice to mix things up a bit. Otherwise, you may come home some Tuesday night and find that you've been burgled."

"Thanks," Angus said. "I'll keep that in mind."

CHAPTER 5

Thursday, November 8

Angus had fallen into his bed exhausted the previous night around 10, but he had woken up around 5:30 AM and been unable to go back to sleep. After the search of her house and storage shed was complete, Maggie had called off their jobs for the rest of the week and taken Jack to Vegas. She had suggested to Angus that he get out of town for a few days, preferably somewhere that would give him an unimpeachable alibi. Angus had also been in touch with Lily on Wednesday. Her day off this week was Friday, so Angus was facing the prospect of an entire day to himself.

The last time Angus had gone out of town was camping with Lily and Jaiden at Eleven Mile State Park, and while it was a bit too cold for that, Angus didn't want to be around people. He wanted to grab his daypack and drive out of town, somewhere like Mueller State Park or Florissant Fossil Beds National Monument. He could just park his truck in a parking lot and go for a wander in the woods, but something stopped him, a nagging feeling that what he did in the next couple of days would have a profound effect on his future. It all seemed rather silly, but he couldn't shake the sensation. His instinct about the Peterson house had been right, after a fashion, but that was how things were for him. He got bits and pieces here and there.

Once he had given up on sleep, Angus had made himself a big breakfast and a cup of tea. He logged onto his email to check the Veterans Hotline volunteer schedule for the week. As always, he was scheduled from 4 to midnight today, but he was glad to note that Mark Herrera was finishing a shift this morning.

Mark had served twenty years in the Air Force as a nurse and had continued working the night shift at an ER when he retired. He was in his late 40s and divorced for many years. After his retirement, Mark had noticed that many of his friends and folks he had served with were having trouble coping with civilian life. He wrote a grant and opened the Veteran Support Center and hadn't looked back.

Angus and Mark had met at a mutual friend's BBQ about three years before and had talked. Angus had found the idea of veterans helping veterans to be very appealing and had come by the Center from time to time. In his first few visits, Angus had spent some time one of one with Mark telling him about his life and his challenges. Mark was one of the few people besides Jack that Angus had told about his "second sight." Rather than mock Angus's insights, Mark encouraged Angus to listen to them; he wasn't much of a believer in the supernatural, but as he always said, you don't look a gift horse in the mouth. Eventually, Angus took some training and started working the hotline one evening a week.

Around 7 AM, Angus checked the toolbox in his truck and headed toward the Veterans Center, which was located in a historic house near Colorado College. The house was divided between three renters. Everyone shared a kitchen and two bathrooms. The other two tenants were psychologists, who each used one of the old bedrooms as an office and another for meeting clients. The Veterans Center used the remaining bedroom as an office and call center for the hotline and the large living room as a place for their support groups to meet. Angus remembered that the faucet in the kitchen was leaking. He had been meaning to fix it for weeks now, but he'd been so busy. Well, no time like the present.

The front door was locked when Angus arrived, so he rang the doorbell. A couple of minutes later, Mark tramped down the stairs and opened the door.

"Angus MacBangus." The balding man with a thick beard and mustache greeted him. "I haven't seen you in a while. What the heck are you doing here so early?"

"Had the day off," Angus said. "Thought I'd tackle that kitchen faucet."

Mark stepped back and let Angus come in. He wore his usual all-nighter outfit - a T-shirt, pajama bottoms, and flip flops. A small paunch stuck out above the waist band. Other than that, he appeared to be in fine shape with muscular arms and a thin face. "That's kind of you, Angus, but the landlord is supposed to take care of that sort of thing. Actually, I gave him Maggie's number a couple of months ago."

Angus shrugged. Most landlords were decent people, but they rarely wanted to pay for a full hour of labor for such a minor job. "I could always get Maggie to send him an invoice." He looked up at the clock on the wall. "Are you almost done?"

"Mostly." Mark pushed some buttons on the portable phone he had brought down with him. "Let me just set up the forwarding to the national hotline. Sheri called last night and said that her work scheduled changed."

"Cool," Angus said. "Hey, on your way out, could you stop by and catch up?"

"Sure," Mark replied. "Why do I feel you have quite a story? More trouble about that burglary?" Angus had talked to Mark soon after the Peterson robbery, but then as soon as Maggie put him back on the job, he'd been too busy to follow up.

"Something like that," Angus said. He turned down the hall towards the kitchen. "See you in a couple of minutes."

When Angus got there, he put his toolbox on the table. While the refrigerator was a vintage Frigidaire, the stove and the sink fixtures had been updated in the 1980s. He opened up the cabinet under the sink and shut off the water. Then he took the faucet apart. The O-ring had all but disintegrated over the years. Angus replaced it with one from his bag and had the faucet back together in a few minutes. He was washing his hands when Mark appeared in the doorway, two cups of coffee in his hands.

"This was left in the pot." He offered a cup that said "World's Greatest Dad" to Angus. He warned. "It's a couple hours old, but whatever."

"Thanks." Angus accepted the cup and took a sip. He grimaced. It was awful, but he'd drank worse.

"There's some milk in the fridge." Mark sat down at the table.

Angus helped himself to some milk, which did little to improve the coffee, and took a seat at the table.

"You wanted to catch up," Mark said. "Do you want to go out and get some breakfast? There's this omelet restaurant on Filmore that ironically makes amazing pancakes."

"Nah. I already ate, and I don't fancy being around a crowd of people right now." Angus took another sip of the coffee to be polite and set it down.

"I'm kind of glad, because I could murder a curry about now." Mark set his now empty cup on the table. Angus marveled at the man's capacity for his own appalling brew.

Angus laughed. "Good luck finding an Indian restaurant open at this time of the morning."

Mark went into the freezer compartment of the fridge and pulled out a box that contained a microwavable Indian meal. He scraped a bit of frost off the package. "Chicken tikka masala! Yum!"

"Yuck," Angus blanched. "Brother, you're a nurse. You know what that crap will do to you. Geez!"

Mark took the meal out of the package and placed it in the microwave. "Yeah, well everyone has a vice, and in a lot of ways, this is your fault."

"My fault? How?"

Mark stood by the microwave as the meal cooked. "About six months ago, you left one of your mystery novels in the office, one about the lady with a fruit name who eats all the microwave Indian meals and lasagna. Talk about gross, microwave lasagna. Anyway, it was a slow night, and I sat down and read the whole thing." He looked at the clock. "You know that my work schedule makes it hard for me to eat out, and I guess that I never realized that microwave Indian was a thing. Well, the next morning I went over to that Indian grocery store on Austin Bluffs, and Bob's your uncle."

"Ok, whatever." Angus shook his head.

"Look, it's not the end of the world. I have one a week and other than that my body is a temple." Mark looked down at his belly and rubbed it. "OK. Well, maybe not a temple, but I try." The microwave beeped, and he removed his food. "Now you were going to catch me up on the latest developments."

While Mark ate, Angus summarized the events of the last couple of days. As he was winding down, he said, "I don't know what to do. Maggie is furious, but I had nothing to do with any burglaries."

"You don't think she will fire you, do you?" Mark threw the container for the dinner in the trash and washed his fork.

Angus hasn't even considered this as a possibility and his heart thumped in his chest. "I hope not. No one else would take me on, but we're always so busy that Maggie practically has to turn away jobs."

"True enough." Mark rinsed his coffee cup out and filled it with the last of the milk from the jug. Then he sat down. "So, are you guys still the number one suspects?"

Angus had told Mark about the anonymous tip and the fiasco with the cameras, but he hadn't mentioned the latter questioning. "I think we are still in the running, but they also seem to be considering the possibility that it's a frame-up."

"I don't get it," Mark said. "It doesn't make sense. Are they trying to ruin the business? If there's plenty of work to go around, why bother?"

"The police haven't shared their thought process with us. However, they asked me about any enemies that I've made, and they questioned Maggie about all sorts of stuff from personal beefs to dissatisfied clients."

"And what enemies have you made, Angus?" Mark couldn't keep a straight face.

While they'd been searching his townhouse, Angus had wracked his brain about the answer to that question. He still felt unsatisfied with his answer. "Not a lot. They asked about my Army days, and there's nothing there. They asked about clients, and my only issues have either been a scheduling issue that I couldn't control or a couple of ladies who have made advances."

Mark nodded. This tracked with his image of Angus. "Yeah, and most house wives don't respond to being spurned by framing the object of their affection for 10 robberies. It's just not a natural progression."

Now Angus laughed. "Yeah, we have to keep it real. They also asked about family and old friends, but who is going to come over from Scotland just to make my life miserable?"

The two men sat in silence for a couple of minutes, each thinking. Mark drank some of the milk and then wiped it from his mustache with a napkin.

Finally, Mark broke the silence. "I bet everyone has a pet theory, but what about this? Knowing that you were implicated in the Peterson robbery, what if an associate of some actual housebreakers called in a tip to the police saying that you had been involved in more robberies to create a distraction?"

Angus considered this. "So, they feed the police bad leads

hoping the police won't turn their attention to the actual crooks?"

Mark smiled. "Not only do they keep the police busy running in circles, but they also add extra false information that keeps the investigators from being able to see the real patterns."

"So, I'm just a convenient patsy?" Angus asked. "But the police found a substantial number of houses I worked on were burglarized."

Mark doubled down. "Chance is a fine thing. They thought they were feeding the cops worthless information, but because of a strange set of circumstances, it turns out that an unusually high number of properties you worked on were actually robbed."

"I think the number is too high to not be deliberate."

"Maybe," Mark said. "Let's run the numbers. How many houses a month do you and Jack work at, maybe 30?"

"Sounds about right."

"And the police eventually looked back over 10 months, so that's about 300 houses." Mark did the mental math. "Ten out 300 is about 3% of the houses that you've worked on. Ok, that's a little high."

Angus stared out the window for a moment. The number was high, but something else was bothering him. "The video cameras," he said.

"What about the video cameras?" Mark asked.

"The cameras at the Peterson house and at a couple other properties that I worked at were smeared with grease before the robbery. That seems to rule out the hand of fate."

"And in all the cases, the robbers knew where the cameras were?" Mark was intrigued by this new information.

"I guess so."

Mark screwed up his face. "Peterson doesn't own a company that installs security cameras, does he?"

"I have no idea." Angus took out his phone. "Let's find out."

Angus opened up his phone's browser and typed Peterson's full name and Colorado Springs into the search engine. A variety of hits came up, including social media profiles and professional photos. When he clicked the News tab, Angus noticed a recent article about a business association giving Peterson an award. He read part of the article out loud. "Mr. Gary Peterson was honored today for his efforts to make tax preparation services accessible and affordable for local businesses and individuals, particularly veterans." He paused. "The guy's an accountant."

"Wish he wasn't such an asshole; I might consider letting him do my taxes." Mark smirked. "Of course, his commitment to veterans could just be a marketing thing."

Angus brought the conversation back on topic. "Don't know," he mused, scrolling through some other hits about Peterson. "From what I can tell, Peterson is an accountant and nothing more. I may not like him, but I doubt he associates with criminals. This is a dead end."

"Well, he works with the IRS," Mark said. He paused, and when Angus didn't laugh at his quip, he continued, "Politics aside, accountants launder and embezzle money, white collar crime. They don't go out and rob people of their jewelry and electronics and then concoct a scheme in which they frame their handyman."

"I certainly hope not." A deep voice boomed from the hall. Dr. Isaac Templeton poked his head around the kitchen door. "Sorry to interrupt, gents, but I have a client due in a few minutes, and I was wondering if you'd move your conversation upstairs."

"Sure, no problem." Mark got up.

"Much appreciated." Templeton looked around the room.

He was a gregarious fellow in his early 60s with a knack for help-ing troubled teens. "Landlord is finally getting that tap fixed?"

"I had the time to get around to it myself." Angus picked up his toolbox and the cup of now lukewarm coffee.

"Good man." Dr. Templeton sauntered off down the hall.

"Want me to make a fresh pot?" Mark asked as they headed up the stairs.

"Nah," Angus said. "I'll make a cup of tea."

The office of the Veterans Center was a crowded affair. A large couch sat against one wall, and a desk and a couple filing cabinets against the other. On a small table by the window, the supplies for making coffee and tea were laid out next to an elec-tric kettle and a coffee maker. A mini-fridge sat under the table. Angus had often wondered how they had never overloaded the circuit on which all the appliances were relying.

"Where were we?" Mark sat down on the desk chair. It was a model designed for people with bad backs, and he was always first to claim it.

"Peterson isn't an agreeable person, but he doesn't seem like a credible suspect." Angus pressed the button on the elec-tric kettle. "Maybe it's someone who installs security cameras or does home security consultations. Well, at least Jack and I don't do that. Maggie has a gal she recommends for home security."

"Well, if I'm wrong, and it isn't random, it still might not be personal." Mark rocked back in the chair. "You told me that the Peterson's security cameras were vandalized while you and Jack were still in the house. Maybe the person saw the name of Jack's business on your trucks and took the opportunity to shift the blame." He sat up straight, feeling proud of himself.

Angus unwrapped a tea bag and placed it in a clean cup. "That's not a bad idea, but why was there a two-week lag be-tween the Peterson robbery and the next one?"

Mark turned to the computer on the desk and looked at the calendar. "Well, the Labor Day weekend is in that timeframe."

"I don't know that criminals observe national holidays," Angus said. The kettle had beeped, and he had added water to the tea bag. He sat down on the couch while it steeped. "In fact, a holiday weekend might mean many people travelling away from home."

"Hmm," Mark said. After his meal and being up for 16 hours, he was getting tired. He considered trying to move the conversation to a list of actions items for Angus when he had a thought. "Maybe they needed time to get access information about the properties that you worked on. Who knows where you are working, anyway?"

"That's all Maggie. Clients call her, and she schedules a time for the repair. If it's a big job, she goes out and does an estimate, sometimes by herself and sometimes with either Jack or I. Most of the time though, she just gives us a list of properties and repairs for the day with whatever details we need."

"And how does she do that, by phone or email?"

"She emails me the list, and I print it out." Angus gave his tea bag a tentative tug, but the tea still wasn't as dark as he wanted it. "For Jack, she just hands him a list."

"And what about tracking your time?" Mark stifled a yawn.

"When we get to a job, we send a text. Same when we leave," Angus said. "We bill in one-hour blocks, so it's not super time sensitive." He paused. "And to anticipate your last question, before I text that I'm done with a job, I fill in a work order with the details. Maggie also shares those files with me by email."

"So, if someone hacked Maggie's email or her computer, they could get both address information but also access to your notes." Mark observed.

"Sure." Angus plucked his tea bag out of his cup and

topped the beverage off with sugar and cream from the fridge. "Or if they just wanted my jobs, they could hack my computer or phone as well."

"I assume you take precautions against that." Mark rubbed his eyes.

"We use virus protection software and avoid dodgy Wi-Fi." Angus blew on his tea. "But I bet if someone wanted to hack us enough, they could. Back to a security professional." He sipped the tea. "I mean, I suppose they could have also put a GPS tracker on my truck, but that some serious tradecraft."

Mark smiled. "You have read too many mystery and thriller novels there, Buddy." He yawned. He couldn't hold it back any more.

"I'm keeping you up." Angus looked at the time on his phone. "I can get going."

"And what are you going to do with you day off?" Mark asked. "Any plans or feelings?"

Angus was glad that he knew Mark took his flashes of instinct seriously. "Big picture, I think that the choices I make over the next couple of days or weeks may have a big impact on my life. As for today, I really don't want to work the hotline tonight, but I feel bad especially since Sheri had to call in."

"Not wanting to work tonight, that's depression or common sense." Mark adopted his best counselor voice. "But if you aren't in the right head space, you shouldn't feel bad stepping back. Take the night off."

Angus drank his tea and considered this. Mark said, "As for the next couple of days, remember what we've talked about in the past. Focus on what you can control. Maybe, just saying, vary your schedule a bit."

Angus nodded. "You aren't the first person to suggest that. Lily asked me if I could take Jaiden to Scouts from time to time, maybe even help at some camp outs and stuff."

"That sounds like a great idea." Mark was bummed at losing the reliability of Angus being there every Thursday, but he would just need to figure that out. "Are things going well with Lily?"

"Yeah, she's been wonderful," Angus said. Lily has been quite supportive of Angus even in the light of Peterson's allegations, and she had encouraged Angus to spend more time with Jaiden, which Angus felt was a sign that she was getting pretty serious.

"I can drop you off the schedule until after the New Year."

"Nah," Angus said. "Take me off for a couple of weeks, and when you put me back on, let's try a couple of different nights."

"Whatever works for you." Mark was glad that Angus might be around for the uptick in phone calls around the holiday season.

Angus finished his tea and placed the cup on the tray of dirty dishes. "I could take these down and put them in the dishwasher."

Mark yawned again. "I'll take them on my way out." He got out of the chair. "You grab your tool box."

The two men walked downstairs, and Angus followed Mark back to the kitchen. "Right after the whole Peterson mess, I showed Lily the letter from my dad to my mom and the picture of them. She suggested I hire a private detective to track him down. What do you think?"

Mark opened the dishwasher and started putting the cups and spoons into it. "You've always said that you wanted to track down your father yourself. Has something changed?"

After his hike in Garden of the Gods with Lily, Angus had used the entire weekend to think. He had always felt it necessary to track down his dad and get some answers before he got married and started a family, but he was starting to wonder if it was that important after all. Lily's points about him making his own life had resonated with him. Also, he realized that his relationship with Lily was progressing to a point where he would need to commit or risk losing her.

Plus, finding his father was overwhelming. Over the years, Angus had made inquiries, but it felt like he wasn't getting anywhere. In the last decade, technology had improved a lot, but Angus felt stymied about where to begin. The simple answer would be to hire a private detective. He could give the person what he had and let them take it from there.

"Angus," Mark said, "sorry, brother, you looked deep in thought. Has something changed?"

"It's just such a big job," Angus said. "When I started looking 15 years ago, it seemed an important part of my identity, but now I'm uncertain if it really matters." Angus paused for a minute. "The problem is if I don't take care of it, I feel like it's going to taunt me, not a deep anguish but an annoying little detail that I'm going to fixate on from time to time."

Mark added soap to the dishwasher and started a new cycle. He took his keys out of his pocket and was ready to leave, but like Angus he knew that this was an important moment, and he had better not brush it off just because he was tired. "How about this," he suggested. "Get out everything you have, lay it out, and look at it with fresh eyes. Heck, have Lily look at it. She's an observant person. While you're at it, organize and scan all of it, so that it's ready if you ever want to give it to a detective. Maybe you'll see a new avenue of investigation, and maybe you won't, but at least you can say that you tried."

"Did anyone tell you that you're great at giving advice?"

"Yeah, I think I took some training in it," laughed Mark. "So, are you ready to face the day?"

"I think I am. Thanks." Angus wondered who he knew with a flatbed scanner.

"Well, thank God, because it's past my bedtime," Mark said

as the two men walked out the front door.

◆ ◆ ◆

"Angus, I think they've mislabeled the people in this picture." Jaiden held up a photo of Sylvester Thompsons's Army unit taken in 1981.

When Angus had left Mark, he had gone home and taken out the box with all his research about his father. He had spent the better part of the day reviewing and organizing the materials with the plan to take everything to the library over the weekend and scan it. When he had texted Lily about his idea, she mentioned she had a digital scanner at home and that Jaiden knew how to use it. Jaiden had helped her mother scan some old family's photos as part of completing the Genealogy Merit Badge for scouting and then had done the same with other family photos to help her make a digital scrapbook.

Jaiden agreed to meet up with Angus after school and help him get started, and Angus thanked him. At first, Angus was intimidated by the variety of file formats and resolution options, but Jaiden had made it easy and had scanned the most important documents and photos. When Angus took over scanning, Jaiden had found the website for his dad's unit historical association to see if he could unearth any additional information.

Angus had just put a letter from the unit historian on the scanner. He hit a button and walked over to the small table where Jaiden was using his computer for internet research. "What are you up to?"

"Well, I had this idea that instead of contacting the unit's historian again, you could contact other guys who served with Private Thompson." Jaiden had several documents and browser windows open.

Angus smiled. Why hadn't he thought of that? "That's a

great idea, Jaiden, but it also sounds like a lot of work."

"Probably." Jaiden nodded. "So, I was making a list of people to contact by going through the picture, and I noticed they have identified this fellow as Sylvester Thompson." Jaiden pointed to a solider with a brown high and tight haircut and large ears. "But the 'Si' in the photograph with your mother has light colored hair and a crew cut."

Angus went back to the computer and brought up both pictures on the photo viewer. He zoomed in the heads of both men, but the resolution of the photographs made their faces fuzzy. "Maybe, or he just changed his haircut. Perhaps when it was shorter, it was darker."

"How often did you change your haircut when you were in the Army?" Jaiden asked. "My dad wore a fade for most of the time he was in. Mom said he tried a flattop once, and it just didn't suit him."

"That's a good point." Angus had favored a high and tight haircut himself, but remembered one disastrous summer when he'd shaved his head and gotten a bad sunburn. "Who do you think they mixed Sylvester Thompson with?"

"Private Simon Tennyson." Jaiden pointed to a soldier a little further to the left in the same row. Tennyson has a light-colored crew cut, normal sized ears, and a square jaw similar to Angus's.

"Wow!" Angus said. Mark had been right. Fresh eyes found new clues. How many times had he looked at the photograph? He'd always looked at the faces and hadn't really looked at the caption. "But it's an understandable mistake; their names are similar. Perhaps they both went by 'Si.' It's a great catch, Jaiden, but I don't see where it gets us."

"It might not get us anywhere," Jaiden said. "But something similar happened with my class picture last year. They mixed me and Jaiden Sullivan up. The thing is it became a bit of a joke and a story that our moms told." He paused and looked at the face that he assumed was Private Tennyson. "You said that no one seemed to remember Private Thompson. I think it's a good bet that Private Tennyson will remember him a little. Might be an idea to reach out to him."

Angus felt proud. Jaiden wasn't his son, but he quite liked the boy. Lily always said that Jaiden was a great kid, and Jaiden's work on this project was reinforcing her praise.

"Sounds good," Angus said. "Let's put him at the top of the list."

"Let me try something." Jaiden brought up a search engine in a new tab on the computer. He typed "Simon Tennyson Fort Stewart," hit enter, and began scrolling through the results. He clicked on one and skimmed it. Then his face went pale.

Angus furrowing his brow. "What is it?"

"It's an obituary in a local paper," Jaiden said softly. "Retired Master Sergeant Simon Tennyson died in January 2000." His voice trailed off, and his body tensed.

Angus tried to remember when Jaiden's dad Christopher had been killed, sometime around when Jaiden was eight. He wondered how appropriate it was to involve the boy in his search for his father.

"Now then, that's a good lad," he said, because he couldn't think of anything else. "It was a good idea, but I think we need a break. Maybe you could go downstairs and see if your Gran will get us a snack."

The comment seemed to snap Jaiden back to reality. "It's too close to supper time to have a snack," he replied in his normal voice. "I'll take a few minutes to put some more names in a spreadsheet, and then I'll go down and help Gran make the spaetzle. It's a two-person job."

"Are you sure?" Angus asked. "I could take care of it."

"Nah," Jaiden said. "I miss my dad a lot, but Mom says you've never even met yours. It just doesn't seem fair. I'm happy to help." He paused and then added. "The article just took me by surprise, you know?"

Angus was touched by Jaiden's simple yet profound declaration. He reached over and gave the boy's arm a squeeze. "I appreciate it, but look, why don't you go down and help your Gran, and I'll finish what you started."

"Ok." Jaiden headed down the stairs to the main floor of the house, clonking at every step.

Left alone in the room, Angus skimmed the obituary. It mentioned that Tennyson's death had been an accident but didn't mention what type. He went back to the search results and looked at a few more of the hits. On the third link, he hit pay dirt. In a short blurb that served as an update to a previous story, a local reporter wrote that police had released the identity of a man who had been struck by a car on the side of the road while helping another motorist change a tire. So, Tennyson had been a good Samaritan. Angus felt a sadness at an opportunity to know a man who both appeared to be a decent human being and would probably have been an excellent source of information. On impulse, he printed both of the articles and added them to the pile to scan. Then he saved Jaiden's spreadsheet and emailed it to himself.

Lily arrived home just in time for dinner, which was jaeger schnitzel, homemade spaetzle noodles, and red cabbage. Lily's mother Hilde served a Riesling wine to pair with the pork dish and baulked when Angus declined a glass. "Wine with dinner is to round out the meal, not get drunk," she chided Angus. It was an argument that they had engaged in many times.

Lily's father, Reggie, ended the argument by changing the

subject. He asked both Jaiden and Lily about their days. Angus attempted to listen, but his head was swirling with different random thoughts brought on by his review of his prior research. He was glad that Reggie didn't ask him about recent events and had assumed Lily had warned him off.

Near the end of the meal Reggie asked, "Are you almost done with your scanning Angus, or do you have a lot left?"

"Maybe another hour." Angus crossed his knife and fork on his plate as his Aunty Ivy had taught him to do when he finished eating. "Will it disturb you if I stay and finish up tonight?"

"Not at all." Reggie stood up and helped his wife clear the table. "In fact, if you end up being here too late, there's a guest room on the first floor. You're more than welcome to stay. Lily can help you find everything you need."

"Thanks." Angus blushed. He has never stayed overnight with the Saunders before. "Let me help with the dishes before I head upstairs."

"We've got this, Angus," Hilde said. She turned to Lily. "There's a glass of wine left in the bottle, dear, why don't you finish it for us."

Lily poured the remains of the wine in her glass and put the bottle in the recycling bin. Then she said to Angus, "Want company while you finish up?"

"Sure," Angus said, as they headed to the office again.

"Have you had any brainwaves?" Lily asked once they were there.

"I've had some thoughts." Angus had jotted down some notes on a pad after Jaiden had left but now wanted to add a few more items. "And Jaiden had some fantastic ideas as well, but I don't know if I want to influence you. Maybe you should look at everything and then tell me what you think."

"Ok." Lily was a little disappointed. She was in the mood

to talk, but Angus made a good point. "Shall I start on the pile that you've already scanned, and when you are done, we can compare notes?"

"Sounds good." Angus handed her a pile of papers. "You can start with these. If you could keep them in order, that would be helpful.

Lily and Angus spent the next 30 minutes working independently. While Angus scanned documents, Lily skimmed through what was in front of her. The last thing that Angus scanned was the letter from Sylvester Thompson to his mother, the one important document that he hadn't given to Jaiden. He even scanned the envelope for good measure. Then he handed the previous items to Lily.

"I'll be back in a couple of minutes," he said, heading toward the bathroom.

Lily took the letter and read it with an eye to details. Parts of it jumped out at her. "Soon after I returned to the United States, I married my high school sweetheart." The statement was vague, but Lily felt like it was truthful and might eventually prove to be helpful. "My father thought that staying with my uncle and cousin for a summer would make me realize that my relationship with Mary was a childish fancy, but it only made me love her more." At first Lily was distracted by the sweetness and innocence of the statement, but then she wondered exactly who Si had stayed with and if they might know where he was now. "I'm sorry that I didn't tell you I was engaged, but I always looked on what we had as a casual fling." *Now that was probably a lie* Lily thought. Of course, the whole letter could be a work of fiction. There might be no Mary, or the uncle or cousin might actually have been a family friend, but the more Lily thought about it, the more she wondered if the way to solve this mystery was to go back to the beginning.

Angus returned and went to add a couple more items to his list. Then he spun the office chair by the desk so that it faced

Lily and sat down. "You look like you've got something there. Want to go first?"

"Sure." Lily had written down her ideas on her own paper. "I've been thinking. You seem to have focused your search on the soldier Sylvester Thompson who was stationed at a particular Army base at a particular time."

"I'm using the information that I have." Angus wondered where Lily was going with this.

"That's true, and a name and place are not insubstantial, but Angus, if anyone should know that a man is more than his name, it's you."

"Aye," Angus agreed. "I feel like I know that better than most people."

"Then I think we need to scour the letter from Si and the photograph and look for clues that will help add to our picture of him." Lily was building up momentum. "With a fuller profile, we might narrow down our search for him."

"Fair enough." Angus brought up the scan of the photo of his mother and Si on the computer "But we don't have a lot to go on."

"We may have more than we think," Lily said. "Let's start by making a list of things that we know for certain."

"Good idea." Angus got out a clean sheet of paper and wrote "Sylvester Thompson" at the top in black ink. "We know he was stationed at Fort Stewart in the spring of 1981 and what unit he was part of."

"And we know he was in Scotland during the summer of 1981," Lily said. "Do we have any dates for his visit?"

"Not that I know of." Angus added this information to the paper. Then he found a red pen on the desk and used it to write "Dates." He looked at the photograph. "So, we also know that Si was blonde with a crew cut. What else do you see?"

Lily examined the picture. "He's fit, not a surprise since he was in the Army. He's got a slim build and a square jaw like you." She paused for a minute. "How tall do you reckon he is? He's over a head taller than your mom, whose wearing flat shoes by the looks of it."

Angus considered this. His mom had died when he was 15 and by then, he had been maybe four inches taller than her. "I'd say she was around 5'5", so, he's maybe 6'. I wish we could narrow it down a bit more."

"Couldn't you ask your Aunty Ivy? Maybe she could help with the dates as well."

Angus sighed. "Aunty Ivy wasn't living with my grandparents that summer," he said. "She and I talked about it when we found the letter and photo years ago. At the time, she could recall vague details, but that was the summer she met her husband, so she was pretty distracted."

Lily took a minute to process this information. "It's too bad. Your Aunty Ivy sounds pretty sharp. You said she does a bit of genealogy research. Do you think she'd been willing to help us out?"

"Probably." Angus thought about his aunt, who was a formidable force despite her love of sweater sets and pearls. "But what can she do? She spent the summer in Edinburgh; she never met my dad."

"It would be very handy to talk to someone who met him." Lily twisted a strand of hair around her finger "I wonder who was there that summer."

"My grandfather and grandmother, both long dead." Angus pictured them sitting at the dinner table in the farmhouse. "Obviously, my mom. Her sister Grace, but she had her first baby that July, so she was distracted. Other than that, I'm not sure."

"Maybe that's something that Ivy would know." Lily

looked at her list and the letter that was still on the desk near her. "And if she knows of anyone, maybe she could talk to them for us."

"Perhaps." Angus considered this. Ivy enjoyed taking day trips with her senior bus pass. She needed little excuse to visit relatives and old friends. "Let's see if there's anything besides dates or height that she could ask people about."

Lily pointed out the passages in the letter that had aroused her curiosity. "As I see it, we need to know where he stayed and who he stayed with. They have probably moved on, but they might be easier to track down than Sylvester."

Angus nodded and let her continue. "We need general impressions and descriptions. Did Si have any clothing with a local sports team or organization or even better a high school mascot? What sort of accent did he have? Did he talk about back home?"

As Lily spoke, Angus made notes in red ink. When she paused, he considered the sentence about Mary. "I wonder." He went over to the computer. A quick search of "Mary and Sylvester Thompson" gave too many hits in the search engine, and adding Fort Stewart to query had the opposite effect.

"Wonder what?" Lily asked, giving the letter and photograph one more glance.

Angus explained to her about Jaiden's discovery of the mislabeled photo caption and then finding the obituary of Simon Tennyson. "I thought I might work a similar magic with a wedding announcement, but either the newspaper hasn't digitized its archives back that far, or they got married somewhere else."

"That would be where a hometown would come in handy," Lily said. "Even if they were married someplace else, their families might have placed an announcement in a paper from their city or area." Then thinking for another minute, she said, "What I can do is use my connections at work to see what newspapers and other publications were in print near Fort Stewart in the early 80s and see if they can find a wedding announcement." She added this her list.

"Thank, Lily. That would be grand." Angus looked at the time on the computer. It was almost 9. He should start thinking of heading home.

"Well, now that we have a list for questions for your Aunty Ivy, perhaps we should get in touch with her," Lily suggested. She folded the letter and returned it to its envelope. "How do you normally communicate with her?"

Angus furrowed his brow. "I call her once a month. I love her to pieces, but she has the gift of gab. We talk for an hour, and then I tell her I have an appointment. Otherwise, we would talk all day," he confessed.

"Does she have email?" Lily asked. She had a similar problem with talking to her mom on the phone when she had lived in another part of the country. While she had always enjoyed listening to her mother's stories and tangents, it wasn't conducive to relaying a lot of information.

"She does." Angus calculated the time difference with Scotland. "If I send her an email now, she'll be up to read it in a couple of hours. In fact, she only checks her email first thing in the morning, so I probably should."

Lily stood up. "While you do that, do you want anything? Tea, hot chocolate, or a night cap?" she yawned.

"Nah." Angus opened up his email on the computer. "I should finish up here and head out."

"You could just stay." Lily pointed out. "I have some more ideas that I want to discuss, but I'm exhausted."

Angus considered this and agreed, "Tomorrow I could help make a big breakfast, and then we could talk some more."

CHAPTER 6

Friday, November 23

Angus and Lily spent a good portion of that first Saturday brainstorming ways to track down Sylvester Thompson, but most of their ideas spiraled back to questions to ask people who either had met Sylvester in Scotland or were in his unit back at Fort Stewart. Aunty Ivy emailed Angus with a short list of people who she remembered were living in his hometown during the summer that Sylvester Thompson had visited. Unfortunately, most of them like Angus's grandfather and grandmother had passed away. Ivy promised to do a bit a research and get back to him.

The weeks leading up to Thanksgiving were a whirlwind for Angus consisting of 14-hour work days and meals eaten on the fly. With three days of missed work to catch up on, he didn't have time for Trivia Night or to visit the Veterans Center. Aunty Ivy emailed from time to time with updates and requests. She talked to her sister Grace on the phone and now had a list of people she planned to visit soon.

Lily's family had invited Angus to share Thanksgiving with them, and Angus enjoyed combining his first day off in over a week with the best meal that he had eaten since the last time he'd dined with them. The dinner was served as a late lunch, and the food and drink had lasted well into the evening. Angus had actually accepted a couple glasses of wine and spent the night.

As Angus sat in his apartment on Black Friday, he was

looking forward to a quiet day. He wasn't a fan of the sales, but Maggie was, so he and Jack had the day off. Lily was also out shopping, but Angus was waiting for the online deals that would come later. He couldn't decide what to buy Lily; it was too early for a ring, but he needed something special.

During the night, Angus's phone had run out of battery power, but he hadn't cared. Very few people needed to get ahold of him, and they all knew how. Aunty Ivy had Jack and Maggie's number, and Maggie and Lily had become good friends. Angus knew he should be better about charging his phone, but he still remembered when people weren't constantly reachable and felt like it wasn't a priority.

Angus had plugged his phone into the charger when he had arrived home and gone upstairs to take a shower. Now, sitting in his bathrobe with a cup of tea and a plan to watch a couple of his favorite Agatha Christie movies on his laptop and then maybe go for a late afternoon hike, Angus wondered if he should check his messages.

He made another cup of tea and looked at his phone. There was a text from Dan wishing him a Happy Thanksgiving, and a second text wished Angus a *Happy Two Weeks Without Having a Client Burgled*. Angus chuckled and sent Dan a silly smiling face. Perhaps his part in that mystery was over, and he could move on.

Aunty Ivy had emailed Angus asking if he knew how to use a video call app and suggesting that they talk at 10 AM. Angus checked the time and realized that it was almost 9:30. He replied to her email and went upstairs to put on a nice shirt and his best kilt.

At 10 AM on the dot, his phone beeped and showed an incoming video call. He answered it, and for the first time since her visit two years prior, Angus saw his Aunty Ivy.

"Angus, it's great to actually see you. How have you been?" Aunty Ivy was sitting in her kitchen. Angus recognized the china cabinet behind her stacked with her beautiful dishes. She was wearing a pale blue sweater set and a string of pearls. Every auburn-colored hair on her head sat perfectly in place. In fact, she looked so good, Angus wondered if his aunt had gone to the beauty parlor to prepare for this call.

"I've been busy, Aunty Ivy." Angus was sitting at his dining room table drinking his third cup of tea. "We lost a lot of time when Maggie and Jack went out of town."

"What a mess," Ivy said. "I hope you didn't let it get you down."

"Not a bit." While Angus was upstairs, he'd found a pen and the notebook he'd been using to keep track of his recent search efforts. He removed the cap from the pen and prepared to take notes. "So, is this just a social call or do you have an update for me?"

"I think I've got quite a good lead." There was a rustling off screen, and Ivy produced a composition book. "I have some additional information, and I think I will have more next week, but I thought I would give you an update." She caught her breath, and her cheeks had a rosy glow.

"That's great." Angus wanted to tell his aunt to take her time, but he was also eager to hear what she had to say.

Aunty Ivy put on her reading glasses and opened the composition book. "As I told you in my first email, the only people living with your mom were her parents," she said. Then she dropped her voice a bit. "Sadly, they're all dead now."

Angus nodded and pictured them, although the image was from around when he was 12 years old. His grandfather, who might have been 75 at that point, was a gnarled old man with white hair and a cane. His wife, who had been in her late 60s, had aged better despite having 8 daughters. She said that having young people around her had kept her young, and she had stayed active and even dyed her hair. Then there was his mother still young and thin with long blonde hair and wearing blue jeans. "Aye," he whispered.

Ivy, who had paused for a minute, looked at Angus. "I'm sorry, dear. I didn't mean to upset you."

"You didn't." Angus's voice had returned to normal. "I just haven't thought about all of them in a long while."

"This had been quite the trip down memory lane," Ivy said, regaining her momentum. "Your Aunty Grace and I had the best chat on the phone, and when I went down to visit her last weekend, we got out the albums and talked about things we hadn't in years."

"Did you have a good time?" Angus asked. Ivy was a tough gal, but he didn't want to cause her any pain to solve his own problems.

"Aye. You forget what times used to be like. Some things were better then; some are better now." Ivy had spent over 25 years as an elementary school teacher and prided herself on her mastery of the Queen's English. However, sometimes, when she had been drinking or was reminiscing about old times, she would lapse back into a heavy Scottish brogue.

Ivy paged through her notes until she found what she was looking for. "So, Grace gave me a list of names of people who were still in town who might remember that summer. There was Bill, the grocer's boy, who is quite grown up." She looked down again. "Siobhan and Rhys, who used to run the post office; they've retired but staying in town." She listed off several more people.

Angus let her talk without making notes. Ivy liked to tell a story, and she eventually got around to her point. He sat back and sipped his tea. When Ivy took a break to breathe, he nodded or made an acknowledging noise.

"Angus, I need you to stay with me," Aunty Ivy said after a while. "I remember how it was when you were in school, head always off in the clouds, but this is important."

Angus shifted in his chair. His aunt was right. He had always struggled in school to pay attention, especially during long, boring lectures. Even so, he had managed decent grades by showing his teachers that he'd understood the lesson. "Sorry, Aunty Ivy. I appreciate all the effort that you are going to. Did you turn anything else up?"

"I'm afraid the remaining townspeople were mostly a dead end," Ivy reported.

Angus groaned. He had tried to pay attention while his aunt went on and on, but in the end, it didn't sound like there was any positive progress from this part of her efforts. She was trying his patience.

"The people I talked to confirmed that after World War II, the family that owned Eagle Hall, as the large estate in the area was called, shuttered the place and tried to sell it," Ivy continued. "Of course, no one had the money to buy it, so it sat decaying for about 25 years."

Angus nodded. He remembered Eagle Hall from his exploration of the area around his grandparent's farm. His recollections from that time were that Eagle Hall had been boarded up and signs had warned that it was unsafe. He remembered one wing was blackened, possibly by a fire.

"Then this fellow with more money than sense bought the place with the idea to restore it and make it a hotel. He ended up fixing up one wing before he ran out of money, so he made the best of it and rented that wing out for various purposes."

"Didn't they use it to shoot a couple of movies?" Angus asked, recalling a story from his childhood.

"Aye, that they did," Ivy said. "They also rented it out for the summer and for hunting parties and such."

"So, there wasn't anyone consistently there from year to year." Angus thought out loud.

"Precisely. Different people came at different times. Some

of them brought their own staff, and some of them hired people from the village."

"And did anyone remember who was renting Eagle Hall in the summer of 1981?" Angus hoped to push the conversation forward.

"Not anyone who I interviewed in town," Ivy said. "You'd think the postmistress would have remembered. She was such a gossip, but I guess time wipes all that away."

"You said you had a lead." Angus shifted in his chair again.

"Yes, yes, dear," Ivy said. "I'm getting there." She continued, "Grace did better with figuring out who might have taken that picture of your mother and Si. Do you remember Colleen McDermott? She was a red-haired girl with an Irish mom and a Scottish dad?"

Angus wracked his brain but couldn't put a face to the name and shrugged his shoulders.

"Well, she was a great friend of your mom, and Grace remembered she has saved up her money to buy a camera. They weren't as common in those days. And when she got one, she went around town taking pictures of all sorts of things."

Angus had forgotten a lot about film photography. It hadn't been something his mom and grandparents were into. He had memories of being hounded to take photos at family gatherings and something called "flash cubes."

"Grace said that Colleen lived in a village a little north of Forfar, and I visited her on my way back to Edinburgh," Ivy said.

"So, you were able to track her down?"

"Aye, but she looked rough." Ivy made a face and shook her head. "Like your mom, she liked a bit of a drink, and time hasn't been kind. She had such lovely creamy skin, and now it's all blotchy, and she's gotten fat."

Angus took a deep breath. There were so many questions

he wanted to ask. Had she taken the picture? Did she have more pictures? What did she remember about Si?

"I showed her the picture on my phone, and she confirmed she took it," Ivy recounted. "She said it was out at the Falls, and that she and her boyfriend along with Heather and Si had gone out there for a picnic."

Angus opened his mouth to speak, but Ivy cut him off. "She says that she took a couple more pictures that day, but the prints and all the negatives were destroyed in a house fire a few years later." Ivy paused for breath. "And that's the only time she met Si."

Angus sighed. This was going nowhere fast.

"However, she confirmed Si was living at Eagle Hall that summer although she wasn't clear about if the person he was staying with was a friend or relative."

"Well, that's something." Angus made a note. "We just need to track down who was staying at Eagle Hall. Maybe there's a property manager or someone."

"We may not need to go that far," Ivy said. "But before we go there, Colleen had one other piece of information. She said that Si sounded like Rhett Butler in 'Gone with the Wind.' That's a Southern accent, right?"

"Aye," Angus confirmed. So, it wasn't just that Si had been stationed in the South, he was from the South. "Anything more specific? Did he talk about a hometown or anything?"

"Nope." Ivy turned to the next page in her composition book. "She didn't remember much about the afternoon. They drank a fair bit, but she said it was only time she'd met someone with that type of accent."

"Fair enough." Angus stared down at his almost blank notepad.

"I headed home and was feeling pretty glum," Ivy said. "So,

I thought I'd call Grace and thank her for the pleasant visit, and we got talking, not like we hadn't talked each other's ears off the day before." Ivy had started talking more quickly. "And Grace said out of the blue, 'What about Bonnie Stewart?'"

Ivy paused for effect and perhaps breath. Angus sat transfixed. "What about Bonnie Stewart?" he asked after a few seconds.

"You wouldn't have known her." Ivy waved her hand. "She'd escaped to Edinburgh by the time that you would have been old enough to remember."

"Ah." Angus wrote "Bonnie Stewart" on a fresh page in his notebook.

"Bonnie and I went to school together." Ivy became more animated. "And she was always so smart and so ready for an adventure. She earned a full scholarship to a teaching program at the University at Edinburgh, and you've never seen anyone more excited." She paused. "But the summer after graduation, her mother took ill, and Bonnie had to stay home and care for her." Ivy stared into the distance and was quiet for a minute.

"Really?" Angus let disbelief creep into his voice. This sounded like something out of a novel.

"Sadly," Ivy said. "Her mother had always had high blood pressure, but she had a minor stroke that summer and wasn't able to take care of herself or her home anymore. And Bonnie only had a brother, and he was already at university, so she did the right thing and stayed home. It was very hard on her."

Angus nodded. He couldn't imagine staying in the small town he had grown up in for his entire life. The prospect sent a shiver down his spine.

"Anyway, I ended up going to Edinburgh and worked my way through a teaching program." Ivy furrowed her brow as she remembered. "I felt so scared and homesick, and it wasn't like it is now. A phone call home was something you did maybe once a week, and it was so expensive. And your gran was never much of a letter writer."

Angus doodled in the margin of the notebook page. He sensed this was going somewhere but knew better than to push.

"Anyway, one day your Gran talked about sitting with Mrs. Stewart, so that Bonnie could run some errands, and when Bonnie got home, she gave her some tea and asked her a million questions about my adventures in Edinburgh, so I started writing to Bonnie. Every time I went somewhere exciting or even a boring museum, I sent her a picture postcard. Every time I went to see a film, I told her about it. And in return, Bonnie kept me informed about every bit of minutiae back home."

"Ah." Angus recalled that neither of his grandparents had been great correspondents. His grandmother had fancied greeting cards, both sending and receiving them, but he was sure that he had never seen a letter that wasn't a bill in the mailbox in all the years he'd lived with them.

"Bonnie and I wrote to each other for many years," his aunt said. "And when I met Rory that summer, I told her all about him." Ivy reached off screen and produced a shoebox of letters. "And that summer she was working during the day at Eagle Hall as a cleaner and general maid and told me all about it."

Angus's jaw dropped as his aunt took a pile of letters, each in its original envelope from the shoebox. "Well, as soon as Grace said Bonnie's name, it all came back to me." She selected a powder blue envelope from the stack and took the letter out. "It was all I could do to end our conversation before I headed to the box room to look for Bonnie's letters."

"Go on," Angus said.

"Well, there's a lot here." Ivy placed the letter on the table and smoothing out the folds. "I was up half the night reading, and I decided to get Charlie to scan the lot and send them to you, as I don't know what might be helpful and what won't be."

Charlie was Ivy's grandson, who Angus recalled was about Jaiden's age. It seemed like a lot of work to give the boy. "Are you sure that's necessary?" Angus asked.

"Aye. His mam caught him vaping and is looking for something tedious to punish him. He's a right little wanker, but don't worry. I'll monitor him."

Angus felt grateful that Jaiden seemed to be a good kid. He also wondered why his aunt had chosen that letter out of the pile in front of her. "Did you have anything specific that you want to tell me?" he asked.

Ivy scanned the letter turning to the second sheet. "Yes, I did. This letter is dated May 28, 1981." She read from the letter. "Mrs. Baker, her who used to be the head housekeeper up at Eagle Hall, came by today to ask if I might want some daily work up at the hall this summer. She said some English fellow named Neal Culpepper is renting the place from June to the end of August and is bringing his family with him. He says he wants a cook, a housekeeper, two cleaners, and a ladies' maid. Actually, she said he doesn't know what he wants as he only just made all his money in some business venture and wants to play lord of the manner. Anyway, your ma said she's look in on mine every afternoon and give her tea, so I said I'd be glad of the work. The money will be welcome, but I am excited to see the trouble those English folks get up to."

Ivy folded the letter and put it back in the envelope "And goodness did she tell me in almost painful detail what they got up to."

"That's amazing," Angus said. "This is even better than I imagined." His heart was pounding, and his head was swimming. He couldn't wait to get ahold of the letters. "Have you been able to get in touch with Bonnie?"

Ivy looked down at the table. "Truth is, we've fallen out of touch," she said. "That was Bonnie's last summer at home. In late July, your gran came over to give Bonnie's ma her tea, and the poor woman was stone dead. The doctor said she must have had a stroke or heart attack while she was napping. Poor thing. Well, then Bonnie was free. She planned to start a teaching course in Edinburgh and gave her notice and to my knowledge has never looked back."

"And you haven't heard from her since then?" Angus asked, trying to picture the challenge of tracking down a woman in the city of Edinburgh. Perhaps, however, the letters would be enough.

"Oh, no." Ivy put the letter back in the box. "We kept in touch for a while. Since Bonnie could finally start her own adventure, we didn't write every week, but she sent the odd Christmas and birthday card. The problem was we both lived our lives. I married Rory and soon your cousin Tess was on the way, and Bonnie married some fellow she met at church. He was older and worked at the University. He used to travel the world collecting plant specimens. She was in heaven."

Angus smiled. It sounded as if Bonnie Stewart had landed on her feet. It was nice that someone was getting a happy ending.

"I'm sure I could track her down given time," Ivy said. "They owned a house in the university district. That's where I plan to start."

Angus considered this. His aunt had a bit of the Miss Marple in her. She felt an obligation to follow through on a problem until she solved it.

"And that's why I don't just want to send you the letters," Ivy summed up. "I thought if I brought them with me when I have time to meet with her, they might jog her memory."

"That's a good idea." Angus shifted in the chair again. It wasn't very comfortable. "You've done a magnificent job so far. When do you think you can send me those letters?"

"Tess said something about putting them 'in a cloud,'

whatever that is." Ivy smiled. "I'll have her get in touch and work out the technical details with you, but our plan is to have Charlie work on it all weekend, so pretty soon."

"Sounds great!" Angus said. He and his aunt talked for another 10 minutes and then disconnected. Angus was energized. His plans to have a quiet day and watch movies went out the window. He sent a couple of text messages to Lily, and then he got out his daypack, got in his truck, and headed to Palmer Park for a hike.

CHAPTER 7

Late November

    With Thanksgiving over, everyone prepared for Christmas. At work, Angus and Jack spent more time outdoors, hanging lights and wreaths. In his downtime, Angus tried to do his holiday shopping, but the large volume of letters that his Aunty Ivy had unearthed kept diverting his attention.

    Charlie had scanned the letters almost immediately after Angus and Ivy talked. The time difference meant that while it had been late morning for Angus, it had been early evening in Scotland. When Angus returned from his hike, he found a mountain of scans in an online folder that Tess had shared with him. Angus had shared the folder with Lily, and the two of them had spent the rest of the weekend reading through the letters. They met Sunday afternoon to compare notes.

    Together Angus and Lily constructed a narrative. Mr. Neal Culpepper has rented Eagle Hall for three months in the summer of 1981. He had come in early June with his wife Bella and their twelve-year-old twins, Nigel and Phillip, and stayed for a couple of weeks. Then he had gone back to London, leaving his family at Eagle Hall. The boys were left in the care of a fellow in his 20s named Ronald Parks, who acted as a combination tutor and babysitter. He kept the boys busy with a variety of outdoor activities that included fishing, archery, day hiking, and painting. Mrs. Culpepper didn't have a constant companion, instead entertaining different friends and relatives every weekend.

    In late June, Sylvester Thompson had arrived and had

stayed for two weeks. The family referred to Si as "our American cousin," although the exact nature of their relationship was unclear. The gossip amongst the servants was that Si had spent 18 months in the U.S. Army and was in love with "an unsuitable young woman" so had been sent to Scotland to help give him perspective.

Bonnie described Si as "quite tall, a full head taller than Mr. Brown," which Ivy had clarified to mean was around six feet tall. She also said that Sylvester "spoke with a funny accent." Nothing was remarkable about Si's clothes, except that Bonnie had an idea that they were all new and purchased for the trip. Si had jeans and khaki trousers for everyday wear and a nice suit for travelling. Apparently, much to the disdain of Mrs. Baker, the family did not dress for dinner.

If Si had talked of home, Bonnie hadn't been privy to it. The young man had mostly gone fishing or hiking or taken one of the estate cars into town. Bonnie recounted talking with Angus's grandmother. The older woman had expressed disapproval of her daughter going about with the American. Angus laughed as Bonnie quoted his gran. "There's something shady about that fellow. Mark my words." His gran had always called things like she saw them, and she had been quite right about Si.

The contents of the letters didn't get Angus much farther. He had definite dates for his father's visit to Scotland, and Bonnie's letters confirmed details he had already surmised. The biggest lead was the Culpeppers. It wasn't a common last name, and with Aunt Ivy's tenacious attention, Angus was sure that she could track at least one of the family down. They didn't need much, just how Sylvester Thompson was related to the family and a way to contact him. Heck, the contact information for any family member in the United States would do. Angus also wondered about Ronald Parks. He would be harder to track down, but he had been around the same age as Si, and Angus wondered if perhaps the men had formed a friendship.

Despite analyzing the letters from Ivy, Angus had finished most of his holiday shopping. He had purchased Jack a utility kilt and some local wine for Maggie. Jaiden was still very interested in cooking, so Angus found him a kitchen apron with hot peppers on it and a cookbook full of simple, hearty recipes. For Ivy, he went to a local used book store and stocked up on vintage Nancy Drew and Trixie Belden mysteries. Ivy was also a mystery buff, but preferred young adult mysteries for their lower body count. Angus also selected a journal with an art print embossed in gold on the cover and a book about the haunted places near Colorado Springs. Ivy was planning a visit next fall, and he wanted to whet her appetite.

For Lily, Angus was at an impasse. He wanted to get her something special but felt it was too early for a ring. Maggie suggested that instead of a gift Angus take Lily up to Denver for a special weekend at a fancy hotel and perhaps take in a concert. Angus felt like an outing of that type was just part of being a decent boyfriend, so instead of making any substantial plans, he just waited for a minor flash of insight.

Friday, November 30

Angus and Jack had spent the entire afternoon decorating one house, and despite the chill in the air, they were both sweating. The job had been a nightmare. They had spent the first hour untangling strings of lights and testing to see which bulb was blown. Once that was complete, they had hung lights on both stories of the home while the owner directed them. Previously, Norman had done all the decorating himself, but this year he had broken his ankle and was forced to hire someone. Angus took little comfort in Jack's assertion that "This is just as tough for Norman as it is for us. Decorating is his favorite part of the holidays." Norman had tried not to be overbearing, but he had sat in a lawn chair in the driveway watching them and talking for the past two hours.

"And then Jenny says to me she wants another sapphire ring." Norman continued a long-winded description of his quest to find the perfect present for his wife. "She already has a big blue one, but apparently they come in every color except red." Norman shook his head, which was barely visible between an enormous hat and an even larger scarf.

Jack had just plugged the lights that were wrapped around a metal reindeer frame into another string and signaled for Angus to turn on the electricity. When Angus did, the lights failed to illuminate, and Jack traced the network back to troubleshoot the connection problem.

"So, she spends all this time looking at rings online," Norman said, staring at the reindeer, "and then she decides on one and insists I buy it that very night. Apparently, they turn over quickly."

Jack worked through the series of plugs, disconnecting and reconnecting them until the reindeer lit up. "Sorry to interrupt you, Norman, but I think that's the last reindeer, so unless you have anything else to add, we'll pack up."

Norman surveyed the display on his lawn for a minute before speaking. "I think that about does it for the Christmas decorations, but if you have a minute, Maggie said you could fix the knob on the kids' bathroom."

"Sure, Norman." Jack took out his phone and checked the time. "What is wrong with it?"

While Angus gathered up their tools, Norman told the story of how his kids had locked the bathroom door and then closed it, leaving no one inside the room. Luckily Mrs. Norman was handy and tried to pop the lock a small tool, as she had done many times. Unfortunately, the lock was old, and the tool hadn't worked, so in a fit of frustration his wife had removed the knob, using various tools and bought a non-locking replacement, which she didn't feel like installing.

"Sounds pretty straightforward." Jack walked towards the front door. "I'll go in and look." He turned back to Angus. "Why don't you get going." Maggie had suggested that Angus limit his time alone in properties with homeowners when it was practical, and fixing the knob would take one of them perhaps five minutes.

"Nonsense," Norman said before Angus could get a word out. "Why don't you both come in. Did Mr. MacBain say something about maybe asking his girl to marry him? I want to show him the ring; give him an idea of what's hot right now." Norman struggled to his feet and then tried to fold up his lawn chair. Seeing his difficulty, Jack came over and took the chair from him.

"I should get going." Angus looked towards his truck with his toolbox in his hand. It never ceased to amaze him how people's mind auto-corrected his name. "I have somewhere I need to be." Angus had volunteered to work a shift at the veteran's hotline.

"Come on, man." Norman stood his ground. "It will only take a minute."

Jack shot Angus a look. He didn't hold with the maxim that the customer was always right, but he believed that if a customer wanted to talk your ear off, you indulged them and then billed them for your time.

"Alright." Angus followed Jack and Norman into the house.

Once inside, Norman hobbled up the stairs and directed them to a bathroom just off the landing. The hole that housed the knob was empty, and a package containing the new knob sat propped against the wall next to it.

"Back in a mo'," Norman said as he made his way back down the stairs laboriously.

"I don't have a good feeling about this, Jack." Angus picked up the knob and removed it from its packaging.

121

"More intel from the fairies?" Jack snickered. Changing the knob was a one-man job, so he just stood there watching Angus.

"You don't need second sight to realize that this guy has told everyone about the ring he bought his wife." Angus loosened some screws and separated the new knob into its two halves. "Honestly, he just wants to share his joy, but let's hope he doesn't tell the wrong person."

"Fair enough," Jack said. His phone beeped, and he checked the text message. While Angus finished installing the lock, he messaged Maggie, assuring her they would leave the property soon.

"Maggie?" Angus asked, taking the remains of the old lock off the bathroom counter and placing them in the packaging for the new one.

"Yup." Jack put away his phone. "Speaking of, she had coffee with Lily the other day. Second weddings came up, and Lily says she doesn't want anything big if she ever gets married again."

"You mean Maggie brought the subject up," Angus laughed. Maggie had taken a great interest in his relationship lately, and while he resented her meddling just a bit, he also hoped to benefit from anything that she discovered.

"Yeah. Maggie talked about how we just went to the courthouse and then went to Vegas, and Lily said she might prefer a small service in a park or something."

"Sounds nice." Angus had been to several large weddings and found them to be an enormous hassle. "As long as Aunty Ivy can be there, I'll be happy, because if she's not invited, she will kill me."

"Angus MacBangus and the Case of the Murdered Bridegroom." Jack suggested.

Angus laughed and then had a thought. Jack and Maggie

had been married for so long that Angus sometimes forgot about Maggie's previous marriage. "Jack, I don't know that I've ever met Maggie's ex-husband, but is it possible that he's the one who is stirring up trouble for us with the police?"

As Jack considered this idea, he glanced down the stairs to see if Norman was coming. "The police asked Maggie about that, and while he's not our favorite person, it just doesn't seem like his style. He's lazy, and unless it's all a coincidence, this frame up seems like a lot of work. Besides, why pick jobs only you were working on?"

"True." Angus looked at their finished work. "Should we just head down and save Norman the trip?"

"Nah," Jack said. "He'll want to see the work."

The men talked for a couple of minutes about Jack and Maggie's weekend plans, hoping that Norman would return soon.

"Done already. Excellent!" Norman declared, huffing and puffing from his latest trip up the stairs. He had removed his coat, hat, and muffler, but he was still quite red in the face from exertion.

"It's easy once you know how to do it," Jack said.

"Indeed." Norman leaned on his crutch with one arm and took a blue velvet ring box from his pocket with the other. He flipped the box open to reveal a ginormous pink sapphire set between two baguette diamonds. "Check this out. Diamonds may be a girl's best friend, but sapphires are the latest trend."

"It's big," Jack said, his eyes like saucers.

"And bold." Angus struggled to find a word that was both accurate and complimentary.

"I agree." Norman turned the box so that he could examine the ring. "It's over three carats, but the wife fell in love with this monstrosity, so what are you going to do?"

Both men nodded being unsure what to say. Norman closed the box and put the ring back in his pocket. "Well, thanks again for your help. I don't want to keep you."

Norman turned around and headed downstairs, and Jack and Angus followed.

"Let us know when you want help to take your decorations down," Jack said when they reached the bottom of the stairs. "Unless you are feeling up to taking care of it yourself." He looked down at Norman's foot that was in a booted cast.

"We'll just see," Norman said, supporting himself with both his crutch and the half wall by the front door. "I should put this foot up."

"Probably so," Jack said. "And maybe you'd better put that ring away somewhere safe." Jack's eyes travelled to an enormous gun safe in the corner.

"Yes, I should, but not in there." Norman followed Jack's glance. "That's the first place the wife will look. I have a much better place to hide it until Christmas."

Jack forced a smile. "Well, OK then, Norman. Happy Holidays!" Jack opened the door.

The two men walked across the street to their trucks in silence. Jack put his toolbox in the back of his truck and then turned to Angus. "So got an alibi, I mean plans, for this weekend?"

"The irony is that I do." Angus opened his truck door. "See you Monday, Brother."

"See ya," Jack said, walking back to his truck.

Saturday, December 1

Angus spent Friday night at the Veterans Center with Mark Herrera. Normally volunteers worked the hotline solo, but

Mark had pulled two double shifts the previous week and had asked Angus to come in just in case he fell asleep. Angus had reheated some stew, and the men had shared it and some bread for a simple dinner. Then they set the burglar alarm, put on a pot of coffee, and waited for the phone to ring.

Unlike most of the holiday season, the night had been uneventful. A woman had called in around 9:30 PM, because she was feeling very lonely. Mark talked to her for about 30 minutes, and after that, no one called. While Mark napped on the couch, Angus tried to stay awake by sitting in the office chair. At some point he nodded off as well and didn't wake until Mark put a cup of coffee in front of him.

"What a night." Mark stretched his limbs and cracked his neck. "I must have needed the sleep."

Angus sipped the freshly brewed coffee. It was decent. "I didn't have that bad of a week. I can't believe I conked out too."

Mark picked up the phone and checked for missed calls. "Well, no harm done," he said. "I'm sure one of us would have woken up if the phone had rung."

"True." Angus stood up and started looking around for the shoes he had discarded the previous evening.

"Omelet place, curry?" Mark put down the phone and reached for a bag that he kept a change of clothes in.

"Nah," Angus said. "Remember, I have plans."

Angus had spent most of dinner updating Mark on the search for Sylvester Thompson. Mark had found the entire process interesting and had asked so many questions that they had talked of little else.

"Fair enough," Mark said. He took his bag to the bathroom.

Left alone in the room, Angus put on his shoes and tidied up. The night before had been chilly. He folded the blanket that he had covered his lap with and placed it on the back of the couch. Then for good measure, he tidied up Mark's sleep space. He went downstairs and collected his containers from the kitchen. He hollered a goodbye to Mark upstairs, turned off the alarm, and walked out to his truck.

On a regular Saturday, Angus grocery shopped and cleaned his townhouse, but today he had a special day with Lily planned. On his way home, he stopped at a supermarket to pick up some things to get him through the next couple of days. His big shopping trip would have to wait. When he was about half a mile from his townhouse, he heard a loud noise and felt the truck lurch. He pulled over and inspected his vehicle. One of his tires had a gash in it from some road debris. Air was leaking out but not quickly. Angus decided it was safe to change the tire later.

He drove home cautiously and parked in the carport that he shared with the three other residents of his building. He unloaded his groceries and called Lily to ask if she could drive. After a light breakfast, he went upstairs, showered, and changed into his fancy dress kilt and nice shirt. He took his lined trench coat out of the closet and waited for Lily to say she was on the way.

Around 9:30, Lily texted saying that she was parked in the carport.

"You shouldn't park in the other residents' spots," Angus said as he got into Lily's car. "Some people get touchy about it."

Lily looked at him and shook her head. "It's just for a minute, and I didn't want to make you stand out in the cold."

Angus felt she had a point, but he also remembered Hank telling him about a 20-minute discussion at a recent HOA meeting about parking. However, since Angus had heard Nick's SUV leave a few minutes before Lily had arrived, he felt no harm had been done.

"So, you said we were going to Manitou Springs and that

I should dress up a little." Lily changed the subject. "Any specific plans?"

Manitou Springs was a small town to the southwest of Colorado Springs at the base of Pikes Peak. It consisted of a main street with a variety of unique shops and several other attractions. There was an old-time portrait studio and a shop that sold only rubber ducks. Just off the main drag, people could take a cog railway up to the summit of Pikes Peak or instead make a similar journey by hiking 13 miles up the Barr Trail. During the tuberculosis epidemic in the late nineteenth and early twentieth centuries, the mountain air had led to the establishment of many sanitoriums in the area. Sadly, while clean air helped the patients, it wasn't a cure for their ailment, and many of them died, leading some people to speculate that many historic properties in the town were haunted.

Angus liked to go to Manitou about twice a year, and it was a great place to take visitors to Colorado. He was always scouting out fresh places to take Aunty Ivy, who visited Colorado every couple of years, and Maggie had proven to be a value ally. A few months ago, a friend of Maggie's had just raved about having tea at a castle in Manitou, and Angus had checked it out. It turned out to be a place where reservations were required, so Angus had booked one for himself and Lily and then sort of forgotten about it with all the drama.

Manitou Springs was a quirky enough place that there was more than one building that referred to itself as a castle, but besides a well-reviewed tea room, Angus and Lily's destination was one place that paranormal experts considered to be haunted. Built in the late 1800s by a French priest, it was haunted by the ghost of a nun or a child who died of tuberculosis or both depending on your source. After he had made the reservation, Angus had stumbled upon a book about the haunted places in Manitou Springs at the library, and while he didn't believe in the supernatural, he stayed up all night reading the book. It was quite interesting, and he knew it would serve as a substantial source of entertainment to his Aunty Ivy on her next visit.

"We have a 1 PM reservation for high tea." Angus put on his sunglasses as Lily drove south toward Filmore Road. "We can take the tour of the historic property that houses the tea room or just walk around town."

"Sounds fun." Lily smiled. "I know it's a day for us, but do you mind if we stop at the vintage jewelry store? Mutti swears she saw a compass in a nice case the last time she was there and thought it would make a great present for my dad, but she can't find it on the website."

Jewelry shopping wasn't Angus's idea of fun, but this was a day for both himself and Lily, so he agreed.

During the 30-minute drive to Manitou Springs, the couple chatted about their week and their remaining holiday shopping. Even though it was early, traffic into Manitou was heavy, and parking was difficult. Lily found a spot at the very western end of Manitou Avenue near the portrait studio.

While Angus paid for parking, Lily looked at the photos in the window. Most of the photos were printed to look vintage in a sepia hue, but some of them were full color. Couples and family groups posed in a variety period costumes from frontier pioneers to Depression Era gangsters.

"I think you'd look rather dashing in that coon-skin cap," Lily said to Angus as he joined her.

"A kilt and a coon-skin cap," Angus contemplated. "I don't see it working."

"You silly goose." Lily quipped. "You'd have to wear the complete costume."

Angus looked at the number of people already milling around the front of the studio, waiting their turns. "Maybe another day."

The couple strolled down the street, passing different

shops, galleries, and boutiques. While they looked in windows, Lily didn't go inside any shop until they reached the jeweler she had mentioned.

A bell rang as they walked in the door, and a small shaggy dog greeted them.

"Hello there, Abby." Lily reached down and petted the mutt. To Angus she said, "Abby is the store dog. She's a good-will ambassador and keeps men from getting bored."

"Hello, Abby." Angus scratched the dog behind her ears. Abby panted happily, but as soon as he stopped, she wandered off towards her bed at the back of the store.

"Well, hello, Lily and friend." A shop assistant greeted them. She was a woman in late middle age with straight white hair that flowed to her shoulders, a floral blouse, and a long skirt. "Looking for anything in particular today?"

Lily approached one of the glass cases that held a variety of watches and men's jewelry. "Actually, Fiona, I am," she said, "But first introductions. Fiona, this is my boyfriend, Angus. Angus, this is the very talented Fiona who always can find five things that I will like off the top of her head."

Angus and Fiona exchanged greetings, and then Lily got down to business. She described the item that her mother remembered in some detail, and Fiona recalled it. "We sold it last week." She tilted her head to the side, remembering the specifics. "But it doesn't matter because it wasn't a compass. It was just a fancy pocket watch with a bunch of weird features and a decorative case."

"Too bad. Mutti's having a such a hard time finding something for Dad." Lily took out her phone to send her mother a text.

Fiona waited for Lily to finish and then asked, "Do you want to see what we've gotten in since last time?"

"Sure." Lily's face lit up.

"Lily loves vintage jewelry," Fiona declared, "but if you think about it, it's kind of recycling."

Angus nodded and followed the women as they walked around the shop. At every case, Fiona pointed out an item or two, and sometimes Lily would try it on. In the back was a case of vintage engagement rings, and Fiona pointed out several new arrivals making comments about Lily's general preferences.

"I don't think we're quite ready for ring shopping yet, Fiona." Lily blushed. "But if we ever have the need, we'll stop in."

Fiona nodded and moved on to another case. After a full circuit of the store, Angus was bored silly, and Abby the dog had dropped off to sleep. The clock over the cash register said it was almost eleven, and he wondered if he should push Lily towards the door or just let her shop.

Lily returned to a case of the oldest pieces and asked Fiona to show her a cameo broach. It was quite large and featured a goddess holding a bundle of grains. "It's quite a delightful piece. We just got it in last week."

Lily turned the broach over in her hands several times and looked at the price tag. Then she looked at the design again.

"It's exquisite, but I don't need it." She handed it back to Fiona.

Fiona looked at Angus and then the broach, and Angus caught her meaning. To Lily she said, "Well, let us know if you change your mind. Remember to remind us you are local if you buy it on the website, so that you can just pick it up."

"OK, thanks, and Happy Holidays." Lily headed for the door.

For the next hour, Lily and Angus browsed the shops up and down the street. Lily stopped to buy some rubber ducks for stocking stuffers but otherwise made no purchases.

Half an hour before their tea reservation, they returned to

Lily's car, drove up a side street, and parked. While the building was large with thick limestone walls, Angus felt that calling it a castle was a bit of stretch. He led Lily down the narrow stone stairs from the parking lot to a door at the side of the building.

The couple entered an opulently decorated room with enough tables to seat perhaps 20 or 30 guests. Garlands and ribbons in red, green, and gold hung above the panoramic windows, and a variety of fancy teapots and cups were on display.

"Good afternoon." A server came up to the couple. "Do you have a reservation today?"

"Two for the 1 o'clock sitting under MacBangus," Angus said.

"Ah, yes." The server led them to a table for two over by the window. "Two deluxe high teas with no allergies, correct?"

"Aye." Angus pulled out Lily's chair for her and then sat down himself.

"My name is Emily," the server said, placing some menus on the table. "Each of you can pick two teas to sample with your four courses. Let me know if you have questions."

"Thank you." Lily picked up a menu and looked through it.

"And feel free to try on any of the hats on offer and take pictures as you like," Emily said before she walked away.

Along the interior wall of the tea room, several racks were laden with large decorative hats. Two mirrors were also provided.

"This place is amazing," Lily gushed. "I think I'll pick a hat after we order."

The server returned a few minutes later and took their order. Lily walked over to the racks and selected a prim and proper yellow hat with a large decorative flower. She put it on and modelled it for Angus, who gave her a thumbs up. Then she changed her mind and picked out a similar hat in dark blue. Satisfied with her selection, she looked through the much smaller selection of men's hats and found a black bowler for Angus.

"Try this on for size." She handed the hat to Angus when she returned to the table.

Angus put on the hat and walked over to the mirror. It looked silly, but what the heck! Returning to the table, he noticed Lily had her phone out.

"Just one selfie," she begged.

Emily returned with their tea pots. "I could take a photo of you two. There's a nice place over here, so that you won't get any glare off the windows." With the manner of an experienced amateur, the server guided them over to a wall covered in wood paneling and decorated with holiday garlands. She took a few photos and when they had returned to their table gave them instructions on how long to steep the tea.

The room, which had been rather empty when they first arrived, filled up and got warmer, but Angus and Lily enjoyed themselves. The server brought them scones, jam, and cream followed by a fruit cup, tiny tea sandwiches, and a variety of desserts. Between bites, Angus entertained Lily by telling her of the various ghosts that were supposed to haunt Manitou. She listened intently.

"So, what kind of feeling do you get from this place?" she asked. Angus had shared some of his experiences with uncanny insights with her, just enough for her to be curious.

Angus considered this for a moment. On his first visit, he had toured the house, and while he had found the displays of period furniture and everyday objects interesting, he had felt absolutely nothing. The whole place reminded him a bit of the vicarage in his grandparent's village. He had visited it a couple times as a boy, but other than nostalgia, the place seemed pretty ordinary.

"I've never been one for ghosts or spirits." Angus took a sip of his Darjeeling tea. "My instincts seem to be centered in the here and now."

"Do you think it would be different if you knew someone who had died here?" Lily asked. She took her napkin from her lap, wiped her month, and set the napkin on the table.

"Maybe." Angus remembered how first his grandfather and then his grandmother and then his mother had all passed away over the course of 18 months. His Aunt Grace and her family moved into the family home after his mother had died, and his Aunty Ivy had whisked him away to Edinburgh. Angus tried to remember if he had been back there since then, maybe once for a weekend. He wondered if he would be able to feel the ghosts of his family in his old home. Probably not. None of them had a reason to haunt the place.

"You just had the strangest look on your face." Lily stretched her legs under the table. "Penny for your thoughts."

"Just thinking that maybe I should visit Scotland again," Angus said, not wanting to go into great detail. "It's been 10 years since I've been back."

"Sounds fun, but isn't Ivy coming next summer? I can't wait to meet her."

Angus smiled. At first, he hadn't been sure how Ivy would react to Lily, but now he sensed they would get on very well. "That doesn't mean I can't visit her as well." Angus looked out the window and noticed clouds had rolled in and darkened. "About finished?" he asked.

"I think so." Lily rose from her seat.

While Lily went in search of a restroom, Angus paid the bill and got out his phone. He looked up the jeweler they had visited earlier and searched their inventory for the cameo. The list price of the item was higher than he would have expected, but as Angus browsed more, he realized he wasn't very familiar with jewelry prices. Angus shared the listing for the cameo with Maggie and asked her what she thought, but she was offline, so he put away his phone and waited for Lily.

Lily walked back to the table. "Sorry, that took a while." She leaned in and whispered. "The gal in front of me was in there forever."

Angus nodded, and the two of them left the tea room. Outside the temperature had dropped, and the air was crisp.

"Looks like snow is on the way," Lily said as they walked to the parking lot. "Want to just head back to my place?"

"Sure." Angus replied. Then he remembered. "But I should change my tire before the storm hits, and the truth is while I know how to change a tire, it's not a job that I enjoy."

Lily considered this as she unlocked her car. "Why don't you text my dad and see if he will help you. He's been wanting to see your place for a while, and then you could come back to our house for dinner."

"OK." Angus took Lily's phone and texted her dad as they pulled out of the parking lot and headed back to the Springs. Lily's dad had spent 20 years in the Air Force, and many people found him intimidating, but he and Angus got along just fine. However, Angus knew that Reggie Saunders would quickly realize the townhouse wasn't big enough for Angus, Lily, and Jaiden. Buying a house wasn't a subject that he and Lily had broached, and Angus suddenly realized that he had a lot of decisions to make.

Traffic back into the Springs was even heavier than it had been in the morning, and by the time Angus and Reggie got back to Angus's place, it was after 4.

"Nice place," Reggie said after Angus had shown him around the townhouse. "I kind of envy you. No lawn. No fence to maintain. Although I could do without the stairs."

"Thanks." Angus had never thought about his neighbor

Hank and Murphey having to climb their stairs every day. "And the resale value is quite good."

Reggie nodded. "Good to see you're thinking ahead."

Angus went upstairs and changed into his work coveralls, and then men went back outside. Nick's SUV was still gone, so they left the truck in its spot and worked on the tire. Angus didn't know a lot about cars, and a couple of years ago he's tried to change a tire and had the jack slip. The whole incident had spooked him, so he was usually more than happy to let his trusted mechanic do all the work on his truck.

As the men finished, a dark blue sedan pulled up and parked behind the carport. Detectives Green and Harrington got out.

"Been a while since I've seen you." Angus wiped his hands on a rag.

"We're sorry to disturb you," Detective Green walked over and stood under the carport. "We just need to ask you about your whereabouts today." Looking down at the jack and damaged tire, she added, "When did this happen?"

Angus spent the next few minutes going through his day for the officers. Detective Green took notes in her notebook. When Angus finished, she asked, "So just to clarify, your truck has been in the carport all day?"

"Aye," Angus said, looking up at Nick's camera.

"Well, that clears that up. We needed to see if we could eliminate you as a suspect in a robbery that took place today. Thank you." Green flipped her notebook shut and turned to go back to the car.

Angus addressed both Green and Harrington. "Out of interest, which one of my clients was robbed?"

"A Mr. Norman Upjohn," Detective Harrington said. "I believe that you and Jack hung his holiday decorations and fixed a bathroom doorknob just yesterday."

"Aye, we did." Angus shook his head. Poor Norman. "His wife's ring been stolen?"

Detective Green consulted a different page in her notebook. "And a new gaming system and some games for his children plus some other small items."

"And, of course, the first person you suspected was the handy man," Reggie commented indignantly. "Can't you just leave the poor man alone?"

"Actually, sir, because of the circumstances of the robbery, we didn't suspect Angus, but we needed to confirm his alibi," Dan said.

"Circumstances?" Angus asked.

Dan looked at Detective Green, who nodded. "Besides the items that we already mentioned, the thief stole a bicycle and made a sandwich while on the premises," Dan explained. "It seems more like the work of neighborhood kids."

A puzzled look came over Reggie's face. "But what would neighborhood kids do with a sapphire ring?"

Green took over the story, "Mr. Upjohn was in the habit of storing his children's Christmas presents in two large duffle bags in the trunk of his car. He's been doing it for years, and it turns out that this was well known by both his wife and his kids." She shook head and tisked. "And half the neighborhood."

Angus's head ached. He'd hoped Norman would have been a bit more cautious.

"Anyway, after he showed you the ring, Norman put it in one pocket of the duffel bag, since he knew his wife had already looked there. He was tired from the afternoon of supervising you two and figured he would move it later," Green continued.

"And he didn't?" Angus asked.

"Nope," Dan said. "Not only did he leave it there, but he

also left his car unlocked in the garage while he and his family took his wife's SUV out to do some more shopping. When he returned home, he noticed the trunk was open and the duffel bags were gone.

"That is awful," Angus said. Norman had been unwise, but the consequences of his actions were pretty harsh.

"If the bike turns up, we might have a chance at catching them." Green looked back at the car. "The kids may not even know that there's a ring in there."

"Well, we've taken enough of your time," Dan said. "Stay safe out there tonight."

The two officers got back in their car and drove away. Reggie watched them go.

"Angus, you're a good fellow," he said. "This has to be taking a toll."

"It's annoying." Angus agreed. "But this seems like a coincidence. At least I can account for my whereabouts. The more often they can eliminate me, the less likely they are to believe I am involved in any of it."

"I guess." Reggie walked toward the door to the townhouse. "I don't think I would have the patience for this."

The men went inside, and Angus changed again. Then he followed Reggie back to his house and had dinner with Lily, Hilde, and Jaiden. Lily gushed about their tea, and Hilde was impressed, but Angus was had trouble paying attention to the conversation. Reggie's words echoed in his mind. He was losing patience with this whole situation. He wished he could figure out who was framing him, but even more than the search for his father, it seemed like too complicated of a problem for him to take on.

CHAPTER 8

Saturday, January 19

Christmas came and went, and Angus enjoyed himself immensely. He gave Lily the cameo she had seen in the shop, and she gave him a new sporran. After spending Christmas with Lily's family, Angus celebrated New Year's Eve with Mark Herrera at the hotline. They drank sparkling cider and wore party hats while they waited for the phone to ring.

Angus took the New Year as an opportunity to finish up old projects and start new ones. After a challenging search, Aunty Ivy had contacted her friend Bonnie Stewart and had arranged a visit in late January. Angus was waiting for the results of that meeting to move forward on the search for his father.

Meanwhile, Angus turned his attention to more practical concerns. Early in the year, he had asked Maggie to walk through his townhouse and suggest some updates. He was considering putting the property on the market either the next summer or perhaps the summer after. She was full of suggestions but felt that remodeling the master bathroom was a priority. Jack agreed, and Angus undertook the project on the next available weekend.

The day dawned cold and cloudy. Angus woke up, had breakfast, and started the demo on his bathtub and shower stall. His plans included putting in new tile that reached the ceiling and changing out the fixtures. Eventually he would replace the toilet and put in new flooring, but he wasn't looking forward to seeing if the subfloor had water damage.

As Angus neared the end of removing the old tile and drywall, he sent a text to Reggie, who had promised to help him with the install. Angus could have done the job himself, but he valued the opportunity to get to know Lily's father better.

While he waited for Reggie to come over, Angus made a snack and a fresh pot of coffee. When Reggie arrived, Angus explained the general plan to him over a cuppa. Maggie stressed to clients that renovations can take longer than expected, and Reggie and Angus experienced this firsthand. The men worked well together, but they didn't finish putting in the tile and fixtures until almost 3 PM. Angus was glad that he had saved the other jobs in the bathroom for another day.

"Well, I don't know about you," Reggie said after he had washed his hands in the kitchen sink, "but I could do with a beer."

"I agree." Angus got out two pint glasses. "But I'll have some iced tea instead."

"Fair enough, but I don't want to take this home." Reggie took a beer out of the six pack he had brought. "You could have one or two."

Angus considered this. He was glad that Lily's family had a healthy attitude towards drinking, but he wasn't the sort of fellow who could share a six pack. "How about we have a couple with my neighbor Hank? He's about 10 years older than you and an Army vet."

"Is that the fellow who was too drunk to give you an alibi for the first robbery?" Reggie twisted the cap off his beer. "Maybe having him over for drinks isn't a good idea."

"True." Angus made no move to pour himself either tea or beer until they made up their minds. "The problem is he's lonely, and the lonelier he gets, the more he drinks." He paused for a few seconds. "And since I stopped going to Trivia Night as much, I haven't been visiting him every week."

"Poor fellow. Maybe we could order a pizza or something. Give him something to soak up the booze."

"Aye, maybe." Angus went back to the utility room behind the kitchen and looked in the compact deep freezer. "Or I could make us a spaghetti dinner." He took out a large plastic container of red sauce.

"Works for me." Reggie took a pull from his beer and waved off the glass Angus offered him.

Angus called Hank to invite him and got to work. He boiled water for pasta, defrosted the sauce in the microwave, and preheated the oven to make some garlic bread. Angus would have made a salad to go with the meal, but his refrigerator was particularly empty.

As Angus was straining the pasta, Hank knocked on the front door and came in with Murphey. The dog barked and tried to jump in Reggie's lap. "Sit, you silly old bastard," Hank ordered. Murphey ignored him but eventually went over and hopped up on Angus's couch.

Hank was skinny to the point of being gaunt. His tan, leathery skin contrasted with his short cropped white hair and neatly trimmed white beard. "Thanks for thinking of me, Angus." He looked across the table at Reggie. "Who's your friend?"

"This is Reggie Saunders, Lily's dad," Angus said. "Reggie, this is my neighbor Hank, and that's his dog Murphey."

The two men greeted each other, and Hank sat down at the table. He placed a small package wrapped in aluminum foil in front of him. "My daughter-in-law gave me some poppy seed cake last week, but she forgets it gets stuck in my dentures. Maybe you can have some for dessert."

"Thanks, Hank." Angus took out some plates and invited Hank and Reggie to serve themselves.

After they had eaten, the men sat back in their chairs and

talked. Reggie and Hank shared their experiences about how the armed forced used to be, and Angus told a couple stories from his deployments. Hank seemed to perk up as the evening progressed.

"You should come down to the American Legion Post with me some time," Reggie said as he handed Hank a second beer. "We have a pretty good time."

"Maybe I will, but I don't like to leave Murphey," Hank said. The elderly dog had woken up long enough to get some table scraps and had then returned to his nap.

"My grandson Jaiden would love to watch him." Reggie looked over at the sleeping dog. "Or so he says. A little dog sitting might be just the thing to get him to stop asking for one."

"Jaiden wants a dog?" Angus asked. This was the first he'd heard of it.

Reggie had been keeping the peace between Jaiden and Hilde for the last couple of years. He welcomed any compromise. "They had a dog when he was little, and when it died, they decided not to get a new one. Then Lily's husband died, and they moved back home, and Hilde says no."

Hank nodded. "He's not much trouble, but Murphey doesn't have a lot of experience with kids."

Before anyone could reply, there was a knock on the door. Angus got up to answer it and found the familiar figures of Detectives Green and Harrington on his doorstep.

"Good evening, Mr. MacBangus." Detective Green could not hide the fatigue in her voice. "We're sorry to bother you, but we have a few questions."

Angus looked back at his guests before he asked the officers inside.

"What is it this time?" Reggie stared at both Green and Harrington as if trying to get a fix on them.

"Angus, what were you doing between 8:30 and 10:30 this morning?" Detective Harrington asked.

Angus thought for a moment. When exactly had he started his project?

"Well, I came over around 9:30 to help Angus with a bathroom renovation project," Reggie jumped in.

"And before that?" Green asked, scribbling something in her notebook.

"I got up around 6:30 AM, had breakfast, and used a sledge hammer to remove some tile and drywall from my bathroom," Angus said. "Then I texted Reggie to come over and help me with the rest of the job."

The two officers looked at each other. Green wrote some more, stifled a yawn, and then asked, "Could you two narrow down those times some more?"

Reggie pulled out his phone. "Angus texted me around 8:55. It took me maybe 10 minutes to get ready and 20 minutes to drive over here."

"And you were at home when you texted Reggie?" Detective Harrington asked.

"Aye," Angus replied. "Although I don't know how I can prove that."

Everyone was quiet for a minute. Then Murphey woke up and started barking at the officers and trying to jump up on Green.

"Well, aren't you an outgoing doggie." Green gently pushed the dog back on the floor. "We've met before, haven't we?" She scratched Murphey's chin and then he rolled over and let her rub his belly.

Hank shrugged, but said nothing.

Angus's phone beeped, and he checked the message. It was from Maggie asking for the before and after pictures that he had taken of the bathtub renovation. Angus was very grateful that Maggie was a bit nosy. He pulled up the pictures from that morning and examined the timestamps. Then he held out the phone for Detective Green, who had convinced Murphey to go back to his nap.

"Here's my bathroom at 7:45 before I got started." Angus showed her the picture. "And here is the shower tile ripped out about an hour later." He showed her the next picture. "So, unless I paid someone else to demo my bathroom and document the process with my phone, I think these photos account for my movements."

"Excellent," Green said. "Just one more thing." She paused. "Was your truck here all morning?"

"I assume so," Angus said. Green had asked about his truck the last time she was here. He wondered why.

"Mr. MacBangus, could we sit down a minute?" Green looked over at the table in the dining area.

"Sure," Angus said.

When both officers were seated, Green flipped open her notebook. "Angus, we've talked about enemies before, old Army buddies, business rivals." Angus nodded. "Well, what about people who live in your townhouse complex? Any issues there?"

Angus took a minute to ponder the question. He tried to be a good neighbor, and he couldn't think of anyone who he had offended. "Not off the top of my head." Turning to Hank, he asked, "Can you think of anyone?"

Hank took a drink from his beer. "Well, Jimmy Kim wasn't happy when you voted against his proposal to put up security cameras in the entire complex, but it was you and more than half the residents, so I don't think he has a particular grudge."

Green noted Kim's name. "He's the fellow who has the camera pointed at the visitor parking area?"

"Yup. A little paranoid, but a decent fellow," Hank said. "Although I know his wife better."

Harrington looked at Green, who nodded. "One idea that we had was that the actual thieves are someone who lives near you, who can keep tabs on you."

Angus wrinkled his brow. "But why?" he asked. "Why go to all the trouble to pin a series of robberies on me?"

"Maybe they saw your truck when they were casing a job, and it gave them the idea," Green said. "Or perhaps the person isn't in their right mind, and they have some sort of unhealthy obsession with you."

"Or it's someone with too much time on their hands who is bored," Hank added.

"Maybe," Harrington said. "By the way, Hank, isn't it?"

"Yup."

"You're at home a lot," Harrington said. "Have you noticed anything suspicious? Someone hanging around Angus's townhouse? Or someone who doesn't seem to belong?"

Hank examined the empty bottom on his beer bottle as if it might hold the answers. "No, not really. I live across the street and don't have the best view, nor do I spent my days sitting at the window keeping watch." He turned the bottle in his hand and looked at it from another angle. "You might ask Mrs. Kim," he suggested. "When she's not outside tending her flowers or bird feeders, she sits on a lawn chair soaking up the sun. Sometimes she carries a small pair of binoculars."

"Thank," Detective Green said. "We just may."

"You know, the person wouldn't have to be home all day to keep an eye on Angus," Reggie said. "It could be someone who works similar hours to him who just monitors him during evenings and weekends."

"I guess that's possible," Detective Harrington agreed.

"That is when most of the robberies take place."

Angus remained silent. He had been against putting up cameras in the complex, because he felt it was an invasion of privacy. Now he wondered if someone was watching him and why. His stomach churned.

"Incidentally, how are you so sure of those times for today?" Reggie asked. "It's a brief window for a thief."

"True." Detective Green consulted her notebook. "The family who was robbed planned to be gone all day in Woodland Park, but about 45 minutes into the drive, their youngest started throwing up. So, they pulled over, cleaned the kid up, and drove home."

"We think the thief just waited for them to leave and as soon as they'd been gone a few minutes, they committed the robbery," Detective Harrington said. "The timing would have been tight for Angus to make it back in time to meet Reggie at his place, but with the evidence of the photos, it just couldn't be done."

"Well, unless Reggie took your phone and provided you with an alibi," Green added. "But it doesn't seem worth it for two tablets, a laptop, and a bit of jewelry."

"And how did I come up as a suspect?" Angus broke his silence.

"We always ask about visitors and tradespeople," Harrington said. "You changed their locks and fixed a running toilet when the family moved in last September."

Angus nodded. That could have been any of several jobs, but he didn't care. He was tired.

"Anyway, we are sorry to have bothered you." Detective Green stood up from the table. "But take care and report anything suspicious to us directly." She took out three copies of her card and gave one to each man.

"Will do." Angus saw the officers out.

Reggie went to the fridge to get himself and Hank the last two beers. Once the door was closed and he heard the officers walk away, he said, "This is ridiculous, Angus! Ridiculous. It's harassment."

Angus looked down at the floor. He had so hoped that the new year would be a clean slate. "They're just doing their jobs, Reggie, but I admit I am weary of this, very weary."

Angus took the package of cake off the table, unwrapped it, and cut it into slices. Then he offered it around. He didn't prepare any coffee or tea, hoping that his visitors would take the hint.

Reggie took a bite of cake and smiled with approval. "It's too bad there's nothing you can do about this," he mused.

"Like what?" Angus had lost his appetite but had tasted his cake to be polite. "I mean, it's not like we can set a trap or something. I kind of wish we could."

"Maybe we could." Hank thought out loud.

"How?" asked Reggie, brushing crumbs off his shirt.

"Simple." Hank looked at the two men. "Next weekend Angus takes Lily to someplace nice for a night or two but leaves his truck here."

"OK." Angus nodded.

"In fact." Hank became more animated. "Angus sneaks out so that someone casually watching thinks he's still at home."

"And then you and some other neighbors keep an eye on the townhouse to see if you can figure out who's watching it?" Reggie nodded his head.

"Exactly," Hank said. "We look for anyone who approaches the front door or anyone with a camera or binoculars, besides Mrs. Kim, of course. I think we should let her in on it."

"I don't know if it's a good idea." Angus didn't see this as a good way to catch his stalker, if he even had one, which he doubted. Although he had been considering taking Lily for a weekend away. He didn't see any harm in letting Hank do some surveillance, so Angus heard Hank out.

"I'm sure that Mrs. Kim would prove quite valuable in your effort, but perhaps you should keep this a one-man operation," Reggie said. "Don't want to take the risk of her letting the cat out of the bag."

"And as much as I am sure Mrs. Kim is a pleasant person and her husband is on the up and up," Angus added, "Mr. Kim owns a business that installs surveillance cameras. There's a chance he is involved tangentially, like maybe someone hacked his camera feed on the parking lot."

"Good point." Hank considered this for a moment. "I hadn't thought of someone using the existing cameras. We'll have to find a way for Angus to get out of his house in a way that doesn't attract attention."

"He could pack now, and I could take his bags home with me tonight." Reggie's energy level had risen, and he had left his beer almost untouched. "And when Lily picks him up, he could wear a disguise."

"A disguise?" Angus looked at both men with some doubt. "Like a ball cap and fake mustache?"

Hank chuckled. "Actually, I think a pair of khaki trousers and a different coat and hat would do the trick."

"Oh, no." Angus raised his voice. "I do not wear pants unless I am working!"

"And that is why it would be effective," Hank said. "If someone is watching your house on a weekend, they are looking for a man in a kilt to come out. No kilt, and they will probably filter you out."

"But I don't own pants," Angus argued. "I don't even own

shorts."

Reggie looked at both men and then at his own grubby jeans. "I don't think either of us can lend you a pair, but I bet you could find some at a thrift store. After all, you won't wear them again."

Angus relented. "Fine, but Lily is driving me back to your house so that I can change. I'm not wearing trousers for one second longer than necessary."

"Excellent," Reggie said. "Now where are you taking my daughter next weekend?"

The men spent the next few minutes discussing potential destinations. Angus suggested a couple of fancy hotels in Manitou or the Broadmoor. Reggie argued Denver was a better bet, because if Angus was going to all this trouble, he might as well have a solid alibi. Hank added that if Angus stayed local, someone might cotton on to the fact that he wasn't at home. Angus selected a hotel in downtown Denver with ready access to museums and galleries, and Reggie recommended a restaurant to make a dinner reservation at.

Hank also ironed out his plans. He suggested Angus come home in the late afternoon on Friday, change into his disguise, and have Reggie or Lily pick him up. That way if the person watching him worked banker's hours, they would just assume that Angus had come home early. Then Jack and Murphey would pretend to come over for dinner, and with the help of light timers, Angus would make it look like he was at home. Angus expressed concern that anyone watching would be suspicious if he didn't go shopping Saturday morning, so Reggie suggested he make a show of coming home with lots of grocery bags Thursday night. After all, Angus hadn't gone shopping this Saturday either.

The more the men flushed out their plans, the sillier Angus thought the whole idea was, but he hadn't ever seen Hank so animated and engaged. Maybe this was just what Hank needed.

From Angus's perspective, the plan worked perfectly. He'd come home from work at 3 PM on Friday and changed into his disguise, an uncomfortable pair of blue jeans he had bought at Goodwill and a leather jacket, hat, and scarf that he had borrowed from Reggie. Then he walked out his front door and met Reggie in the visitor parking lot. Reggie had driven him back to his house, and Angus had changed and waited for Lily to get home from work.

Driving up to Denver in Lily's car had taken longer than he would have liked, but driving from Colorado Springs to Denver and back was always slow. The route had been under construction for as long as Angus could remember, and even with addition lanes and streamlined interchanges, the traffic got no better.

Angus and Lily had checked into a hotel room that featured a jacuzzi tub and spent a quiet night. Angus had bought a bottle of champagne, which he took a polite sip of and let Lily enjoy. They had slept in and had a large breakfast before heading to a natural history museum. The couple were looking at dinosaur skeletons when Angus's phone buzzed. Seeing the name "Detective Dan" pop up on the caller ID, Angus stepped into a hallway and picked up.

"Angus?" the caller asked.

"Yes," Angus said. "What's up, Dan? Another burglary?"

"Yes." Dan didn't use his usual "just a couple of questions" tone. "The good news is that you aren't a suspect. That bad news is that it's your townhouse that was broken into, and when he tried to interfere, Hank was injured."

"Is he badly hurt?" Angus felt his stomach drop and his pulse quicken.

"It looks like a sprained ankle and some bruising from a fall," Dan said. "But the paramedics are taking him to the hospital just to be safe." Lily had come out of the exhibit and was giving him an inquiring look. Angus covered up the microphone on his phone and mouthed "Hank." Lily's face went pale, and she stood near Angus trying to hear the conversation.

Angus breathed a little easier. "And what about Murphey?" he asked.

"The little dog that likes to jump on people?"

"Yes." Angus felt horrible. He had thought that nothing would come of Hank's plan, and now Hank had been hurt.

"He's with your neighbor, Mrs. Kim, right now," Dan said.

"Good." Angus let out a breath he hadn't realized that he'd been holding. Hank could be bristly and brusque, but he loved his dog and would be upset if anything happened to Murphey while he was away. "So, tell me about the burglary."

There was a pause and the rustling of paper on the other end of the line before Dan summarized what he'd learned from various people at the scene. "Apparently, as you planned to be away for the weekend, Hank was watching your townhouse to see if anyone was snooping around. He was sitting outside having an iced tea and talking to Mrs. Kim, when he saw someone approach your door. He pointed the individual out to Mrs. Kim, and they watched as a person, who was dressed in a black jogging outfit, first knocked on your door and then took something out of a fanny pack and used it to open the door."

As Dan paused, Angus jumped in, "Did they jimmy it or pick it?" Angus had never really believed in the theory that someone was watching him and trying to set him up. It was just too fantastic, but now he wondered if perhaps it wasn't. Or maybe it was just his turn to get burgled. Colorado Springs had a problem with property crimes.

"Picked it," Dan answered. "Hank and Mrs. Kim were

using her bird watching binoculars to observe your door, so the intruder didn't know they had been seen."

"Oddly professional," Angus observed, realizing that they would need to pack up and go home.

"Quite, and it gets weirder," Dan continued with his account. "Hank told Mrs. Kim to call 911 and went over to your townhouse to investigate. He found the burglar in your office going through your boxes of photos. According to him, he confronted a woman, and she pushed him into the bathroom and ran down the stairs. Mrs. Kim confirms she saw a thin figure in the black jogging suit run out the front door and away from the road a minute after Hank entered your townhouse."

"Did you catch her?" Angus asked. The townhouse complex was bordered by some sandstone bluffs on one side and a busy roadway on the other. The only straightforward way in and out of the community was a two-lane road that had townhouse buildings on each side. Surely the woman would have had to return to the main road through the townhouse complex at some point.

"No. It's like she vanished without a trace," Dan said. Angus could hear the frustration and annoyance in his voice. "Perhaps into a townhouse in the complex. We still haven't reviewed all the security camera footage. By the way, you don't know if Nick fixed the camera that points at everyone's front doors, do you?"

Angus tried to remember his recent conversations with Nick, who had been laid off and was doing some freelance work from home. Since the man's cameras had provided him with an alibi, he had made a greater effort to get to know him. He said, "I don't think he has."

"We'll know soon enough," Dan said.

"So did Hank see the burglar take anything?" Angus was glad that he had digitized most of his family photos and documents. Even if some of them had been taken, he would at least have a copy.

"No. In fact, remember how I said that it got weirder?"

"Aye." Angus was just about done with life being unpredictable.

"You will need to confirm this, but it doesn't look like she took anything," Dan said. "Quite the opposite. She appears to have left a watch and a ring in the box of photos of Clan MacBangus."

"What?" Angus's jaw dropped. People didn't break in and leave items, unless....

"The watch and ring were reported stolen during two robberies in October that you didn't have a firm alibi for, but after they occurred, we did a thorough search of your vehicle and property," Dan added.

Angus wasn't sure what to say. His mind was reeling.

"Given the circumstances, it looks like the burglar broke in to plant the items," Dan said. "On an interesting note, while they look fancy, the ring was costume jewelry, and the watch wasn't particularly valuable. Also, we've dusted them, and there are no fingerprints on them."

"So, being unable to sell them, they used them to shift the blame to me?" Angus speculated.

"That's what we think. Look, we need you to head back here as soon as you can to confirm nothing was taken."

"Alright." Angus looked over at Lily, who had her phone out. "It may take a while."

"I understand," Dan said. "Hank gave Mrs. Kim your spare keys, so we'll lock up when we're done. Call me when you get home."

"Will do. Bye." Angus ended the call and turned to Lily. "I know you heard my half of things." He summarized what Dan had told him. "I'm afraid we'll have to check out of our hotel and head back to Colorado Springs," he concluded.

The couple returned to their room and packed up. As they merged onto I-25 South towards the Springs, Lily asked, "So, to be clear, the police think that someone has been surveilling your townhouse and committing robberies of your clients while you are home alone with no alibi?"

"Apparently." Angus signaled and moved over to the far-left lane.

"And now that person has broken into your townhouse while you were out of town to plant worthless items to further implicate you in the robberies?" Lily shook her head.

"Aye." Angus tried to concentrate on the road. He'd already been through this several times in his own head and was still having trouble processing it. "And on a weekend when I tried to make it look like I was at home by sneaking out."

"So maybe they are watching you pretty closely," Lily said. She paused for a minute. "Do you think it could be one of your neighbors?"

Angus gazed at the horizon and went through the people he knew from his complex, one by one. "I don't know; I really don't," he said. "My neighbors are older folks or young professionals. I don't see any of them moonlighting as burglars, but I guess you never know."

"Maybe you should move." Lily stared out the car window at the mile markers on the side of the highway.

"I've been considering it for a while," Angus said. This didn't seem like the time for a discussion about moving in together, but he didn't want to spend the next hour and a half listening to the radio and brooding. "I guess I should finish the updates that Maggie suggested and start looking for a house."

"Where were you thinking of buying?"

For the next half an hour, the couple talked about the property market in Colorado Springs. Lily discussed the best school districts, while Angus shared what he knew about the quality of the building in each neighborhood. His least favorite neighborhood was the one that was built on the old municipal landfill where the grass didn't grow in random places, and he often wondered why.

"I guess you just need to find a house that you like, and if Jaiden and I move in, we could just use school choice to get him into the school we want," Lily concluded. She looked over at Angus with a tentative smile.

Angus smiled back. "That sounds like a sensible solution." Lily had opened up a possibility, so Angus pushed it a little farther. "Maybe you can help me look at some properties."

"I'd like that," Lily said. "We used to rent, so I've lived in a lot of different houses and know what works and what doesn't."

"Cool," Angus said. He stared at the next exit sign and calculated that they still had at least another 45 minutes on the road.

Lily turned up the radio, which was playing light, upbeat music, and the couple sat listening to it. Lily had always found that moments of stress could lead to moments of clarity. She liked Angus's townhouse, but it wasn't big enough for three. Besides, she was eager for some resolution of this whole "framing Angus for burglaries" situation. If moving made the burglaries stop, it was a step in the right direction.

As they approached the exit for Palmer Lake, Angus's phone beeped with a message from Hank. The text read. *Doctor says I need to stay off my feet for a couple days. Nothing broken. Home tomorrow.*

"Well, that's a relief," Angus said after sharing the news with Lily.

"It certainly is. So, are you going to tell Dan about how

you planned this weekend?"

"I should," Angus said. Over that last couple of hours, he'd felt the adrenaline bleed away and be replaced with fatigue. Knowing that Hank wasn't seriously injured helped get rid of some of his guilt. "It was a stupid thing to do, but I didn't believe that anything would come of it, and I am just so sick of sitting around having things happen to me. I wanted to do something."

Lily considered this for a moment. "It was kind of stupid and super cheesy, and I still can't believe you wore jeans, but Hank's going to be OK. That's all that matters."

"I suppose." Angus's eyes burned, and his head ached. He just wanted to get home and see if anything was missing.

When Angus and Lily pulled into the visitor parking space across from the Kim's, Mrs. Kim rushed out to meet them. After Angus shared the news with her that Hank would be home the next day, she calmed down. Her husband didn't like dogs and had insisted that Murphey stay in Hank's townhouse, where he had been alternating between sleeping and howling. Angus went over to Hank's and took the dog, some food, and his water bowl over to his townhouse.

Angus wasn't sure what to expect as he let himself and Lily into his home. Fingerprint powder lingered on the front doorknob, but his key worked. As soon as they entered, Murphey jumped up on the couch and made himself at home. Angus and Lily stood in the doorway, looking at the first floor. Nothing seemed disturbed.

Angus's office was a different matter. One box of photos had been knocked onto the floor, and the contents were scattered everywhere. The other box sat open with its cover on the desk. Angus took a few minutes to examine the contents before he came to the same conclusion that Dan had; nothing had been taken. Just to be sure, he and Lily looked through the rest of the rooms on the second floor before they called Dan.

Dan arrived about 20 minutes later. He needed Angus to sign some paperwork about the burglary and gave him a copy of the police report for his records. While the men took care of their business, Lily made a salad and took out some bread and butter. She realized that she and Angus hadn't eaten since their late brunch.

"Let me get this straight," Dan asked after listening to Angus's account of his weekend. "You snuck out of your townhouse in disguise to set a trap for anyone who was watching the place?"

"Pretty much," Angus admitted. He had accepted a bowl of salad from Lily, but he was picking at it.

"Well, that explains why we didn't spot you leaving on either Nick or Mr. Kim's camera." Dan laughed. "We were looking for a tall man in a kilt." He stirred some sugar into the coffee that Lily had offered him. Then he said sternly, "Angus, no more playing detective. Leave that to Green and I. You and Hank took a big risk, and things could have been much worse."

"Aye." Angus hung his head. "I didn't consider the risk. I just wanted to do something proactive."

"Fair. If you want to be helpful, you can try to figure out where the burglar came from and disappeared to."

"Didn't the cameras show you that?" Angus asked. He looked over at Lily, who had sat down at the table and was listening intently.

"Not really." Dan reached for his notebook but then seemed to decide against it. "Nick's carport camera didn't see anyone enter, leave, or approach your townhouse's back door after you came home yesterday afternoon." He recounted. "His front door camera still isn't working, but Mr. Kim's parking lot camera shows a blurry image of a figure approaching from the direction of the bluffs just before we see Hank follow them into your townhouse."

"So, she approached my door not from the street or sidewalk but from the side of the property that runs up against the sandstone bluffs?" Angus tried to picture that area. He didn't go back there often and had a vague notion that between the building and the bluffs there was a simple fence comprised of periodic posts with two wooden beams connecting them. There was enough room for a person to walk comfortably between the building wall and the fence, but the person would still need to get into the townhouse complex.

"Apparently Mrs. Kim called her husband as soon as she got off the phone with 911, and he came home right away. He was so frustrated that he called a couple of his clients in the complex and got permission to access their video feeds. The long and the short of it is that we don't see the intruder on the road into or out of the complex either on foot or in a vehicle during the appropriate time frame."

"What did she do then?" Angus asked. "Bushwhack across the back of the complex?" He was pretty sure that wasn't possible, but necessity was the mother of invention.

"I guess that's one way," Dan said "But we checked some other cameras along that route, and it doesn't look like it. We think she may have gone into a townhouse, and that takes it back to one of your neighbors."

"That's crazy," Lily chimed in. "Did you do a house-to-house search?"

Dan shook his head. "We don't have that kind of time and money, Lily. We only checked for fingerprints and spent so much time on the videos, because Angus has been implicated in a series of robberies, and honestly we are stumped."

"Could she have climbed the rock wall?" Angus asked. It was that, or she vanished into another townhouse or thin air.

"I doubt it," Dan said. "Again, we had a quick look, and maybe there's a way up, but not one we could easily find. As someone who had lived here a while, do you know of one?"

"I don't," Angus said after thinking about it for a while. "I can ask around, but if there was a path, I feel like people would use it. Heck, people make their own paths all the time. Just look at Palmer Park."

"Maybe." Dan stretched in his chair. "Oh, and one other thing. Remember that last robbery where the family came home because their kid was puking?"

"Yeah," Angus said. "What about it?"

"Well, last week we got a call from a neighbor. She reported that she'd seen a female jogger enter the house by the back door around 8:50, but she had just assumed that it was the wife coming back from a jog. The outfit was similar. It wasn't until the wife told her about the robbery that she realized what she'd seen."

"Interesting," Lily said. "So, the thieves may use jogging as a cover to case and then break into properties?"

"It would explain a lot," Dan said. "The small volume of goods taken; just enough to fit in a small backpack."

"And it's Colorado Springs," Lily added. "There were joggers everywhere all day long. Nobody pays attention them."

"It's one theory. The problem is that the wife had gone out for a jog earlier in the morning before they left, so maybe the neighbor mixed up the times. I don't know. The more clues we get in this case, the less it seems to make sense."

Lily and Angus both nodded. "Do you have any advice for me?" Angus asked. He shared Dan's frustration.

Dan sighed. "Common sense. Lock your doors. Change up your routine. Check in on your neighbors. Don't play detective." He listed off his suggestions and then looked at his watch. "Well, Angus, I've been off duty for the last hour. I'd better get going. I hope I don't see you in an official capacity again for a long time."

"The feeling is mutual." Angus got up to show Dan out. "Maybe I'll see you at the Veterans Center though."

"Probably," Dan said as he walked out the door.

"Do you really think you won't see Dan again about more robberies?" Lily asked after Angus had closed the door and sat back down to face his uneaten salad.

"There's always a chance," Angus said. "Maybe being caught in the act will make them back off."

CHAPTER 9

Saturday, February 16

The big day had finally arrived. Aunty Ivy was going to meet with Bonnie Stewart at her house, and they were going to do another video call with Angus and Lily. Aunty Ivy had told the story of her search for Bonnie in a series of apologetic emails. Bonnie still owned her house, but when her husband had died a few years ago, she had converted it to a rental and found a small apartment to use as a place to stay between adventures. Since Bonnie was a largely absent landlord, her tenant had directed Ivy to an estate agent, who was initially resistant to sharing Bonnie's contact information. However, the agent's young and impressionable administrative assistant had been quite helpful after Ivy had taken her out to tea and given her the short version of Angus's story. Upon returning to work, the young woman had called Ivy and given her a contact number for Bonnie.

When Ivy had called the number, she hit another hurdle. Bonnie had been vacationing in Australia after spending an entire summer working on an archeology dig. She was planning on staying with various friends, former colleagues, and relatives of her husband and not returning to Scotland until early February. Bonnie had grown weary of Scottish winters and preferred warmer climates. Nonetheless, she was tech savvy and agreed to download the scans of her letters from the cloud and read them to prepare to meet with Ivy. Aunty Ivy arranged the meeting for mid-February to give Bonnie some time to get settled back into her apartment.

Angus and Lily had some exciting news of their own to

share and had decided to wait until the end of the conversation, so as not to distract the ladies.

"Did you get the app working on your computer?" Lily asked Angus as she brought him a cup of piping hot tea. It was early morning in Colorado, so she had also brewed a pot of coffee for herself.

"Thanks," Angus said. "I think so." Given that multiple people were going to be involved in the conversation, Angus and Ivy had agreed to use laptops instead of phones. Bonnie had recommended a video call app, and Angus had installed it on his computer. He approved of Bonnie's choice, noting that he could even record the conversation, which he planned to do.

Lily sat down next to Angus on the sofa. They had placed the laptop on a stack of books, so that the webcam captured them, but their hands were free. "I'm so excited." Lily wrapped her hands around her warm coffee cup. "Do you think Bonnie will remember anything helpful?"

"I don't know." Angus had been asking himself that exact question for the last several weeks. "I hope so." He looked at the computer's clock. It was almost time. "Remember what we talked about. Just let Ivy talk. She takes her time, but she always gets around to her point in the end."

Lily nodded, and the laptop chimed, showing an incoming call. Angus accepted it, and a window on the screen opened showing a rather dingy living room and two elderly ladies sitting on a scuffed leather couch.

"Hello, Angus," Aunty Ivy greeted him. She was sitting on the left wearing her usual uniform of a sweater set and pearls. Despite the formality of her dress, she seemed happy and relaxed. "Let me introduce you to my old friend Bonnie Stewart." She looked over at the woman next to her.

"Nice to meet you, Bonnie," Angus said. Bonnie wore a brown turtleneck and a camelhair blazer, which matched her lined, somewhat leathery skin and contrasted with her long white hair that was braided over one shoulder. A large amber necklace containing some preserved plant matter completed her ensemble, and when she opened her mouth, Angus noted her teeth revealed a lifetime of NHS dentistry and tea drinking.

"You as well," Bonnie smiled. "Ever since Ivy got ahold of me last year, I've been intrigued with your story. Going all the way to America to find your father. Fascinating. And ending up in Colorado. Do you get out to the mountains much?" She and Ivy appeared to share a high level of energy. Perhaps it was because they were both retired teachers.

"As often as I can," Angus said. Then he put his arm around Lily. "This is my girlfriend, Lily Saunders. She and her son Jaiden have also been helping me with my search for my dad."

"Hi." Lily waved in greeting.

"Oh, Lily, I have heard so much about you," Ivy gushed. "It's wonderful to meet you even if it's on a video. Well, I guess I'll see you in person soon enough."

"Indeed, it's nice to put faces to your names." Bonnie cut in as soon as Ivy stopped for breath. "Now that we have introductions out of the way, perhaps we should get down to brass tacks. When we've finished our business, we can make some further plans and get to know each other."

Angus took an instant liking to Bonnie. He couldn't steer the conversation this way without seeming rude, but an old friend of his aunt's had more latitude. He gave an acknowledging nod.

"Too right, dear," his aunt said, although no one was sure if she was talking to Bonnie or Angus.

"This has been a trip down memory lane." Bonnie took over. She consulted some notes on a pad of paper. "It seems a million years ago that I was working as a housemaid. The letters were almost painful to read. I can't believe that I found all those details interesting at the time." She paused. "But I guess I hadn't seen very much of the world."

"Just tell us what you remember to the best of your ability," Angus said. "Any little detail could be the clue we need."

"Alright." Bonnie sipped an amber liquid that looked like Scotch on the rocks. "I'll tell my tale, and you can feel free to interrupt. I've had my fill of university lectures in my day."

"Fair enough." Lily had been surprised to see the woman drinking at this time of day but then recalled the time difference.

Bonnie cleared her throat and began, "You've both read the letters, so you know the big picture. Neal Culpepper made a packet of money in the market and decided that his family should spend a summer in the country, but he wasn't a fellow with any social graces or class. He thought he ran the house, but Mrs. Baker actually ran it, and she got what she wanted. It was pretty simple work once the husband left, because when the wife's friends came down, they didn't know anything about servants either. As long as they got three meals a day and the drinks didn't run out, they were happy."

"And what do you remember about Si?" Angus took Bonnie at her word when she said to ask questions.

Bonnie took another sip of her whiskey and collected her thoughts. "His visit, that was a little different. He wasn't down for just a weekend. He came for two weeks, perhaps because he came all the way from America."

She paused and looked at Angus. "I know the information that you want, but I'm afraid I can't help you much, and I'm sorry. Si, that's what everyone called him, wasn't around the house much, so he interacted with the family very little. He usually got up early in the morning and went out for a walk or to go fishing or to go into town. The person who talked with him most was the cook, Mrs. Wallace, who was pretty ancient even then.

163

She served him an early breakfast and sent a picnic lunch with him. Some days he didn't even come back for dinner. He was on his own program, and I don't think I spoke over five words to him in the two weeks he was there."

Angus's stomach lurched, and his chin dropped. After waiting for months to have this conversation, he felt like it had been a waste of time. Perhaps he should have just hired a detective and turned over all his information. Maybe if he'd gone in a different direction, he'd already have an answer.

Seeing Angus's reaction, Bonnie raised her voice a bit. "I said I don't have a lot of information, not that I can't help you at all. I led with the bad news, son."

Angus perked up a bit. He took a sip of tea to fortify himself.

"Just because I didn't talk to him doesn't mean that I didn't hear the family talk about him," Bonnie said.

"And what did they say?" Angus asked, looking at Bonnie and wondering what gossip she had heard. "I notice you didn't write much about it in your letters."

Bonnie nodded. "As I remember it, I called him 'the quiet American fellow.' Truth was, he wasn't that interesting. Not when folks were coming from Edinburgh and London, drinking all night, and breaking things. The wife's friends were rough around the edges, and they were never boring."

"Tell him about how the family knew him." Aunty Ivy spoke for the first time in a while. Angus was amused that she could be impatient when it wasn't her telling the story.

"Ah, yes." Bonnie finished her drink and set the glass on the table. "The problem with what I'm about to tell you is that I don't remember it clearly, because at the time, I didn't think it was important enough to write down." She looked at her pad of notes. "So, you know Si was sent to 'visit family' in Scotland, because he was engaged to a girl, whom his family thought was unsuitable." Bonnie made finger quotes in the appropriate place. "Well, I don't remember his last name, but I'm sure it wasn't Culpepper, so that makes me think he was related to the wife, Bella."

"And any clue how he fit into Bella's family?" Lily asked. Like Angus, she had gone through the cycle of being disappointed and now was getting excited again.

Bonnie furrowed her brow, as if trying to recall the information. "I have a vague recollection of a story of an English nurse meeting an American soldier in Korea, but Britain didn't send many troops to Korea, so I don't imagine that they sent many nurses either." She shrugged her shoulders. "Anyway, the American solider came from a long line of soldiers, and when they got married, they moved back to America."

"Any idea where in America?" Angus asked. A multi-generational family might be easier to trace than a soldier in a family of civilians, but it was still an intimidating search.

"No," Bonnie said. "Being in the military, they moved around a fair bit. I got the impression that they had been stationed in the southern United States. The cook remarked on Si's 'Rhett Butler' accent."

"Ach," Angus said. This wasn't really news, although the involvement of an English nurse might make tracing the family easier. "Out of interest, do you know Mrs. Culpepper's maiden name?" It was a longshot.

"It was Smith," Bonnie said. "She made a big deal of it when one of her sister's visited, because her sister had married an unrelated fellow with the last name of Smith and hadn't had to change her name." She giggled.

"I wonder how many sisters Bella had." Lily thought out loud.

"It's a good question." Bonnie couldn't suppress her teacher voice. "Just the one visited, but it wasn't at the same time as Si. I think it was before, but I'm not sure."

"Remember from the letters," Ivy cut in. "The Smiths were some of the first visitors. They may have even come while Mr. Culpepper was still there." Ivy was excited to add to the conversation.

"Perhaps they were scoping the place out for Bella's other sister," Bonnie speculated. "I guess we'll never know. Unless you can track down a Smith in Edinburgh, Ivy dear."

Ivy shook her head. "I don't think we'll need to." She paused for effect. "I think we can probably get the information from one of the Culpepper's children, whom I have located. I don't think searching for more family members is worth it until I've talked to the others."

"You've tracked down some of the family members?" Lily asked. "Why haven't you talked to them yet?"

Ivy looked down at her hands. "Well, I only just recently found the twins, but I thought I would wait to see what Bonnie remembered before I talked to them. I wanted to go in with the fullest picture possible."

"I think that was an excellent strategy," Angus said to his aunt in a calm voice.

"Yes, I'm sorry to be impatient." Lily followed his lead. "It's just exasperating how long this is taking."

"It's alright," Ivy acknowledged. "I don't know if it would have been easier 20 years ago, but even then, the memories weren't exactly fresh." She paused. "Would you like me to tell you what I found out about the Culpeppers now?"

"In just a moment." Angus mentally reviewed to his own research. To Bonnie, he asked. "So, Si's last name wasn't Culpepper. Could it have been Thompson?"

Bonnie took a moment to answer. "I think it started with a T, but Thompson doesn't sound right."

"What about Tennyson?" Angus thought back to Jaiden

looking at the unit photograph.

"That doesn't sound right either," Bonnie said. "I feel like it might have been Trussell or something similar." She shrugged. "It was a long time ago. Why do you ask? I thought you had a letter from Private Thompson."

"Just an off the wall idea that Lily's son Jaiden had," Angus said. Jaiden was probably right. The photo had just been miscaptioned, but he was grasping at straws at this point.

There was a pause in the conversation as everyone took that in. Finally, Lily spoke. "Why don't you tell us what you found out about the Culpeppers, Ivy?"

Ivy took out her battered composition book and opened it to a page marked with a sticky note. "Neal and Bella Culpepper are both dead." She let that sink in. "Neal committed suicide in 2008 when he lost heavily in the stock market, and Bella died of breast cancer in 2005."

"That's horrible," Bonnie said, "but I guess not surprising. I got the impression he had come from a very poor background. Perhaps the thought of having to return to it was too much to bear."

No one commented, so Ivy continued, "The twins both did rather well, at least until recently. Nigel in an osteopath in London." When she saw the look of confusion on Lily's face, she clarified, "That's something like a chiropractor." Then Ivy continued, "Phillip was a prominent barrister until he was implicated in a sex scandal about 18 months ago."

"So, what's your next step then?" Angus asked. Doctors and lawyers were busy people and rarely listed their contact information publicly.

"This is one place where I have been able to help." Bonnie beamed from ear to ear. "Over the years, I've run into Ronald Parks a few times. He teaches at an Edinburgh boys' school now, has for years, but sometimes he likes to use the university library. We were never very close, but I tracked him down and took him out to tea last week. He kept in touch with Nigel because of a mutual interest in hiking, and he has already contacted him."

Ivy summarized the plan, "He's coming to Edinburgh in six weeks for a conference and has agreed to meet with me."

"Does he know what you want to talk about?" Angus asked. Six weeks was a long time to wait just to have someone say they couldn't remember anything helpful.

"Ronald gave him the details," Bonnie confirmed. "But considering all the terrible publicity his brother is experiencing right now, Nigel is hesitant to discuss anything over the phone. I think he wants to make sure that he's talking to a harmless old lady and not a reporter trying to dig up dirt on his brother."

"Probably wise." Angus wondered if a private investigator would have better luck. He could afford one, but Angus also sensed that Nigel would be more willing to talk to a friend of an old friend. Perhaps it was best to wait to see how this played out.

"And what about Ronald Parks?" Lily asked. She was on her second cup of coffee and feeling energized.

"Indeed," Bonnie said. "We must remember Ronald, although he's a quiet fellow and people tend to forget about him. According to him, no one ever said anything indiscrete about Si, perhaps because there was nothing indiscrete to say about him. Well, other than Si's unsuitable fiancée."

Angus looked at Ivy and knew that they were both thinking the same thing. Si had left Angus's mother pregnant. There were some negative things to be said about him, but perhaps his English relatives hadn't known them.

"Did he at least have any unique impressions of Si?" Lily continued to push.

"Ronald's take on Si was that he had come to Scotland with his mind made up to return to America and marry his girl," Bonnie said. "And with that idea, he had considered Scotland to be a vacation, nothing more. He enjoyed himself, had one last fling, and went home."

She paused and then added, "That agrees with the village gossip at the time. Si came into town for drinks one night and met your mom. They spent some time together, and then he left."

"What about my mother's impression that Si was shady?" Ivy asked.

"Well, I guess it's a matter of perspective," Bonnie said. "Si seemed to make it pretty clear up at the house what his plans were, but I'm not sure what he said to Heather. Maybe he told her what he was up to and she ignored him, or maybe he just said nothing."

Bonnie's comments hung in the air. Angus and Ivy knew Heather had been a flawed person, and Angus has always suspected that his mother had been looking for a way out of town. The only other conclusion to draw was that Si was a big jerk, who had lied to his mother and left her. Either way, it didn't paint a pretty picture of Angus's parents.

Lily looked at Angus. "Should we share our news?"

"Oh, goodness, I had been wondering." Aunty Ivy's introspection turned to joy like the flip of a switch.

"You have that look Lily, glowing," Bonnie added. "Is there a baby on the way?"

"Bonnie!" Aunty Ivy rebuked her friend. "Why would you think such a thing?"

"Well, with a name like MacBangus..." Bonnie started but thinking better of it, she changed to. "It's a modern world Ivy, and Lily's been married before. There's no need for them to wait."

Angus blushed deeply. His aunt's friend seemed rather

worldly. "I've asked Lily to be my wife, and she accepted," he announced.

"Congratulations, Angus!" Ivy almost shouted. "That's wonderful. When's the wedding?"

"We were thinking of having it coincide with your visit," Lily said. "I don't want anything big, so it shouldn't be hard to arrange."

"I had been meaning to talk to you about my visit." Ivy was literally on the edge of her seat. "But we can get there in a minute. Is there a ring?"

"Not yet," Lily said. "Angus knows I want something vintage and unique. When I see it, I'll know."

"Good girl." Bonnie had briefly gone off camera and returned with another Scotch and what appeared to be a glass of sherry. "I believe a toast is in order. Do you two have something suitable?"

Angus considered what he had on hand. Someone had given him some sparkling cider before New Year's Eve, but it was sitting on a shelf in the pantry. The only other booze in the house was a bottle of vodka and another of brandy, neither of which he liked. "It's a bit early for us over here, Bonnie," he said.

"Just fill your glass with something besides tea," Bonnie urged. Lily went into the kitchen, open the fridge, and produced a bottle of orange juice, which she poured into glasses. She brought them back to the living room.

Bonnie raised her glass, and everyone else followed suit. "To Angus and Lily, may they enjoy many happy years."

"To many happy years," Ivy echoed, and everyone took a large drink. Ivy's face puckered at the taste of the sherry, and she set her glass down. After she took a moment to compose herself, she asked, "When did this happen?"

Angus set down his juice glass and put his arm around

Lily again. "I meant to propose on Valentine's Day. I had it all planned. A nice restaurant, flowers, a little custom cake, but then at 10 AM on the big day, it started to snow."

"It was one of those blizzards that we'd known was coming for a few days, but the system moved slower than we thought," Lily said. "It was supposed to hit Wednesday night, but the storm hit Thursday right before lunch."

On the other end of the video call, both ladies nodded as if they perfectly understood the vagaries of Colorado weather.

"Anyway," Angus took over. "By two PM everything was closing down. I picked up Lily at the library, and we headed to my place. All my plans had gone sideways, but I proposed anyway over lasagna out of a box and a bottle of wine that someone brought to a party two years ago."

"I had kind of suspected the proposal was coming and was so glad that he didn't wait," Lily finished the story. "I was so happy, but the wine was terrible, Angus."

The couple laughed, as did Ivy and Bonnie.

"Are you willing to have your wedding in October?" Ivy asked. "I mean, if you'd prefer a summer wedding, I could change my plans or stay longer."

"I would have been willing to go to the court house as soon as the roads were clear. I don't want anything fancy, but summer is too soon. We need to buy a house and sell this townhouse in addition to planning a wedding, and the Colorado Springs real estate market is hot. It's going to be a lot of work," Lily said.

"I'll take your word for it." Ivy turned to another page in her composition book. "By the way, Angus, I haven't thanked you for your wonderful Christmas presents. I especially liked the book about the haunted town. Is that close enough to drive to? Didn't you and Lily have tea at one place mentioned in the book?"

The change in topic was a bit odd, but Angus felt relieved. He agreed with Lily. He would have gotten married sooner rather than later, but there were practical concerns, like Jaiden finishing the school year and his townhouse not being built for three people. "It's very close to Colorado Springs," he said. "In fact, the entire area has grown together. Lily and I had tea in Manitou Springs before the holidays. We can get reservations there over your visit."

"How exciting!" Ivy loved a good high tea. "If I change my departure, can we go to the coffin races they have to commemorate that poor woman whose casket slid down the mountain?"

Bonnie appeared to choke on a swallow of whiskey and when she composed herself, she asked, "I'm sorry, did you say coffin racing? Has all that marijuana given them brain damage?"

Angus had never ventured into Manitou Springs during their annual coffin races. He wasn't a big fan of crowds. He let Lily field these questions.

"They aren't actually coffins," Lily clarified. "Just racers that are designed to look like them. Teams build them and race them up Manitou Avenue. The event was inspired by the mostly true story of a woman who wanted to be buried on a nearby mountainside but whose coffin came rolling down the slope some years later. The town does it as a tourist draw, and it's a unique experience." She paused. "And if you want to Ivy, we can help make the arrangements. It's worth your time."

"Oh, I very much do," Ivy replied. "We can work out the details later."

"It sounds fascinating," Bonnie said. "I haven't ever been to Colorado. I'm not asking for anyone to put me up, but would you mind if I tagged along, Ivy? It sounds like quite a lark."

"I certainly don't mind. We've never gone on a proper adventure together," Ivy said to Bonnie. To Angus, she asked, "Do you mind? Maybe Bonnie and I could get a short-term rental or something."

Angus realized he hadn't considered where his aunt

would stay during her upcoming trip. Previously, she had stayed in the other bedroom of his townhouse, but he and Lily hadn't gone into detail yet on what type of house they would buy. While he was sure they would have a guest bedroom, he wasn't sure they could afford or wanted a house with two extra bedrooms. However, he didn't want Bonnie to feel unwelcome. He got the impression that she was a low maintenance guest. "We can figure something out," he said.

They spent the next five minutes on trivial conversation. Once Bonnie and Ivy had signed off, Angus got up and stretched his legs. Then he walked over to the electric kettle and flipped the switch.

"Your aunt and her friend aren't boring." Lily twisted her hair around her finger absentmindedly.

"Indeed, they aren't," Angus agreed. He put another tea bag in his cup, but didn't sit down. He had been sitting too long. "I just wish we had more answers. It seems like for every two steps we take forward, we take one large step back."

Lily crossed the room and hugged Angus from behind. "That's how research usually goes. You wait for a long time and get your hopes up, and then with every answer you get, it spawns two additional questions."

"So, do we wait on Nigel?" Angus asked.

"I don't think we have much of a choice." Lily disengaged her arms and walked over to the coffee pot. It had turned off at some point, but the liquid was still warm. She poured some in a cup and microwaved it. "If he can give us the name of his aunt and her husband, we may be able to trace them more easily than Si." She thought for a minute and then frowned. "The problem is that with their age, we may end up finding their obituaries, but those usually list where the next of kin live, so that would be another starting point."

Angus looked at the electric kettle and considered this.

Thinking of obituaries make him think of Simon Tennyson. What if the reason that he couldn't find Sylvester Thompson was that he was dead? What if he was too late? "I guess," he said.

The kettle beeped, and he made a cup of tea. The day had been a letdown, so he let Lily talk a bit. Discussing buying a house during the video chat had whetted her appetite, and she listed features she was interested in. Angus didn't consider himself very fussy. He wanted a place for that Lily approved of and a school district where Jaiden would learn what he needed to succeed in life. His highest priority was a structurally sound house. Angus didn't mind doing some minor fixes, but at the end of a long day of working on other people's houses, he didn't want to come home and start demoing parts of his own home. As Lily talked, he decided he was glad to be moving on. The townhouse didn't feel much like home anymore, and only part of it had to do with having Lily there more often.

CHAPTER 10

Sunday, February 24

"Let me get this straight. This started off as a bet?" Isaac Templeton asked as he spread a generous helping of buffalo chicken dip on a cracker.

Isaac and his wife Cassandra were sitting around Angus's dining room table with Lily, Maggie, and Dan. The afternoon gathering of friends had taken on a festive atmosphere with appetizers and tasty beverages, but its original purpose had been to see if a friend of Maggie's named Sandy could sneak into the townhouse complex without being caught on camera.

Jimmy Kim and Nick Swartz were sitting side by side on a couch in the living room staring at a large monitor, on which Jimmy was displaying the video feeds from several cameras in the complex. In addition to their efforts, Angus had spent the last 20 minutes standing by the front window of his townhouse, scanning the sidewalk.

"Actually, it began with a conversation on a long hike a couple of weeks ago." Maggie went into the kitchen, where bottles of hard liquor and various mixers were sitting on the counter. "My friend Sandy and I were doing an eight-mile hike on the Air Force Academy, and I spent the most of the time telling her about Angus's recent adventures with the law. When I mentioned the burglar had stumped the police by getting into the townhouse complex and avoiding the cameras, Sandy became even more interested." As she told the story, Maggie combined gin, vermouth, and olive brine with a little ice in a cocktail shaker. She paused her narrative to cover the shaker and mixed the contents with a few pumps of her wrist.

"When I told her that a witness had seen a jogger at the last burglary, Sandy's face lit up. She asked me to get her some specific information like Angus's address and the location of the cameras and then suggested our little wager," Maggie continued as she poured her murky concoction into two martini glasses and garnished them with green olives. Finished with both her story and the drinks, she offered the second glass to anyone at the table.

"Thanks, Maggie." Lily accepted the drink. The women clinked glasses, and then Maggie returned to her seat.

"What's up for grabs if she wins?" Dan asked. Angus had sent him a text late last week asking him to attend this get together if he was available, and while he felt that the Sandy's chances of success were low, he had the day off and decided that it sounded like a fun way to spend the somewhat chilly and blustery afternoon.

"If she wins, she gets a bottle of her favorite Irish whiskey, and if I win, I get two bottles of cheap white wine." Maggie pointed to three bottles by the hearth. "It's all in good fun though; both of us agreed to share our winnings with the all the guests."

"Well, this is certain the most interesting party that I have been to in quite some time." Cassandra spoke for the first time. She was a woman of late middle age with wavy, closely cropped gray hair and a cheery disposition to match her husband's. Cassandra Templeton loved puzzles and mysteries, and while she enjoyed reading both the classics of the genera and modern thrillers, her genuine passion was watching British murder mysteries on television. Many an evening, she sat down with her knitting and spent two hours trying, usually unsuccessfully, to figure out who done it. Sometimes Isaac joined her, but within the first 20 minutes, he was asleep in his chair. Like clockwork, he would wake up for the last 10 minutes and somehow know who the murderer was along with their motives. While this phenomenon frustrated her, as a psychologist Cassandra found it fascinating and wondered if she could work it into a research paper. She added, "While I appreciate the invitation, how did settling a bet become a social occasion?"

"I think it is the number of people who needed to be here," Lily said. After an initial sip, she left her drink untouched. "We needed Jimmy and Nick to monitor the cameras, and Angus, because it was his house. Right, Angus?"

Angus hadn't moved from his surveillance position and appeared not to hear Lily.

"Angus, what are you doing?" Lily raised her voice to see if she could get Angus's attention.

"Oh, just waiting." Angus came back to the present. "Figured Sandy would be here soon." Then he returned his gaze to outside and his thoughts elsewhere.

Lily felt a little embarrassed that Angus wasn't being the best host, but then she looked around and saw that everyone was having a good time. Considering the recent stress Angus had been under, she let it go. She continued her narrative, "And I wanted to be here, because I wanted to see Sandy's explanation."

"And I needed to be here to verify that Sandy won the bet." Maggie took a large swallow of her drink and poked at the olives with a toothpick. "Plus, to get all the people together at the right time and have decent weather, we realized we would have to plan ahead."

"Sandy picked the weekend day with the best weather forecast, and we made sure everyone was available and arranged for food and refreshments," Lily concluded the story.

"Well, thanks for including us." Isaac demolished the appetizers on his plate and sipped a glass of scotch. "It's too bad that Mark is out of town at a wedding."

"And that Jack got called out on that plumbing emergency." Maggie shook her head and then popped an olive in her mouth. "I see Hank gave it a miss as well."

Lily nodded. "He said something about not wanting to leave Murphey at home and not wanting the little fellow to jump all over everyone. Honestly though, since the burglary, he's been a little gun-shy."

"Understandable." Cassandra got up to refill her cucumber and mint infused water. "Even though it wasn't his house that was broken into, it was still a traumatic experience."

"I also don't think parties are his speed," Lily said. "My dad wasn't interested in coming either, so he brought Jaiden over to hang out with Murphey and Hank. Jaiden wants a dog, and Hank needs someone to watch Murphey from time to time."

Cassandra had returned to her seat and scoffed. "Just get the boy a dog, Lily. It's Colorado; everyone has a dog. It's like they issue them to you at the DMV when you register your Subaru."

Before Lily could reply, Isaac mumbled, "Dogs, why didn't the dogs bark when the burglar broke in?" He looked over at Dan. "Did the homes that Angus is accused of burglarizing have dogs?"

Dan thought for a minute. He'd worked a lot of robberies in the last six months. The ones that Angus had been implicated in seemed like a long time ago. "A few of the families had dogs, but they either took the animals with them or arranged for them to stay with friends." He paused. "Of course, the burglars could have selected houses based on factors like whether there would be a dog at home. It's a good point though."

"So, Dan, you're a police detective?" Cassandra asked. Having finished her refreshments, she had taken out a partially complete glove from her bag and had started knitting the thumb. When Dan nodded, she asked, "What about Sandy? Is she also an investigator by the trade?"

"In a manner of speaking," Maggie said. "She teaches high school forensic science and physics, so she has some familiarity with police procedures. Although today she's using her extensive experience as an urban hiker on this particular puzzle."

"So, she's going to hike in, not jog?" Isaac asked. "Is that completely fair?"

"In what way isn't that fair." Cassandra looked up from her knitting and shot her husband an icy glance. "She's going to get here on foot."

"Well, yes," Isaac acknowledged, "But hiking is different from jogging, different pace, equipment, shoes." He tried to keep his remarks jovial. The assembled crowd seemed to consider this.

"There's a sport called trail running where people run along hiking paths." Cassandra set her knitting aside on her lap. "I don't know whether they wear hiking boots or running shoes or some hybrid footwear, but it seems to be that if Sandy can get here on foot without being seen, then so could other people, so it counts." Cassandra seemed agitated with her husband.

"I suppose." Isaac looked down at his empty scotch glass. "Guess I don't get to count her in my tally of female joggers though."

"Not unless we see her jog up." Cassandra picked her knitting back up as if to give a note of finality to her remark, but she didn't resume her work. "Isaac and I have a mostly friendly debate about whether more women or more men are joggers. It's been going on for years now, and we have taken it to the point of calling out when we see them," she explained to everyone.

"Like punch buggies?" Lily asked. Isaac and Cassandra seemed a happy couple. She wondered if she and Angus would be like them in the future.

"Something like that," Isaac replied sheepishly. "I think there are more female joggers, and Cassandra disagrees."

Before Cassandra could comment, Dan glanced at his empty beer and then his watch. "When did Sandy say she planned on making her grand entrance?" He walked over to the fridge and grabbed a second brew.

"She said that she would aim for about 3 PM." Lily looked at the clock on the stove, which read 3:05.

"But she also planned to make a substantial hike out of it, so I would give her a grace period," Maggie said. "She says there's no point in getting out your day pack for under five miles."

Outside a gust of wind whipped through the tree branches. "She's better hurry," Cassandra remarked. "It was quite nice earlier, but the forecast says the weather is about to turn."

Angus was still staring out the window and drinking a cup of tea. Lily didn't feel like disturbing his reverie, so she turned to Jimmy and Nick. "Do you fellows see anything yet?"

Jimmy looked up from the monitor. He had dressed for comfort and warmth in flannel trousers and sandals with thick wool socks. "Nothing much," he said. "There hasn't been a lot of foot traffic all afternoon, and the wind has been picking up in the last 15 minutes."

Isaac stood up and made his way to a buffet table that had been set against the wall. He helped himself to another plate-ful of food and poured a little more Scotch in his glass. "Does anyone else feel like they are in a production of 'A Murder is Announced?'" he asked. When no one responded, he said, "I'm at the juncture of that and feeling like we have all gathered in the library and soon that French detective with the funny shaped head and mustache will unmask the murder."

Angus, who had walked away from the window long enough to refill his cup, laughed out loud. "Aye. If only it were evening, we could say that it was a dark and stormy night."

Dan had also cracked a smile. "Luckily we aren't dealing with an actual murder, just a series of burglaries."

"And that detective takes great pains to point out to everyone he is Belgian," Angus said.

When Isaac looked a bit taken aback at the criticism, Cassandra stepped in. "It's alright, dear. We got your meaning. You've just been mixing up your detective and plots." She paused for a second to concentrate on her knitting. "But you might not want to compare Sandy to that detective. I'm just guessing, but I feel like she does not have as impressive of a mustache as our favorite Belgian detective."

"You're complete right," Maggie confirmed. "She has some crazy mad scientist hair, but no mustache."

Everyone had a good laugh, but eventually returned their glances to either the kitchen clock or the men on the couch. Then the doorbell rang.

The postman always rings twice Isaac thought, but refrained from saying it out loud.

"That's probably her now." Angus walked over to answer the door.

The woman standing outside was about five feet tall dressed in a well-worn polar fleece pullover, tactical cargo pants, a stocking cap, and dusty trail runners. Despite the cloud cover and chilly temperature, she smelled of sunscreen and was practically vibrating with energy. It took a few seconds for Angus to recognize her. "Angus, Angus MacIver, it's great to see you again!" Sandy greeted him with unbridled enthusiasm. "Did I make it without getting spotted?"

It perplexed Angus how Sandy always got his name wrong. They were acquaintances and had been introduced multiple times by Maggie. Oh well, could be worse.

"Hey, Sandy. Why don't you come in and ask the guys watching the video feed?" Angus opened the door a little further and motioned for her to come into the living room. "Fellows," he called. "Meet Sandy Musgrave."

As Sandy approached the monitor, Nick stood up and offered his hand. "Congratulations. We didn't see you until you were at the front door and then only from Jimmy's camera across the street that covers the parking lot. How did you manage it?"

Sandy removed a thick glove and pumped Nick's hand. "I came in the back way," she stated matter-of-factly. To the assembled crowd, she said, "I want to meet all of you at some point and don't want to be rude, but if you guys want to see the route I took to get in here, we better get a move on. The temperature is dropping, and the wind is picking up."

"Sounds like a plan," Dan said. The rest of the room murmured their agreement.

Sandy looked over at Angus, who had dressed in one of his sport kilts and knee-length socks for the party. "I don't want to offend your sensibilities, Angus, but it's rather blustery out there, and I don't need confirmation that all you wear under that kilt is socks, so I will wait long enough for you to put on some pants."

"Pants." Angus thought back to the last time he had worn pants outside of working hours. "Thanks for your concern, Sandy, but I've lived in Colorado long enough to have a contingency plan for this." He walked over to the closet and took out a lined London Fog overcoat and began buttoning it up. "If anyone needs them, I have an extra parka and some random hats and gloves that have been left here over the years."

The party took a couple of minutes to don a variety of warm garments. When she was satisfied that everyone was bundled up, Sandy led the entire party behind Angus's townhouse building and pointed upwards. "What do you guys see?" she asked.

"A sheer wall of white sandstone," Isaac said, as if it was the most obvious thing in the world. Everyone else nodded in agreement.

"Very good," Sandy said, using her best teacher voice. "But what's in front of the wall of rock?"

"A fence and some trees," Nick Swartz offered, looking for confirmation to Sandy, who gave an encouraging half nod.

Angus examined the area behind his building. He realized that he rarely came back here, and why would he? There was no sidewalk or even much of a path around the back of the building. If he wanted to go to the mail boxes or the community pool, he took the sidewalk that ran along either side of the main road. "At the base of the rock wall, there is a ledge of flat rock," he observed. "But the one thing that I don't see is a path."

Sandy's grin lit up her face. "Or is there?" She paused for effect. At that moment, a gust of wind shook the tree branches, and several people shivered.

As soon as they recovered, everyone gave the area a second look. Dan walked about 10 feet down the fence line in each direction before returning to the group. "I can't find one. Anyone else?" he asked.

When no one else stepped forward, Maggie spoke up. "Oh, come on, Sandy, you have kept us in suspense long enough, and we are freezing our butts off. Just tell us already!"

Sandy continued to smile. "Before I show you how I got past the cameras, I want to say that I spend quite a bit of time hiking, as I know several of you do. I think we can all agree that the key to finding and staying on the path is a matter of experience and perspective."

Besides Sandy, the hikers with the most experience were Angus, Lily, and Maggie. All three of them nodded. "I can't tell you how many times I have been hiking in Palmer Park and suddenly realize that I am at the edge of a cliff and have lost the path," Angus said. "I mean half the time I backtrack and discover that I just wandered off the main path, but one time I thought I was going to have to wait for someone to come the other way."

Sandy laughed. "My point exactly. You backtrack to change how you are looking at the trail, but sometimes the only way to really see the trail is to come at it from the opposite side." She furrowed her brow and stared into the distance. "When I first started hiking in the southern part of Garden of the Gods, I would always get lost. I would head west from the High Point Overlook and take a wrong turn onto a bushwhacked trail and eventually end of at the Girl Scout Huts, not understanding how I got there. However, one time I hiked around the park counterclockwise. Using the official trails that sort of follow the curve of the road, I actually found the true path to the overlook and haven't gotten turned around since."

Another gust of wind whipped through the trees, and Jimmy Kim shivered in earnest. "Could we hurry this up?" he asked. "Some of us prefer the great indoors."

"Certainly." Sandy focused her attention back on the rock wall. "Let's change our perspective on the path." She swung her leg over the split rail wooden fence. Looking at Isaac in particular, she said, "Wingtips, it's a bit of scramble near the top, so you may want to sit this one out."

Isaac looked down at his leather dress shoes and sighed. Then he looked at Jimmy's sandals and asked, "Fancy another drink, Jimmy?" Jimmy grunted his ascent, and the two men headed back to Angus's apartment. Cassandra, who had anticipated taking part in Sandy's explanation and had worn shoes with deep treads, shook her head in dismissal at her husband.

Meanwhile, Sandy had walked along the shelf of rock that sat in front of the wall. The slab angled upward gently as she continued. She motioned for the others to follow her.

"Since there is a church and a major road a quarter of a mile south of here, all of you know that this rock formation doesn't continue on forever," Sandy said as she strolled up the incline. As the party got higher, the winds became more intense, but they plodded on. "What you don't know, because it is hidden by a grove of trees, is that this ledge comes to a peak just a little past the edge of the complex and then the terrain descends into a park."

"So, there's no way to get to the top of the main bluff, but this ledge wraps around it?" Dan asked. He'd had the sense to wear a pair of old hiking boots, but the tread was worn and he was spending most of his time looking at where he placed his feet. He was also regretting not wearing thicker gloves.

"That's about the size of it." Sandy stopped and turned around. "If you all look back towards the complex, you will see how we got here. Then I invite you to look down at the park, which to be frank has seen better days."

The party took in the view. Dan was the last to ascend and then spent a minute taking pictures with his cell phone. "What street is over there?" he asked Sandy.

"I'm not sure," Sandy said, after a moment's thought. "I got to this neighborhood by taking the Homestead Trail from parking lot of the High Chaparral Open Space. After that, I took a local side trail to get to the park. I try to avoid walking on sidewalks and streets as much as possible."

Dan's numb fingers somehow opened the mapping app on his phone. He dropped a pin and decided it was time to head back to Angus's.

"Sandy, that's over five miles!" Maggie exclaimed. "Why on earth did you walk that far in weather like this?"

Sandy looked past the park to the trail. "When I started, it was a bit nippy but still a pretty nice day for hiking, and the forecast claimed the weather wouldn't change for three more hours." Just then, the wind howled and shook the nearby trees. "Guess the meteorologist was wrong. Let's go back down and crack open that bottle of whiskey."

Taking care to keep their descent as successful as their ascent, the group swiftly made their way down the rocks and back to Angus's townhouse. While Sandy still exuded her boundless energy, everyone else seemed deep in thought.

At the front door of Angus's property, Sandy paused. She had spent some of her trip down looking over the complex to note the changes that had taken place over the years.

"They've repainted since the last time I was here, but they have done nothing about that fence," she commented in a low voice, almost to herself.

"You've been here before?" Angus looked toward the fence and realized that it could use some attention. The wood was damaged in several places and looked shabby.

"A fellow teacher lived here some years ago," Sandy said. "Sometimes she would watch my girls for the afternoon. One day they had a bunch of pine cones and leaves when I picked them up and wanted to show me where they got them from. She had learned about the path to park at some point and took them there a lot."

Sandy squinted at something in the distance and started walking towards the neighboring building. "It goes back to the experience part of my strategy. I already knew there was a path into the complex, because I had been on it."

Angus followed Sandy, who had tilted her head at an odd angle. "I've never seen anyone use that path before. How do you think your friend found out about it?"

Sandy shrugged. "No idea." She didn't seem to pay much attention. "Teaching doesn't pay much, especially at the beginning, so she did a lot of babysitting on the side. Maybe one of the other families she worked for showed her, or heck maybe she found the park and put two and two together."

Sandy's voice trailed off, and she looked up at the eaves of the building. She clicked her tongue and pointed upward. "Is it just me, or is that a camera pointed straight at your front door, Angus?"

The cold and wind forgotten, Angus followed her finger with his gaze and was surprised to notice a small black tube mounted to the underside of the rain gutter. Walking around in front of it, he saw the winking glint of a lens. "How did you ever see that?" he asked, looking at Sandy in disbelief.

"They replaced the gutters since the last time I was here," Sandy said matter-of-factly. "They look like they are a lot better quality. I was admiring them, when I saw something shiny. It didn't fit, so I went to check it out."

"Maybe it belongs to the owner of this townhouse." Angus hadn't taken a lot of time to look at the cameras that Jimmy had installed in the complex, but he knew that part of Jimmy's strategy was to have cameras that people could see to act as a deterrent. That had been part of his sales pitch to the HOA. This camera was barely visible. It didn't seem his style.

"What are you two up to out there?" Dan called from inside Angus's apartment. "Come in from the cold and get a hot drink."

"Wrap Jimmy up in my parka and bring him out here," Angus shouted back. Dan had a point. If this hadn't been so important, Angus would have left it for another day and gone inside for a hot cup of tea.

Jimmy stomped out the door a minute later, wrapped in a parka and fleece blanket and sporting a knitted hat with a garishly colored pompom, which had been left behind by a guest long ago. Angus always wondered if it was an accident or on purpose, but no one had ever claimed it.

"What's the big idea?" Jimmy asked as he made his way across the lawn with Dan behind him.

"Oh, I think you will want to see this," Angus said, with a glimmer of amusement in his voice. "It looks like you have a competitor for the home security market in the complex."

Jimmy rummaged in his pocket for a pair of glasses and

failing to find them, took out a cell phone. He handed it to Angus. "You're tall. Snap some pictures of the camera for me. See if you can get a serial number in particular."

Angus did his best, but he wasn't a skilled photographer, and the light was failing. When he returned the phone, Jimmy took a quick glance at the photos. He whistled. "This is very high end. I don't even bother to stock this camera."

"Really?" Dan had been standing back and observing the situation. "Can you think of anyone local who does?" he asked as he followed Jimmy across the lawn.

"I can make some calls on Monday, but there's an even chance that whoever installed it bought it online." Despite all his layers, Jimmy's teeth were chattering. He opened the door and returned to the warmth of the living room.

Dan turned around at the front door to wait for Angus and Sandy. "Hey, can you send a copy of those photos you took to Green and myself?" he asked Angus, who had followed behind them. "We'll see what we can turn up about them on Monday."

"Sure thing. I'll share them as soon as I get a hot drink." Then Angus turned around to look for Sandy. "Where the heck did that woman go?" he asked, looking at Dan.

"I thought I'd see if there were any more cameras around the back," Sandy called. She was just about to go around the corner of the building. "It's just a hunch."

Angus felt he had no choice but to follow her. When he and Dan caught up, they saw she was inspecting the area around the mailboxes for the complex and muttering to herself. She circled the mailboxes one more time and then shouted, "Aha! There you are, you sneaky little bugger!"

Sandy didn't wait for anyone this time. She pulled a cell phone out of one pocket of her cargo pants and a small, high intensity flashlight from another and began taking pictures of an object underneath the eave. Then she pulled a key chain from her jacket. Sandy had so many keys that Angus wondered if she was moonlighting as a janitor, but after a minute of fumbling, she found a laser pointer and held it up just below the black tube she had discovered and turn the beam on. An instant later, Angus saw a red dot on the license plate of his truck. "Bingo," Sandy exclaimed and snapped another picture.

"You've got to be kidding me," Dan said, staring at the red dot. "Whatever made you think to do that, Sandy?"

"Well, I'm a physics teacher and lasers are cool," Sandy responded glibly. "But I saw it on some forensics show."

While Dan and Sandy took a few more pictures, Angus shivered and reached out for the building wall. It was probably just the temperature dropping, but still. Angus could not believe that someone had gone to the trouble of pointing covert cameras at his front door and parking space. And in a small way, he also found the variety of equipment that Sandy carried around to be a bit intimidating. He almost expected her to produce fingerprint powder and starting lifting latent prints.

"Hey, Angus, are you doing ok?" Dan shifted his focus away from the camera.

"I just don't understand," Angus said, shaking his head. "Why would someone spy on me with cameras?"

A particularly icy gust of wind blew past the trio. "Let's not worry about that now." Dan led them towards Angus's back door. "We'll mull it over after some hot drinks.

When they opened the door, the sudden rush of warmth reminded Angus how quickly weather conditions could change in Colorado. Lily, who had been watching all the activity, met them. "Are you ok, Angus? You look pale."

"I think we all need a hot drink." Sandy took over. To Angus, she said, "You go sit down in the living room, and I'll make us some hot, sweet tea." To Lily she threw a look that said, "He's had a shock, get him to sit down and keep him warm."

Lily led Angus to a large armchair and helped him out of his coat. She found the remote for the gas fire and turned it on. Then she picked up the bottles of wine and whiskey and went out to the kitchen to check on Sandy and Dan.

Sandy had filled the electric kettle and taken down several cups. While she monitored the temperature display on the appliance, she put tea bags in the cups and had found the sugar bowl.

"What happened?" Lily whispered to her, setting the bottles down on the counter.

"We found another camera pointed at the back door." Sandy made an attempt at a quiet voice. As much as Angus was in shock, she was still quite amped. "Looks like a similar make and model to the one out front." She let her statement sink in.

"It may mean that someone is watching Angus to make sure that he is home alone while they go out and commit the burglaries." Dan tapped the screen of his cell phone. "Or it might be unrelated."

"I find a coincidence like that highly unlikely, don't you?" Lily asked, sneaking a look over at Angus, who appeared to be getting some color back in his cheeks.

The kettle beeped, and Sandy poured steaming water into three cups. "The former makes the most sense to me." She looked at Lily. "That also explains why they knew the house was empty when Angus tried to sneak out. A man entered the back door wearing coveralls and then maybe 15 minutes later exited the front door wearing jeans. It doesn't take a rocket scientist to put two and two together."

Dan had only been half listening to the conversation. He remained focused on his phone screen. "Green wants me to call her. Please excuse me." He took his cup of tea and walked up the stairs to the second floor of the townhouse.

As Sandy waited for the other cups of tea to steep, Isaac

joined them in the kitchen. "What happened out there? Angus looks pretty rattled."

Sandy gave Isaac an update, and then removed the tea bag from one cup, strained it, and added three spoonfuls of sugar. "He's a man with a good head on his shoulders; let's get this in to him, and he will be right as rain in a minute." She handed the mug to Lily to take to Angus. "But while you are here, Wingtips, would you mind opening that bottle of whiskey?"

Isaac laughed hardily. "Isaac Templeton." He held out his hand.

"Sandy Musgrave," Sandy said, taking it.

Isaac picked up the bottle of whiskey and opened it. He poured himself another small measure and handed the bottle to Sandy, who poured a substantial amount into her tea. The pair clinked glasses.

"By the way, you are rubbish with names." Isaac took a sip of his drink. "Angus's last name is MacBangus, not MacIver, although with his occupation I can see where you mixed it up."

"Seriously?" Sandy asked in disbelief. "MacBangus cannot be an actual name. I mean, what clan is that? What does the tartan look like?"

"No idea, but that's his name, for better or worse."

"Oh, dear." Sandy shook her head and blew on her hot tea. "I wonder if Lily will take his name when they get married. Maybe they should just change it to something like MacIver. It might even be good for business, make people think he is extremely handy."

"It just might be." Isaac contemplated his glass, which was once again empty. He set it aside. "Wait, did you say married?"

"Yes," Sandy said with a look of regret on her face. "Crap. I assumed you knew. I had suggested to Maggie that we buy some champagne and have a toast to the couple, but she said Lily doesn't want a big fuss."

"Well, mums the word then."

Sandy took a sip of her tea and let the warmth wash over her. She relaxed her muscles a bit and looked towards the living room. "I had a long hike and a great deal of excitement today. I think it may be time for me to get off my feet. Please excuse me."

As Sandy took a seat in front of the fire in the living room, she noted that word of the second camera had reached Jimmy and Nick. The men were having a vigorous conversation.

Dan returned from upstairs and joined them. "Green wanted to know if those cameras could have been installed a few years ago and been forgotten about," Dan said to Jimmy.

"Absolutely not." Jimmy zoomed in on the picture on his phone. "This camera uses cutting edge technology. It was manufactured in the last 9 months and was professionally installed by the looks of it."

"Besides," Nick added, "Jimmy has lived here for 10 years. He would remember if someone else had installed cameras."

"The presence and placement of these cameras leads to several questions," Dan said. "Mr. Kim, do you have any other thoughts or insights?"

"None of this makes sense. The cost of these cameras is substantial. Why install them to frame someone for a series of relatively low value burglaries?"

"Maybe it's personal," Nick said.

"Or maybe the first one belongs to the person who owns the townhouse across the way, and the other one is just a coincidence." Angus had been sitting quietly sipping his tea but suddenly came to life.

"Then why are they pointed at your front and back doors?" Dan asked, raising his voice.

"I wish I knew," Angus almost shouted. He paused and then said in a calmer voice, "Sorry about that; I'm just so frustrated by this whole thing. I mean, I am glad that Sandy figured out how the woman who broke into my house could have gotten in and out mostly undetected, but now doesn't this put me back in the frame?"

Dan considered this for a moment. "It definitely complicates matters."

"But the fact that the woman broke in and left behind worthless stolen property points to someone else being involved." Lily sat on the floor at Angus's feet, warming herself by the fire.

"And why would Angus host a party to show how he could have done it, if he had done it?" Sandy asked. "God, this is ridiculous."

"The discovery of the cameras and a way to enter the complex virtually undetected adds a new angle to this case," Dan said.

"Or maybe it lets us see it through a new lens." Jimmy quipped. When his joke fell flat, he said, "Surveillance humor."

"Green and I will follow up with each of you next week." Dan took copies of his card out of his wallet. "In the meantime, if you think of anything relevant, call or email." He passed them out to everyone in the room. "Our primary interest at the moment is the cameras, specifically who owns them and when they were installed. The serial numbers may help, but if you remember anything about seeing someone who could have installed them, maybe someone dressed as a utility worker or cable installer, get in touch with us. And no amateur investigations," he warned.

Cassandra put Dan's card in her wallet and packed up her knitting. "Detective, is it correct that the burglaries stopped for a while and then resumed again and then stopped?" she asked.

"I'm sorry to ask, but I've heard the story third hand."

"That's an accurate description." Dan knew Isaac and Cassandra were both psychologists and might be valuable resources, but he didn't want to impose. This was a series of petty thefts, not a serial killer investigation.

"Have you considered the thieves might have stopped for a while because they were in jail or otherwise occupied?" Isaac inquired. "It seems odd that they would just quit and then start up again."

"It is something that we have considered," Dan lied. Police work wasn't like it was on television. He and Green didn't have the time and resources to explore every possibility. In the Robbery Unit, they focused more on how, when, and whom than why. The why was usually financial. Nonetheless, he decided to see where this was going.

"Or perhaps some of their robberies weren't reported," Cassandra mused as she looked for her coat. "Perhaps some victims didn't want to deal with law enforcement for one reason or another."

"Oh, I doubt that," Maggie said. "Our clients are regular, respectable folks. I try very hard to screen out people or projects that seem shady. And we don't get a lot of those sorts of inquiries. Our biggest issue is people who want to do a substantial renovation that would overextend them financially."

Dan waited to see if anyone else offered a pet theory. When they didn't, he picked up his coat and gloves. "Well, I think I'll leave before the weather gets worse. Anyone need a ride?"

"I wouldn't mind one, as long as it's not too far out of the way," Sandy said. She had finished her tea.

"No worries." Dan took his keys out of his pocket.

Sandy got up and went over to Angus. "Well, I'm sorry to have caused you more trouble, Angus. Since you already had an alibi for a couple of the robberies, I didn't see any harm."

Angus considered this for a minute. "It's alright, Sandy. Jimmy's camera pointed at the visitor parking lot saw you, so it would have also seen me if I'd tried to sneak out." He paused. "But with an escape route not covered by cameras, it's less likely that my burglar lives in my complex. That's something."

"I guess it is," Sandy said. "See you soon, Mr. MacTavish!" She put on her coat and followed Dan out.

Within 20 minutes, everyone had made similar excuses leaving Angus and Lily to clean up after the party.

"I'm sorry," Lily said as she threw disposable plates and cups into a trash bag. "This was an awful idea."

"Aye." Angus packaged up the leftovers. "I agreed to it, because I really didn't think that Sandy could pull it off, but Dan is right, Sandy's success leads to more questions than answers. I feel that as far as the investigation goes, not a lot has changed."

"What about the cameras that Sandy found?" Lily stopped her work and looked at Angus. "Don't tell me that doesn't change anything."

Angus sat down in the living room. "I don't like to admit it, but those cameras pointed at my door; that freaks me out. I love this townhouse. It's the first place that's felt like home since Scotland, and now that feeling is ruined. Part of me wants to pack a bag and move out tomorrow." He sighed.

Lily joined Angus. It was disturbing to think that people could watch her and Angus come and go. "Well, if you're serious, you can use our guest room until we find a house we like. I'm sure my parents would understand."

Angus ran his fingers through his hair and shook his head. "I appreciate the offer, but I think I better just stay here. Green and Dan will look into the cameras, and you never know; they may belong to someone, or Jimmy might be mistaken about their age."

"But what if they are still watching you?" Lily pressed.

"After two months without a robbery? My guess is that no one has looked at those feeds in a while. Why would they? Of course, then why haven't they come back and taken them down if they cost so much?"

"Maybe they don't want to take the risk of being observed removing them, or maybe getting caught breaking in spooked them."

"Perhaps," Angus said. "No, I think our best bet is to stay with the plan we had. Look for a house, buy it, sell this place. We don't want to make things worse by rushing into things. Those cameras were pointed at my place long before we knew about them. In a lot of ways, nothing has changed."

CHAPTER 11

Friday, March 8

As jarring as the revelation that Angus could get in and out of the townhouse complex on foot had been, the next two weeks proved even more frustrating. Jimmy had inquired with all his competitors about the make and model of cameras pointed at Angus's place, but no one in town stocked them. One company said they could special order them and quoted Jimmy a ridiculously high price. Since Nick was working from home, he had asked several neighbors about the cameras, but no one claimed to be their owner. Dan called the manufacturer with the serial numbers, but they refused to give him any information without a warrant.

The silver lining in this cloud of uncertainty was that after the cameras proved to be a dead end, Detective Green nodded and told Dan that while it was all very interesting, unless there were more robberies, she had no plans to act on this new information. "The goods are long gone, and the insurance has paid out on them," she said. "We don't have the time and resources to waste on yesterday's news. We need to pursue more recent cases."

While Angus had been relieved when Dan texted him with this news, he still couldn't shake the feeling of unease that came with the possibility that he was still being watched. However, today Angus had to deal with that something made almost every American anxious; he had to file his income taxes. Maggie knew how much Angus dreaded the entire process, so she tried to make it as painless as possible. She did as much on her end as she could and then gave him a list of specific information and forms to bring her before she dropped them off with her accountant. All Angus had to do was show up and sign the papers, which he still despised doing. Somehow, no matter how much work the preparer did ahead of time, the computer would run slow or something would need to be reviewed, and the signing appointment would end up taking a good portion of the afternoon.

This year Angus was particularly peeved. Maggie had not confirmed the address of their appointment and had changed accountants in the last year, so he had shown up at the old office and then had to drive across town to get to the new one. The extra drive time meant that he was 20 minutes late.

"I'm so sorry about this," Maggie said as Angus sat down on a couch next to her in the waiting area. "Luckily the appointment after us was early, so they just switched us."

"No worries." Angus tried to sound good-natured. In actuality, he was fuming. He hoped they wouldn't have to wait too long. He browsed the small selection of magazines including one aimed at female business owners and found nothing of interest.

"I really thought that I told you about switching firms." Maggie broke the silence. "Don't you remember how we got audited last year, and I was furious, because the fault lay not in our records but in how the accountant filed the paperwork?"

"Maybe." Angus had a vague recollection of Maggie huffing and puffing about their business taxes last year, but when she started talking about money, he tuned her out. "Do you like these guys better?"

"Very much so." Maggie smiled and put her magazine down on her lap. "Not only did these guys get things straightened out with the IRS, they went back and looked at our tax filings for the last five years. They found a couple of errors in our favor. I couldn't be more pleased."

"I'm glad," Angus said. It paid to keep Maggie happy.

Angus and Maggie sat in relative silence for the next 15 minutes. Angus read a couple of news stories on this phone and then checked in on social media. Old friends and acquaintances shared their weekend plans freely, and he shook his head. Sometimes he felt foolish for having fallen into a routine that someone had taken advantage of, but at least he wasn't announcing to the world that his house would be unoccupied.

A young woman walked out of an office and called for "Maggie Evans and Angus….MacEnroe?"

"Close enough. Just as long as you actually spelled it right on my taxes." Angus stood up and followed the young woman, who introduced herself as Melanie Purcell.

It turned out that all of Angus's information was correct, and Ms. Purcell was efficient and concise. After offering her clients coffee and asking the administrative assistant to fetch one for Maggie, Ms. Purcell got down to business. For once, Angus signed all his forms electronically without a delay and was ready to go in 20 minutes.

"Thank you so much for your time," Maggie said as they got up to leave.

"You're welcome." Ms. Purcell stood up to show them out. "If there's anything we can do for you in the future, anything at all, please call."

"Actually, I thought we were going to be meeting with Karen. Is she out today?" Maggie asked.

"Yes, she's indisposed at the moment." Ms. Purcell walked the towards the office door and opened it.

"Well, I hope she is well. She's been so busy lately that I've had a hard time getting ahold of her."

Ms. Purcell glanced out the doorway and kept her voice low. "She said you were a favorite client of hers, so I don't think there's any harm in telling you that Karen's boyfriend proposed to her last night, and they are spending the weekend in Denver to celebrate."

"Oh, how exciting!" Maggie smiled. "Please pass on my congratulations to her."

Angus was pleased that Maggie did not mention his recent engagement.

"I certainly will." Ms. Purcell was acting more like a teenager that an accountant. "Next time you come in, ask to see her engagement ring. The main stone is over a caret and has so much sparkle."

"Wow," Maggie exhaled. "That sounds like quite a ring."

"It sure is." Ms. Purcell recovered herself a bit. Her voice returned to its normal pace and tone. "And as I said, if you have any questions, please give us a call."

"Thanks, we will." Maggie left the office. She looked over at Angus. "Well, I'm glad that's over with. Fancy grabbing a bit of lunch?"

Angus checked the time. It was only 1 PM, but Maggie hadn't scheduled him for any jobs for the rest of the day. "Ok. Any place in particular you want to go?"

"I'll go wherever." Maggie scanned the hallway and finally found the door she'd been looking for. "While I visit the ladies' room, why don't you decide."

While Maggie was away, Angus contemplated his choices. He didn't feel like driving across town to go to Macduff's, but there was an all-day breakfast place a few blocks away. Some eggs and bacon would hit the spot. His decision made, he located the unisex restroom at the back of the office and noticed that the firm had hung a plaque featuring a reproduction of a positive newspaper article. The practice of displaying reviews and other such pieces near a business's restroom baffled Angus, but felt oddly compelled to read them. He was most of the way through when his thoughts were disrupted by the flush of a toilet and water running in the sink.

As Maggie emerged from the restroom, her cell phone rang. Looking at the display, she furrowed her brow and answered it. Angus only heard half the conversation. "Maggie Evans, how can I help you?" There was a long pause while Maggie listened and twirled her left hand in a "get on with it" gesture. "I understand you're in a pinch, Larry, but this sort of thing happens. You could just delay the closing." While Angus couldn't make any words out, he could hear a very agitated voice on the other end of the line, talking rapidly. Maggie breathed in deeply and exhaled slowly and then interrupted the caller. "Ok, I'll see what I can do, but you owe me a huge favor, and I plan to call in it this summer," she said as calmly as she could muster. "I'll call you back in five minutes." She hung up and shook her head.

Angus was glad he didn't deal with this side of the handyman business. He knew from Jack's stories that Maggie fielded at least one or two panicked calls each day. Typically, the person was just upset and wanted something minor done immediately, but when it was an actual emergency, Maggie could usually talk the client through a short-term solution like turning off the water to the house and either schedule a same day appointment with Jack, Angus, or another firm. Based on Maggie's reaction, Angus wasn't sure where this situation fell. "Everything ok?" he asked.

Maggie sighed. "Angus, I hate to impose, but that was a realtor who gives us a lot of positive recommendations. He just did a final walkthrough on a property, and they discovered that one of the bathroom sinks won't stop dripping. Even though it's a minor repair, the person buying the house wants it fixed before they sign the closing paperwork today at 5:00 PM. It's unreasonable, but Larry doesn't want to delay closing over the weekend." She looked at Angus with weary eyes. "I know we were going to do lunch, but would do this job instead, please?"

Angus's stomach growled, but he was used to his day not going as planned and kept some protein bars in his truck for just this contingency. "Sure, Maggie," he said. Maggie and Jack had done a lot for him over the years, so he had no issue indulging her. "Can you text me the address?"

"As soon as I get it." Relief washed over Maggie's face. "From what Larry said, it's in Black Forest, so if you head that way, I'll forward it to you." Maggie started typing a text, but then she looked back up. "Thanks, Angus, I appreciate this. Let me know how you like Larry, because I can probably convince him to be very helpful when you start looking at houses." She returned to her phone.

"Will do." Angus nodded. He has never been a big fan of realtors, but it might be nice to have one who had some loyalty to him. When he had purchased his townhouse, the realtor who handled the sale had been in her late 50s and smelled like an ashtray. She'd managed the paperwork competently, but Angus hadn't liked her and wondered if she was even still alive. "I'll head that way now."

Angus went out to his truck and took Woodman Road heading east. When he was just passing under Powers Blvd, the address came through. Not being familiar with the exact location, he put it into his phone's mapping app and followed the directions. The job took less than 15 minutes, and when Angus finished, he headed home and made his own omelet.

For the rest of the afternoon, Angus found himself in the unusual position of having unexpected time off, so he did his weekly shopping and cleaning his townhouse. He even went to price new flooring for his bathroom, but he still couldn't face ripping up the old floor just yet. Instead, he settled in for an early night with a collection of mystery short stories.

Saturday, March 9

Angus woke with a start about 5 AM and couldn't get back

to sleep. On a day that promised to be tranquil and carefree, he couldn't calm his thoughts. After a cup of tea, he tried to return to his book, but he couldn't focus. If he's been talking to someone, Angus would have felt like there was a word or phrase on the tip of his tongue. In reality he had an inkling, really more of just a notion that he had seen or heard something important in the last couple of days, but he could not pin it down. His predicament wasn't surprising. Angus had always had a tendency to retreat into his own thoughts when a conversation got boring or a person droned on and on. His attention issue was not helped by a slight loss of hearing from all the loud explosions during his years of training.

Angus make a cup of hot milk and sat down with a pen and paper. He mentally reviewed the last couple of weeks going through each day and each job in turn. Sometimes he referred to the timeline on his phone to remind him of what he'd done. While he sensed he hadn't gained any insights while painting a wall or ripping up carpet, Angus didn't completely dismiss the idea. When he zoned out, he let his mind wander and sometimes the connections that he made were very useful.

If he excluded the jobs that he'd worked in the last couple of weeks, Angus only had a few events to work with. Friday, he had signed his taxes and gone shopping. Thursday night he had done a shift at the veteran's hotline, during which no one had called in. Sunday Angus had gone hiking at Pulpit Rock Park with Jaiden and Lily. During none of these events had he discussed the robberies or the cameras pointed at his front door. In fact, in an effort to move on, Angus had looked forward and refrained from rehashing the events of the last few months. He chided himself for not making firmer plans to rip up and replace the bathroom floor. The sooner that task was done, the sooner he could sell his townhouse. However, he reminded himself that nothing stopped him from going to the hardware store today.

Angus looked at the clock and noted that most stores would not open for at least an hour, so he returned to retracing his steps. When he reached the day of the "How I Would Have Done It" party, he recalled the twin realizations that he could leave the townhouse complex undetected and cameras were pointed at his house. These facts were so earth shattering that he wondered if they had obscured and overshadowed some other important detail. Angus went over the party in his head and racked his brain but got no further.

Thinking of the party made him think of Isaac Templeton. At some point, Cassandra had told the story of how Isaac could always guess who the murdered was in a mystery program even when he slept through most of the action. She speculated her husband was very good at accessing his unconscious mind. It made Angus wonder if perhaps Isaac could hypnotize him and help him find the missing clue.

Contacting Isaac seemed to be a long shot, but Angus got out his phone and sent him a text anyway. Then he went to take a shower. As he was toweling off, he heard his phone ring.

"Hello." He managed to pick up the phone without getting it wet. He noted it was Isaac and put it on speaker.

"Good morning, Angus." Isaac Templeton's voice boomed out of the phone's speaker. Angus wondered how the man's gregariousness was transmitted through a telephone signal. "I hate to burst your bubble, but hypnosis doesn't work like that."

Angus nodded to himself. "I figured it wouldn't be that easy," he said, taking the phone with him to his bedroom to pick a kilt for the day.

"I assume you've tried going back over the last couple of days or weeks."

"Aye." Angus looked over his choices. The one thing he hadn't done the night before was laundry. He only had two kilts left and neither would be suitable for home improvement work. He went over to dig through the hamper. "I can't seem to nail it down to anything recent. I feel like someone said something minor at the party a couple of weeks ago, but why did it just occur to me now? It's been two weeks."

There was a pause while Isaac processed this idea, and Angus found an older kilt that had a couple of small spots of worn fabric on it. He sometimes used it for lounging around the house. Maybe it could become a working kilt.

"I think it likely that several relevant things were said at your party and then something happened recently that helped you make a connection between them." Isaac finally spoke.

The men spent five minutes discussing the last two weeks with little success. Eventually Angus said, "Maybe if we recreate the party, we could figure out what I missed."

"Hmm." Isaac considered this. "It's an idea with merit, but I think I'd like to try something else first. What do you have on your schedule today?"

After dressing, Angus had moved back to bathroom to tidy up his towels. He looked down at the linoleum floor. It could wait another day. "Nothing in particular. Why?"

"Let's try a technique I sometimes use in my practice to access thoughts and feelings that are bubbling just below the surface," Isaac said. "I find people open up a bit when they engage in some sort of physical or mental task while talking through a problem. I once ran a teen support group where we played UNO and other games while processing the events of the week. The mind sometimes lets its guard down that way."

Angus pictured sitting in Templeton's office and playing cards. It beat sitting on a leather couch, but he had doubts. Isaac was great at getting teens to make progress. "What did you have in mind?" he asked.

"We could do a lot of things. I think perhaps a hike but someplace where we won't get distracted by the terrain. How about Black Forest Section 16? It's a loop."

Angus recalled Templeton's wingtips from the party and

wondered if the man knew what he was getting into. "It's four miles, Isaac. I'm up for it, but are you?"

"I'll be fine," Isaac chuckled. "It's been a couple of years, but I used to take a patient out there every other week."

The men arranged to meet at the trailhead in an hour. Angus make a simple breakfast, checked his daypack, and headed out the door.

Isaac was a few minutes late and when he exited his 1990s bottle green Mercedes sedan, Angus wondered what was older, the car or Isaac's heavy soled hiking boots. While many people had transitioned to lighter trail runners, Isaac appeared to have remained loyal to a bygone style. The boots looked both well cared for and well used. Angus thought about commenting but decided Templeton had enough experience to make his own decisions.

Isaac followed Angus's gaze. "It's irrational, but I just can't seem to throw these boots away," he acknowledged. "I have others, but I keep coming back to these."

"Suit yourself." Angus took his daypack out of his truck and locking the doors. Despite the early hour, the parking lot was already three quarters full. He was glad that Isaac hadn't been further delayed.

"I always do." Isaac placed an overlarge hat made from synthetic fabric on his head, grabbed a bottle of water and a granola bar, and locked up his car.

The Black Forest Section 16 Trail was situated inside a "country block" just west of Vollmer Road in Black Forest, a wooded area near northeast Colorado Springs. The main parking lot was on Burgess Road. From there, trail users could go either west or east. Either way, after four miles, they ended up back where they started. The terrain was flat with a few hills and many trees. In 2013, the Black Forest Fire had destroyed count-less homes, but the trees along the Section 16 trail had been largely unaffected.

The men hiked the trail in a clockwise direction, which led them west. They started their conversation by exchanging pleasantries and talking about the weather, which was predicted to be gorgeous. As they turned north with the trail, Angus wondered when they would get down to business. When he asked Isaac, the psychologist said, "Oh, we've already started. Talk about whatever you like, the weather, the trail conditions, the flowers, plunging a toilet. We'll see what comes into your mind and out of your mouth."

Angus liked Isaac Templeton, but he suddenly felt like this was a wild goose chase. At least he was getting some exercise. He'd spent at least two hours going over every detail of the last two weeks in his mind, and he didn't see how an in-depth discussion of plumbing was going to shed any light on his dilemma.

After a long silence, Isaac took another tack. "If you don't want to talk, how about you ask me some questions?"

"Ok." Angus considered his options. He supposed they could compare strategies for helping clients in crisis, but he dismissed the idea of "shop talk." Instead, he asked, "So, how do you do it? How do you sleep through most of a two-hour movie and then know who did it in the end?"

Isaac stopped the crest of a small hillock and gazed at a stunning view of Pikes Peak. He seemed to be deep in thought. "Can you keep a secret?"

"As long as it doesn't hurt anyone." Angus wondered what Isaac Templeton had to hide.

"Well, the truth is that the winter I was 15, I broke my leg rather badly skiing," Isaac began. "I spent about eight weeks in bed and read a huge number of classic mysteries, Sherlock Holmes, Father Brown, Hercule Poirot, Miss Marple, the whole lot of them."

"What about school?" Angus asked as the men continued on down the trail. "Didn't they send you work to do?"

"School was always easy for me," Isaac chuckled. "I had a teacher who joked that they should just let me take the final exams and excuse me from the work, which I never did anyway, because I was bored silly. So, when it came to putting together packets of work for me, that teacher sent me the final exam from the previous year, and I sent it back the next day. When I got an A on her final and didn't do any of my other classwork, the rest of the teachers followed suit."

Now it was Angus's turn to laugh. "That's quite a good deal all around. They didn't have to put it together or grade it, and you got out of a semester of school work." He took a sip of water. "But how did you get all the mystery novels? And why did you read them if you hated to do busy work?"

"That same teacher who just gave me her final both loved and hated me." Isaac smiled as he remembered. "I was a disruptive clown in her classes, but she also understood why. Good old Miss Harelson. She was also a huge mystery fan. She visited me and brought some of her classic mystery collection. Once a week, she would come by and we would discuss the similarities and differences. It was then that I discovered I have a photographic memory for written text."

Angus wasn't sure what impressed him more about the story, that a teacher had made house calls for one of her hardest students, or that Isaac used his superior memory to affect a parlor trick with his wife.

"Cassandra knows about my photographic memory," Isaac clarified. "We met in medical school, and it annoyed her how I didn't have to study as much as her."

"But she doesn't know about eight weeks of reading mysteries?" Angus guessed.

Isaac took another sip of water as if to ponder the best way to answer this. Despite the chill of the morning, he was looking red in the face, and Angus wondered if perhaps they should head back before they hit the halfway point in the loop.

"I hope someday you know what it is like to be married for over 20 years," Isaac finally said. "You feel you know everything about your partner, but they lived a good portion of their life before they even met you, and it's not like you sit down and compare notes systematically."

He closed the cover on his water bottle. "I hadn't thought about that winter in years, and then one evening we were watching television and I fell asleep and then I woke up and knew who did it. It was the Belgian detective's last case; everyone knows how that ends. Anyway, I think we'd just gotten a subscription to a streaming service or something, because we watched a mystery a night for a couple of weeks. Cassandra made me a sweater and the entire time got more and more frustrated."

When Isaac paused, Angus asked, "And you, who had a photographic memory, didn't remember reading all those novels years before?" It didn't seem credible.

"Well, it's kind of like that modern version of Holmes where he talks about how he feels like he has run out of room in his memory to store extraneous information. I didn't think about it until a friend from high school shared Miss Harelson's obituary on social media. Then it all came back to me in a flash."

"I wish I could have that kind of epiphany." Angus felt a stab of jealousy.

"And you will eventually." Isaac used his most reassuring practitioner voice. "You will either figure out what's bothering you or life will move on and it won't be important anymore."

Angus nodded. "I suppose, but why haven't you ever told Cassandra?"

"Well, I guess the time was never quite right." Isaac confessed. "At first, I didn't want to talk about Miss Harelson, and

Cassandra finished the sweater and didn't feel like starting anything new, so we stopped watching mystery programs for a while. One of our kids was going through a rough patch, and then by the time things calmed down, I felt like the moment had passed." He paused. "Besides, Cassandra has a lot of fun telling the story. It seems a pity to ruin it for her, although I might have to if she seriously considers writing it up for publication."

"It's not lying, just omitting." Angus tried to be supportive. He didn't totally agree, but he understood.

"Something like that," Isaac said and then changed the subject.

They had been walking at a slow but steady pace for perhaps 50 minutes. As they were approached the midpoint of the hike, Angus felt no closer to solving his problem, so he let Isaac talk. He wondered if since Isaac listened to patients talk all day, the man didn't need to prattle on a bit with a friend.

Isaac was recounting the tale of a semester in Italy when he was in college and a beautiful woman who had taken him out for snails and wine when they came across one of several benches along the trail. Angus liked how the benches with splendid views were placed throughout the loop, but he didn't take advantage of them often.

"She didn't speak a word of English, and my knowledge of Italian was much better for reading ancient and Medieval texts." Isaac continued his story. Seeing the bench, he took a seat. "Anyway, after a couple of bottles of wine, it didn't matter. Our bodies knew a more universal language."

Angus, who had placed his daypack on the bench and was rooting around looking for an apple, blushed.

"I'm sorry, dear boy." Isaac's grin contradicted his words. "I forgot you prefer the PG version of stories." Isaac unwrapped his granola bar and took a bite.

"It sounds like quite an adventure." Angus rubbed his

apple against his kilt to remove an invisible speck of dust. Slowly his face returned to normal. "I sometimes wish that I had gone to college," he commented to keep the conversation going as Isaac made quick work of his snack. "But I don't know that I would be suited to a career that requires a college education."

"It seems to me that you are in the right place." Isaac folded up his empty wrapper and put it in his pocket. "Hey, do you mind if we sit a little longer? I could use a break."

"Sure." Angus bit into his apple and sat down on the bench next to Isaac. "A little more challenging of a hike than you remember it?"

Isaac agreed and then launched into descriptions of all the hikes he and Cassandra used to go on. Angus wondered why they had stopped but held his tongue. While he was familiar with many of the trails, he was also feeling fatigued from his early wake up. He let Isaac talk and just zoned out.

"And then, we ended up on a side trail that wasn't on the map," Isaac droned on. Abruptly he added, "Female jogger! And we didn't get back to our car until it was almost dark."

The sudden change in tenor of Isaac's voice jolted Angus back to reality. His heart beat faster and he had an odd tingling sensation that was more mental than physical. "What did you just say, Isaac?" he asked following his intuition.

"I was talking about a time that we got all turned around in Palmer Park," Isaac said flatly as he realized Angus hadn't really been listening.

"No." Angus tried to cling to the sensation that already seemed to be dissipating. "In the middle of it, you went off in a different direction."

"Ah, I was just noting that a female jogger went past us. Cassandra and I..."

"Female jogger!" Angus cut him off. Suddenly it all became clear. "Female jogger," Angus repeated, as the pieces of the puzzle fell into place. "A female jogger."

"Yes, Angus," Isaac said in frustration. "A female jogger. Are you criticizing me for cataloguing joggers based on their biological sex?"

"Isaac, shut up for a minute." Angus hated to be rude, but he needed to flush his thoughts out. "I have to look something up, and then we can talk."

Angus pulled out his phone and was surprised that he had a signal on the trail. He searched for the article on Gary Peterson that he'd looked at the previous fall. It didn't take long to find it and note the name of Peterson's firm. Angus also realized where he had recently seen the photo that accompanied the article. It had been on the plaque by the restroom at the tax firm. What were the chances? A few more taps brought up the website for Peterson's firm and a list of accountants who worked at each location. The employees at the office he had visited yesterday were listed as Rodney Cunningham, Karen Peterson, and Melanie Purcell. It was a solid connection between the Petersons and Maggie, Jack, and Angus, but how had he jumped from jogging to accountants?

Angus turned back to Isaac. "Sorry I interrupted you earlier. Can you explain to me why you notice joggers by biological sex?"

"Well, it's a longstanding debate that Cassandra and I have." Isaac seemed confused by this interaction but also recognized the signs of a breakthrough. "I claim that jogging is more prevalent amongst women, while she claims the numbers are about equal and women just jog in places where they are more visible, for safety."

"Hmm." Angus considered this statement. He felt like he had heard it before, but the problem with recurring discussions or running gags was that they came up frequently. "Did you discuss it at my party?"

Isaac thought back. "Almost certainly. I think we got talking about it, because we discussed that the woman who broke into your apartment was dressed as a female jogger." As he said the last sentence, he slowed down the words and began to realize the implications. Then he shook his head as the next point in the line of reasoning evaporated.

"Who amongst the people involved in this case is most likely to be a jogger?" Angus asked, more to himself. He cast his mind over the major players.

"Angus, this is Colorado Springs. Everyone is a potential jogger. Heck, every morning I see the same overweight man jog past my house," Isaac said with exasperation in his voice. He felt like this was a red herring.

"Fair point," Angus said. "But we are looking for a young to middle age female jogger who is thin." He paused. "That takes Gary Peterson out of the picture. He's too heavy. And I have a distinct feeling his wife wouldn't be able to scramble over rocks to get away."

Isaac nodded. "Who does that leave?"

"Their daughter Karen, who did Jack and Maggie's business taxes and my personal taxes last year."

"It could just be a coincidence." Isaac played the Devil's advocate.

"I guess," Angus admitted. With a little more to go on, he tried to remember what Mrs. Peterson had told him about her daughter. Middle-aged women loved to talk to him, and he largely tuned them out, but what was it she had said? "At one point, Mrs. Peterson talked to me about why they didn't just go with the original plan of renting a townhouse," Angus recalled. "I think it was dawning on her how much the renovations were costing, and as much as Mr. Peterson is an unpleasant person, he has a point. Karen would need to live in the basement for a good amount of time for them to break even. Mrs. Peterson said something about Karen loving outdoor activities and wanting her to be in a safe neighborhood. At the very least, she sounds like a healthy gal who might go jogging."

"I suppose it's possible." Isaac stood up. He took a couple of stiff steps, inhaled deeply. "What's our next move?"

"I think the best thing would be to get you home and then talk to Maggie."

Using the mapping app on his phone, Angus figured out where they were about a mile and a half from the trail head parking lot. Isaac still looked peaked, so Angus left him sitting on the bench and power walked to his car. Along the way, he called Maggie and arranged to come over. Once he had ferried Isaac back to his car, Angus headed for the Evans' house.

On the weekends, Maggie tended not to be a morning person, so she looked a bit disheveled when she let Angus in her front door at 9:30 AM on a Sunday morning. Angus removed his shoes and followed her into the dining area.

"I'm sorry not to be a better host." Maggie stifled a yawn. "But we were up in Denver late at a concert. I wouldn't have even considered seeing you this morning if you hadn't made it sound like it was life or death."

"It's not quite life or death, but I feel like I have a solid lead." Angus noticed the kettle was hot and his cup and a tea bag were already laid out, so he poured the water and waited for the tea to steep. "Chances are you'll shut it down, but if not, it's worth exploring."

Maggie walked over to the coffee pot and refilled her cup. Then she padded her way over to a couch in her slippered feet. Baxter, her mutt of a dog who was mostly golden retriever, snuggled up next to her. "Well, if we're going to explore some theories, you might as well get comfortable." Maggie invited, scratching Baxter behind his ears.

Angus finished prepping the cup of tea and joined Maggie in the seating area that bordered her dining room. He picked an armchair and got comfortable. "Do you remember where you first heard about A5 Accounting?" he began. He didn't want to influence Maggie by letting her in on his idea too early.

Maggie took a minute to think of her answer. "Um, a friend of mine from the gym. She also runs a small business, and when I complained about my last accountant, she gave me their card. She said they had a reputation for helping military service members and their dependents."

"And when did you start using A5?" Angus sipped his tea.

"Late April, early May," Maggie confirmed. "It took a couple of weeks to get things sorted out with the IRS, but they were very thorough."

"Hmm." Angus mentally reviewed the facts. Gary's daughter had moved back in late August or September - too early to have helped Maggie through the audit. "And did you always work with Karen?" he asked, knowing the answer couldn't be yes.

"No, not at first," Maggie recalled. "At first I worked with a fellow, Cummings maybe."

"Cunningham?" Angus remembered the name from the website.

Maggie hesitated. "Could be. I'm not sure. Seriously, Angus, what's with the questions?"

"One more question," Angus said, thinking how he wanted to phrase it. "When did your working relation with Karen begin?"

"Sometime last fall." Maggie took a sip of her coffee. She paused to think and eventually said, "I can't remember precisely when. We had so much going on. Is it important?"

Angus was shocked that Maggie hadn't made a connection between the accountant Karen Peterson and the client Gary Peterson, but then Peterson was a very common name. He laid everything out. "Remember the Peterson job that started this entire mess?"

Maggie nodded.

"Well, Gary Peterson is an accountant." Angus watched Maggie's face for the moment of realization. "He owns A5 Accounting, and according to his firm's website, he has a daughter named Karen, who joined the firm as soon as she graduated from college." He showed Maggie on his phone.

As Maggie processed this information, her look turned from puzzled to pissed. Her cheeks flushed, and she tightened her grip on his phone. "But she was so nice," Maggie said through clenched teeth. "I can't believe that I never connected Karen to Gary Peterson." She handed Angus back his phone. "And she was so helpful, going through our records and taxes for the last five years to look for filing errors."

"Almost too helpful." Angus thought of Karen going through their invoices, looking for his name. "Tell me about the process for the records review."

"Well, as part of resolving our IRS audit, A5's accountant offered to conduct their own audit," Maggie began. "At first that Cunningham fellow just wanted copies of old tax returns. It seemed reasonable."

Leaving Angus to think about this, Maggie excused herself and went upstairs to get her laptop. She placed it on the coffee table and booted it up.

"That seems like an appropriate course of action," Angus said as the computer made various noises. "So, when did Karen enter the picture?"

"I feel like it was early September. Let me check." Maggie spent a couple of minutes on the computer. "I got an email from

A5 on August 28th asking me to make an appointment to discuss my audit," she confirmed.

"From which accountant?" Angus tried to remember his conversations with Mrs. Peterson about when her daughter was moving back.

"From Cunningham, but when I called, they said not to come in until after the holiday weekend. That suited me fine as I had plans, so I came in the next Wednesday."

Angus was still waiting to hear when Karen came into the picture, but his mind was racing. Were Karen and her dad in this together, and why? Did Gary Peterson have an expensive habit to finance? What was Karen getting out of this?

"The meeting was with Cunningham," Maggie said. "We sat and talked for perhaps 20 minutes, and his conclusion was that everything looked fine, which annoyed me. They could have just told me that on the phone."

Angus could sympathize with Maggie. Their time was valuable.

"We were wrapping things up when there was a knock on the office door. In walked this young woman impeccably dressed and well made up." Maggie's voice sounded dreamy. "Cunningham went to introduce her, but she just interrupted him and said her name was Karen and that she was the new general manager of the branch."

"And she just introduced herself as Karen, no last name?" Angus had wondered how Maggie hadn't clued in on the same last name between Karen and her father, but perhaps Karen's approach to people was as subtle and her father's was brusque.

Maggie took a minute to think back. "Yeah, it seems so weird in retrospect, but Karen has so much personal magnetism that I just accepted what she said."

Angus wondered what sort of insights he would get if he met Karen. Perhaps it had been propitious she was unavailable for their appointment. "What happened next?" He tried to push Maggie's story forward.

"It's weird. It's like trying to remember a dream." She paused to collect her thoughts. "Cunningham tried to give Karen a quick update, but she cut him off. Gosh, I didn't think about it at the time, but she was quite rude to him."

Angus thought back to Sandy's lecture about changing your perspective on the terrain to find the trail. Maggie was interpreting events in a different light. "Then she invited me to her office saying that she had an exciting opportunity for me."

"Well, if a life of crime doesn't work out, perhaps she could sell Tupperware," Angus laughed. "Let me guess, no name plate on her door."

"I don't honestly remember, but it was odd. She was so beautiful and sophisticated. I just listened to what she said but didn't really comprehend it."

"What was the amazing opportunity?"

"Karen said that she had studied both accounting and computer programming in college and that she had developed an auditing program for small businesses." Maggie's face turned sour. "She thought it would help small business owners avoid the problems that I had encountered, and she asked if I would like to be part of beta testing it."

"I feel like she wasn't going to take no for an answer," Angus said.

"It was odd. I genuinely thought it sounded like a good idea. In fact, I still think it is a good idea, but now I suspect it was just a way for her to have access to our business records."

Angus hated to break it to Maggie, but software of that type probably already existed to help small business owners. Nonetheless, it was a creative hook.

"Anyway." Maggie sighed. "She told me that if I was part of

the pilot program, she would do our business and personal taxes for free this year. I signed a piece of paper, and then she asked me a bunch of questions about how I kept our records. In the end, she installed the program on my computer and assured me that if the test went well, it would be the best decision that I ever made."

"What did the program do?" Angus asked.

"Beats me. In theory it tracked our invoices and quarterly tax payments and make sure everything was kosher. In actuality, it meant that Karen and her dad could access our records whenever they liked." She hung her head. "After a few weeks, I forgot about it."

Angus nodded. It had been a hectic year. "Didn't you say though that A5 did an audit and got you back some money from the government?"

"Yeah. They got me back like $1500. That was kind of nice. Karen said that with more information at her disposal, she went back and found some mistakes."

"Well, wasn't that considerate of her?" Angus snarled.

"Maybe it was part of her trying to establish a relationship," Maggie said. "It was strange. Karen and I didn't meet at the office after that. We had a couple of lunch meetings, and I ran into her at the gym. She even tried to get me to join some sort of running club. She's fantastic at working that 'it's hard to be a woman in the business world' schtick."

"Do you think she was using the occasions to pump you for information on clients?"

"Maybe," Maggie took out her phone and opened an app. "I know I have said it several times, but it was weird. I think it was just about maintaining a connection. At one point we became friends on social media." She showed Angus a profile with the name Karen Anne. "You can see why I never suspected that she was Peterson's daughter. I don't know that I had ever heard her last name."

"Did she post a picture of her ring?" Angus asked out of curiosity.

After two or three clicks, Maggie whistled and showed Angus a picture. "You've been looking at engagement rings with Lily, how much do you think that monster would run?"

Angus examined the picture of a woman who bore little resemblance to either of her parents showing off a ring with a massive colorless stone. He hadn't paid a lot of attention while looking at rings, but he had never seen one that size. "Maybe it's fake," he suggested.

"Maybe it's stolen," Maggie joked. "Nah. She's way too smart for that."

"Although one wonders where two young people just out of college, one of whom is living in their parent's basement have the money or the credit to get a ring like that," Angus pointed out. "Hey, while we are looking, what's the finance's name?"

"Jonah Simmons." Maggie clicked on his profile. "He lists the same college as Karen but with no graduation date. That doesn't mean much though." Maggie scrolled. "Wait a second. He works at White Knight Security Solutions, LLC. Wonder if they install cameras. Should we call Jimmy?"

Angus felt his stomach flip flop. You didn't need to be psychic to see where this was going. "I think it's time to call Dan."

When Dan didn't answer his phone or texts, Maggie took some screen shots of Karen and Jonah's profiles and forwarded them to Angus. Then Angus emailed Dan with a summary of their discoveries. He knew he should have felt elated to have found a connection, but he just felt restless. It was like the feeling you get when your furnace stops working at 4:45 on a Friday afternoon, and you know you will either need to pay for an after-hours call out or wait until Monday to get it fixed. It was a dangerous sort of mood to be in. Angus recalled a homeowner who had tried to light his oil heat himself because he couldn't stand the waiting and almost burned down his house.

"You know Dan would tell us to not do anything rash," he said as a warning.

"Oh, I won't do anything rash." Maggie's mood seemed to have oscillated back to fuming. "This woman and her father have done their best to ruin your reputation and my business. While it might be nice to see their tax office burn to the ground, I would rather see us vindicated in court."

Angus took a moment to analyze her statement. "What if Gary isn't in on it? What if it's just Karen? He's not exactly a smooth operator."

"Maybe he needed money for drugs or gambling debts. How would we know? That's something that Dan could find out."

"Even so, I see the gears turning in your mind," Angus said. Maggie was a plotter, and Angus was concerned as their previous plans had not gone as expected. "Promise me you won't do anything stupid."

"Alright," Maggie said. "I won't put any plans in motion until we hear from Dan."

CHAPTER 12

Tuesday, March 12

On Sunday, Dan had called Angus to apologize for being out of communication. He and Green had just busted a crew that had been working a neighborhood stealing cars and trucks, and they had been filling out a mountain of paperwork. Dan promised that as soon as he came up for air, he would share Angus's information with Green and look into it.

As Angus was driving home from work on Tuesday, he got a phone call. The caller ID showed it was Dan, so Angus answered it.

"I have --------- for you," Dan said. The connection wasn't great, but Angus could sort of make out what Dan was saying.

"What's that, Dan?" Angus was about to cross Powers Boulevard and knew that his reception was pretty bad here. He was stopped at a red light. If he drove a block further west, he'd be back into an area with good signal strength.

"--------- information --- you," Dan repeated.

Angus got the idea. Dan wanted to talk, but they couldn't make any plans until the light turned. Angus hung up and texted *Call you in 5.*

When he got home, Dan was waiting for him with a six pack of Guinness. "Mind if I come in?"

"Go for it." Angus opened the back door and let him come through.

Angus took out two pint glasses and allowed Dan to pour

him a beer. It wasn't his favorite, but it seemed the thing to do. "Sorry about that. You know how network cuts out in places here."

"Yeah." Dan nodded. "Sometimes it feels like being in one of those cell phone commercials from 2005."

"You had some news?" Angus asked, taking his beer and sitting down in his chair by the fireplace.

"I do, good news and bad news."

"Good news first." The room was a little darker than Angus liked, so he turned on a lamp and returned to his seat.

"Well, Karen is Gary Peterson's daughter," Dan confirmed, consulting a notebook.

Angus raised his eyebrow. This wasn't Dan's normal MO. Seeing Angus's reaction, Dan said, "Look, some of this is official and some of it is unofficial, got it?"

"Aye." Angus sipped his beer.

"Karen Peterson has a degree in accounting and computer programming from a Colorado university," Dan said. "She has all her appropriate professional licenses, and she is the general manager of a branch of her father's company."

"That sounds quite official," Angus said. This was nothing new to him.

"Unofficially, I touched base with Mrs. Peterson. I gave her a line about some new information, and then I just let her talk. According to her mom, Karen's branch of the business is doing very well. Lots of new, happy clients. Online reviews back that up."

"Sounds like sunshine and lollypops." Angus struggled to keep the contempt out of his voice.

"It's not all good news," Dan said. "While Gary and his wife are pleased about their daughter's engagement, Gary is hopping mad that he paid so much to have his basement renovated for his daughter to move out after six months."

"He could always rent it out. That place might go for as much as $1000 a month." Angus had worked with a lot of home owners who had converted their basements to apartments. If you didn't need the room, it could be a nice source of supplemental income. "Speaking of money, did you check his financials?"

"He's had no unusual activity since the robberies; no large withdrawals or deposits except the insurance check, but Karen's accounts are another story. Her salary, which is quite generous, gets deposited and then almost immediately her balance is down near zero. No idea how she affords the fancy clothes and trips. Also, she doesn't seem to use credit cards, so either she uses cash, or it's on her boyfriend's dime."

"Fiancée." Angus corrected and laughed. "What about him?"

"Jonah attended the same college as she did but never graduated." Dan consulted his notebook. "Dropped out sophomore year after he got in trouble for academic dishonesty and underage drinking."

"Really?" Angus asked. "Doesn't everyone drink in college? I mean, I never went to college, and I'm not a big drinker, but I feel like that is a given."

"Well, that's what the university claims," Dan said. "But I talked to a recent graduate who is trying to make a name for herself in journalism, and she claims it was more like he was selling tests and papers to other students and the administration wanted it hushed up. They busted him for the alcohol, because it was convenient."

"Ah. Does he happen to install security cameras?"

"I'm getting there." Dan looked at the beer he had left untouched on the coffee table, and as if to emphasize that he was in control of the discussion, he took a sip before he continued. "Jonah's major was computer science, and apparently he got his merchandise by hacking the college's cloud drive."

"Nice," Angus said. Jonah was looking more like Karen's accomplice than her dad.

"After he 'dropped out,' he floated around to several jobs." Dan made air quotes in the appropriate place. "Then last spring he came back to the Springs and started working for White Knight Security Solutions."

Angus recalled a conversation from over the weekend. "Jimmy says they are shady."

"Yeah." Dan ran his fingers through his hair. "We've dealt with them before. If you want someone to install security cameras around your house, there are much better places to go, but if you want to stalk your ex-girlfriend or spy on your business partner, they can hook you up."

Angus shifted in his chair. "Isn't most of that stuff illegal?"

"There are a lot of grey areas, and White Knight Security rides the line." Dan took a long pull of his beer. "I didn't interview anyone from the company, because they have never been cooperative, but it's the sort of place that Jonah could buy or perhaps even steal high end security cameras."

"So, he and Karen could be working together?" Angus asked. "What are his financials like?"

"Virtually non-existent. While he has a bank account, there isn't a lot of activity. Maybe he stays with a friend and pays in cash. His only asset is a pretty sweet vintage Corvette, but he bought that in cash when he was still in college."

"Sounds like a fine upstanding citizen who can afford to give his fiancée a giant rock." Angus's voice dripped with sarcasm. "Don't tell me he paid for that in cash."

Dan shook his head. "Actually, Mrs. Peterson told me it was his grandmother's ring, and then I showed the picture of the ring to Green, and she said it was modern. I don't know; I am not a jewelry expert."

"Neither am I." Angus had thought about showing the ring to Lily, but he didn't want her to get ideas. Well, that wasn't completely true. He and Lily had looked at several vintage rings, but none of them had seemed right. Perhaps he didn't want to taint their search for the perfect ring.

"You look deep in thought there," Dan said after a minute. "What's on your mind?"

"Just wedding stuff," Angus said. "It's so weird to me that Lily and I are getting married at the same time as the people who may have made the last year of my life a mess. How weird is that?"

Dan got up to get another beer. "The year I got married, there was a big wedding on one of those sitcoms that everyone loved, so half the time I felt like my wife was comparing our plans to their unrealistic ones. It was a trip."

"So where do we go from here?" Angus realized he hadn't really heard any bad news yet.

"Well, that's the problem." Dan opened a second bottle of Guinness and poured it into his glass. "There's a lot of circumstantial evidence but nothing concrete." He walked back to the couch. "I know it must be frustrating, but there's no evidence that Karen and Jonah were part of the robberies."

Angus frowned. "What about Hank? Couldn't he identify Karen as the person who broke into my house?" even as he said it, it struck Angus that he hadn't heard from Hank in a while. He knew that Hank and Reggie had been hanging out more, but he hadn't seen Hank in several weeks, not since he had invited him to the get together with Sandy.

"Thought of that," Dan said. "Hank's description was pretty vague, so we had him look at a photo lineup. He didn't pick Karen out. And the image on Jimmy's video isn't clear enough to identify the burglar."

"But the spyware on Maggie's computer," Angus countered. Maggie had mentioned that Dan sent a technician to look at her computer.

"While it gives Karen access to Maggie's business records, that is all it does," Dan said. "Besides Maggie signed a valid if somewhat vague waiver. Again, shady but not illegal."

"And since they do everything in cash?"

"Definitely suspicious, but unless they deposit significant amounts of cash without an explanation, there isn't a lot we can do." Dan finished his thought.

Angus got out of his chair and started pacing the room. "So, we know who probably robbed all these people, but there's nothing we can do?" he asked.

"We'll monitor them," Dan sighed. "The way they go through money, it's only a matter of time before they need an influx of cash, and if they get it by illegal means, we'll be in a better position to gather evidence."

Angus was usually a pretty easy-going guy, but he was working himself into a lather. He and Lily were decent, hardworking people, and through the actions of others his reputation had been sullied. Meanwhile, the people who they suspected were responsible not only were living off their ill-gotten gains but were free to do it all over again. It didn't seem fair.

"Any advice for me?" he asked. "Either as a friend or as a cop?"

Dan settled back into the couch, sipping his beer. "We advised Maggie to sever her relationship with A5 Accounting and get her computer professionally scrubbed. That cuts off the flow of data about your clients to Karen."

Angus shook with rage. "Karen's not stupid. She could have all our records back up somewhere." He spat.

"Yeah," Dan agreed. "She might, but if she's smart, she'll move on to someone else. Look, there hasn't been a robbery of one of your clients in a while. Maybe she's already moved on. "

"So now she's messing with someone else's livelihood and life. That doesn't sound any better," Angus muttered.

Dan could see that Angus was upset, and he was frustrated as well. One of the computer techs had accessed Karen's profile, and he has spent an hour looking at her posts about clothes, hair, and make up and wanted to puke. "But they are on our radar now," Dan said, more for himself than Angus. "At some point they'll screw up like the folks we caught over the weekend, and we will nail them."

Angus went over to the kitchen sink and poured the remains of his beer down the drain. He has lost his taste for it. Without even thinking about it, he turned on the electric kettle and placed a tea bag in his cup. Dan held back and let him make the tea and come back to his chair.

"Better now?" he asked after Angus had drank a few sips.

"Not really," Angus said. "But I think it's going to be awhile before I am."

"Well, I told you what we are doing as cops. Now let me tell you as a friend that I think you've already started down a good path."

"Really?" Angus held his cup in both hands, letting the warmth sink in.

"Yeah," Dan said. "The best thing is to leave the entire mess behind you. Sell this place. Get married. Move on."

"True." Angus still felt bad leaving Karen and Jonah to prey on others with only the possibility of being caught.

Dan finished his beer and put the glass on the coffee table. "When are you putting this place on the market?" he asked, changing the subject.

"We were thinking early May. I don't think that we will have found a house yet, but there are places I can stay."

The men talked for another 30 minutes, and then Dan headed out. He hoped he had talked Angus down from doing something rash. It was a cliche that cops hated dealing with amateurs, but that was because civilians took stupid, unnecessary risks. Dan wasn't worried about Angus as much as he was about Maggie. When the technician had offered to uninstall the software from her computer and scan for further spyware on his own time, Maggie had declined. She had said something about having a friend who was a computer nerd, but Dan had other suspicions.

Wednesday, March 13

Angus tried to take Dan's advice to heart as he began his day. Like the new year, a new day was a chance to start again and move in a different direction. However, when he studied his list of jobs, he was taken aback to see Sandy's address listed as his first appointment.

Sandy and her husband Greg lived in Cimarron Hills, a neighborhood in eastern Colorado Springs. They had bought the house seven years ago, because it was near the high school where Sandy taught and far enough away from the university where Greg worked. Even though the house was only 20 years old, the previous owner has undertaken some enthusiastic but haphazard renovations. Angus liked to refer to the style as "when DIY goes wrong." He once remembered coming to the property to find the light fixture in the master bath hanging by a single electrical wire. The fixture contained five bulbs and globes and had only been secured by half inch screws. Sandy had at least had the good sense to turn off the current to the circuit.

As the house and the shoddy workmanship aged, small things broke. Since neither Sandy nor Greg were particularly house proud, they waited until they had a list of several repairs and then called Maggie. Maggie had owned the house next door before Jack had retired, so they were old friends, and she put Sandy on the schedule pretty quickly. It had been about 9 months since he'd been to Sandy's house, so Angus wasn't surprised that she needed some work done. He was just a little miffed at the timing.

When Angus arrived at Sandy's house, she answered the door holding a cup of coffee and looking like she had been up for hours. Unlike her normal pony tail or bun, her hair was down, and static electricity was wreaking havoc with it. "Morning, Angus." She moved aside so that he could come through the front door.

As she closed the door, the lever handle jiggled loosely in her hand.

"Need me to tighten that again?" Angus asked. This wasn't the first time and wouldn't be the last.

"Please," Sandy said with a sigh. "If it was just a knob, I could fix it. I hate this style, but it's what came with the house.

"You could always get a new door." The front door knob was a perpetual source of frustration for Sandy, but Angus also knew that she was hesitant to spend a lot of money on the house's cosmetic features.

"Maybe I will get Maggie to price one for me." Sandy turned inward toward the main body of the house. "But right now, let me show what else there is."

Angus nodded and followed Sandy to the basement. She directed him to the bathroom at the foot of the stairs and pointed to a towel bar that had been pulled out of the wall. The bar and one of the mountings were sitting on the vanity.

"What happened here?" Angus asked, noting that the bar had been installed much higher than was standard. He also saw the poorly patched and painted drywall below it where the original bar had been attached.

Sandy shook her head. "My mother-in-law was in town last month, and one evening we heard one hell of a clatter and her screaming. She says that she was trying to pull her towel off the rack when it just fell down. After all the stuff I've broken in this house, I believe her."

Angus inspected where the mounting had been ripped out of the wall. He observed that the current bar was wider than the first one and that the mounting hadn't been screwed into a stud. "This wasn't installed very well. My guess is that since it doesn't get used much, it took a while to break."

"Fair enough," Sandy said. "What are my options?"

"Cheap or expensive?" Angus looked at the rest of the bathroom. He saw the mounting bracket for towel ring above the sink and next to it, a cheap plastic hook. "Hey, what happened there?" he asked, pointing the hook.

"When we got here, there was a towel ring there. Then my mother-in-law went to open the medicine cabinet and the ring feel off. Someone had placed it so that it blocked the cabinet door." Sandy frowned as she recalled her frustration. "She went through the cycle of putting it up and knocking it down a few times, before I hid it and put the hook up. It works."

Typical "when DIY goes wrong" mistake Angus thought. Someone wanted a different style of towel ring and didn't use the medicine cabinet, so they just put it up and didn't realize the implication. "I could move the mounting bracket."

"Nah. This works, and as you pointed out, it's not like it gets used much." Sandy looked over at the broken towel bar. "What's a cheap solution that allows us to hang a bath towel there?"

Angus considered this for a minute. He got out his stud finder, took a few measurements, and finally spoke. "I suggest replacing the current bar with a narrower one and moving it back to where the original one used to be installed." He pointed to the poor patch job. "Then I can either patch and paint the wall or you could find a piece of art to cover the mess."

Sandy glanced at the wall, which was painted a soft coral color. "I'm guessing matching the paint is going to be a pain."

"Aye. If I were going to paint, I would suggest repainting the entire room."

Sandy wrinkled her nose. "I think I would rather put some sort of picture over the damage," she said matter-of-factly. "I can probably get something from a secondhand store, and besides I don't have anyone coming for a couple of months."

"Fair enough," Angus said. "Anything else?"

Sandy showed him a closet door that had gone off its track and then left him to work. After a quick trip to the hardware store and about an hour of work, Angus was finished and ready to head out, so he popped his head into her office. "All done?" Sandy asked, looking up from a stack of student papers.

"Pretty much," Angus said. "Just thought I would let you know I was heading out."

"Thanks," Sandy said. "I'll come downstairs with you and lock the door behind you."

The rest of the day was pretty routine. Angus helped hang some blinds at one property and replace a showerhead at another. He ended the day by unclogging a drain and augering a toilet in the same property.

When he finished with his last job, Angus texted Maggie to let her know. It was only 2:30, and he mentioned he had time for another minor job, if anything came to mind. Sometimes Maggie put small repairs on the equivalent of flying stand by. Maggie texted back saying that she and Lily were having an impromptu dinner party and invited him to meet them at her and Jack's house around 6 PM.

Angus headed home and took a shower. The weather was

unseasonably warm for March, so he put on one of his nicer kilts and a collared shirt. He spent an hour reading his latest mystery, and then he brushed and polished his shoes and set out for Maggie and Jack's.

As he pulled up to their house, Angus didn't see a lot of cars besides Lily's. To him, a dinner party implied multiple guests, but perhaps what Maggie had meant was that she was hosting himself and Lily for supper. Angus picked up the four pack of alcoholic ginger beers that he had bought on the way, went to the front door, and rang the bell.

Jack answered the door and told him to, "Come on in and join the party." And despite the lack of vehicles, it was quite a party.

Angus took off his shoes and headed into the Evan's kitchen cum living room and was surprised to see both Detective Green and Dan as well as Sandy and Greg sitting around on the sofa and loveseat. Lily was helping Maggie in the kitchen. She brought Angus a lemonade, gave him a kiss, and then put the ginger beers in the fridge. Angus turned to face the assembled group. "What the heck is going on here?"

"A Sting is Announced," Detective Green said and then frowned. "That sounded a lot better in my head. Anyway, Maggie came to me today with a plan, and while Dan and I rarely involve civilians in police matters, I had the distinct feeling that if we don't cooperate, she'll just do it anyway, so there you have it."

Angus was confused. What sort of plan could Maggie have hatched? How had she gotten Detective Green to go along with it?

"Why don't you have a seat, and we'll explain." Maggie left the kitchen to stand by the fireplace. "In fact, why don't we all sit down and talk through the plan before we eat."

After everyone had found a place, Sandy joined Maggie near the fire place, and Maggie began. "We suspect that Karen

Peterson and her fiancée Jonah Simmons have been involved in a series of burglaries preying specifically on clients that Angus has done work for, but we don't have any concrete evidence."

"And since there hadn't been a robbery that's been associated with Angus in a couple of months, we assume they have either stopped or moved on to a different way of selecting victim," Sandy said. Everyone in the audience nodded.

Jack shifted in his chair. "If they've stopped, I don't see why we don't leave well enough alone. Sever your connection with Karen's accounting firm and move on."

"Jack's making a great point there." Dan looked at Maggie and then at Detective Green.

"It would be if you believe that they've stopped for good," Sandy said. "But I work with young people, and my instincts tell me that this wasn't a onetime thing. They robbed some houses, got some cash, and then, by the looks of it, they spent most of it. They just came back from a weekend in Denver and have a wedding to plan. You don't need much imagination to think that they won't fall back on what's worked to get them easy money in the past."

"So, what's the plan?" Angus agreed with Sandy. Karen seemed to have an insatiable need for money, and he didn't see her suddenly settling down and following a budget.

"I'm so glad you asked," Maggie said. "Angus, I sent you to work at Sandy's house today, because they had a couple of minor jobs, and I wanted a record of you visiting her property recently."

"Why?" Angus asked. "I go to Sandy's once or twice a year."

"True, but you haven't been there 'since my grandmother passed away and left me a bunch of vintage jewelry.'" Sandy made air quotes with her fingers.

"And when did all this happen?" asked Greg, who was as much in the dark as everyone else.

"If anyone asks, it was a month ago, but I've been putting off getting the items valued, because I have been busy with other things." Sandy directed her response to Greg. Then to the group, she clarified, "There's no heirloom jewelry in my family, but as some of you may know, I love vintage jewelry, and over the years, I've collected a good number of items. A few of them are quite nice but most of them are lower quality or costume. I don't buy items for investment value. I buy them to wear. Some days I walk out of the house wearing four carets of sapphires, and sometimes I just wear a paste broach that I quite fancy the design of. Bottom line, I have enough in my jewelry box to attract Karen's attention, especially if she is looking for a big score."

Several heads nodded. Greg's was not one of them. "But how will Karen know about all our jewelry? I do our taxes."

"That's where I come in," Maggie said. "I have an appointment with Karen on Friday morning ostensibly to discuss my taxes, but with the gigantic engagement ring on Karen's finger, it won't be hard to steer the conversation towards jewelry."

Sandy jumped in. "Then she's going to ask Karen if she's had the ring appraised and work in that I'm looking for someone to value my grandmother's jewelry."

"What if she wants details?" Dan asked. Green had gone over the bare bones of the plan with him, but he had a few concerns.

"Sandy sent me some pictures of her collection," Maggie said. "I'm planning on also working in that Sandy is a client who got talking with me about her jewelry after we booked an appointment to get some work done in her house."

"Smart." Lily took a sip from a glass of wine. "Although won't it seem suspicious that Angus was there just today?"

"I don't think so," Maggie said. "It's all just a series of lucky coincidences: Karen getting engaged, Sandy needing that towel rack fixed, Sandy inheriting a bunch of jewelry. Heck, maybe she mentioned it when I was talking about Karen's ring. Don't think too hard about this."

"And then let me guess, Maggie is going to mention that we're driving down to New Mexico to see my dad and stepmother." Greg chimed in.

"Bingo." Sandy snapped her fingers. "You're starting to get it, Greg."

"You're planning for our house to get broken into this weekend!" Greg was visibly upset. "What if they damage something, and what about Mr. Pigglesworth?"

Everyone focused their attention on Greg. "Who in the hell is Mr. Pigglesworth?" Dan asked.

"He's our hairless guinea pig," Greg said. "He's very sensitive to the cold. What if they leave the door wide open?"

"That's where Dan and Officer Miller come in, if I can get Dan to agree to it." Detective Green stood up and made her way to the fireplace. "You and Sandy are planning on leaving very early Saturday morning, but Sandy is planning on having Dan hide in her car when she comes home from running errands on Friday afternoon. He'll stay at your house the whole time you are gone in case someone breaks in. Meanwhile, Officer Miller will be across the street in a van monitoring the situation outside."

"But what about the HOA rules about parking on the street?" Greg searched for an excuse to put an end to the plan.

"We can arrange to park in a driveway," Green assured him.

"But won't someone notice that Dan is in the house?" Jack asked.

Green took a sip of a diet soda and looked out over the assembled crowd. This was quite a group of problem solvers.

"Dan's going to stay in the basement," Green clarified.

"And all the windows in the basement have blackout curtains, so no one will see that he's there," Sandy said. "He'll only go upstairs if he hears someone and perhaps briefly to feed Mr. Pigglesworth."

Dan looked down at the ground. "So, I am spending my first free weekend in a month hiding in someone's basement and babysitting their guinea pig?"

"Oh, it's not as bad as you think," Sandy said. "The basement is like a little apartment with a kitchen and a television, and now we have a functional towel rack in the bathroom."

"Besides, if the burglars stick to their pattern, they will rob the place sometime Saturday when Angus will be at home cleaning his townhouse," Detective Green added.

"But how will they know we are out of town?" Greg didn't seem to buy in.

"Let me take care of that," Maggie assured him.

"It's doesn't seem like a bad plan," Angus admitted. "But it's last minute. What if they don't hit the place this weekend? Doesn't that open Sandy and Greg up to getting robbed in the future?"

"Maybe," Maggie said. "But the pictures I have will lead Karen to think there's a lot of jewelry there, enough that she might take the risk."

"And if she doesn't, Maggie can just touch base with her next week to thank her for her advice and mention that I sold the entire collection, because it's too emotionally painful for me to wear it," Sandy said.

"So, Dan, are you willing to be a part of this?" Green gave Dan an intense look.

Dan thought for a minute and sighed. "I'll do it," he finally said. "I'd like to clear all these cases." Then he turned to Greg. "What do you think Greg, are you up for it?"

When Greg said nothing, Sandy added, "Come on, Greg,

these people messed with Angus's reputation. We can't let them get away with it."

"Fine," Greg begrudgingly agreed.

CHAPTER 13

Friday, March 15

Maggie hadn't been nervous until she woke up the morning of her appointment with Karen. The plan was well thought out and already in motion, but as Maggie sat in front of her untouched breakfast, she considered cancelling the appointment and calling the whole thing off. Jack was sitting across her and noticed that Maggie's skin looked chalk white. "It's a good thing you are doing, Maggie," he said. "As scared as you may be right now, think how much you will regret it if you don't go through with it."

Maggie looked at him and smiled. "You're probably right." She gave her oatmeal a stir. "I'm just worried about how much Karen has been able to manipulate me in the past. I'm afraid that she will take control of the conversation, and I won't be able to get a word in edge-wise."

Jack laughed. "I find it hard to think that anyone could talk circles around you, girl, but now you know that you are dealing with a master manipulator putting on a show. She doesn't realize that. You have the advantage."

"That's a good way to think about it." Maggie got a little something in her stomach and headed over to the A5 office.

When she arrived, Karen came out to the waiting room to meet her. "Maggie, darling," she said breathlessly. "How are you doing? It's been so long since I've seen you."

"I'm well. Thanks," Maggie said as Karen led her into the office and closed the door.

"Coffee, tea, water?" Karen offered as she sat down at her desk.

"No thanks." Maggie wasn't sure if she could hold a cup of coffee without shaking.

"So, what can I help you with today?" Karen opened up a manila folder with Maggie's name on the tab. As she did so, she rested her left hand on the flap of the folder, and her engagement ring sparkled in the light.

"Ah," Maggie stammered. She had a couple of bullshit questions prepared, but she wasn't sure if she wanted to start with her taxes or her actual agenda. As she considered her options, her eyes were drawn to Karen's ring. The pictures on social media didn't do it justice. The large stone possessed a fire unlike any diamond she had ever seen.

Karen followed Maggie's gaze to her ring and smiled. She loved all the compliments she had received over the last week. Maggie's reaction was a little over the top, but she wasn't the first person who was lost for words when she saw it. "Stunning, isn't it?" she said, hoping that this might spurn Maggie to speech.

"I've never seen anything like it," Maggie said, which was true. "I guess congratulations are in order."

"Thank you." Karen looked down at her ring and rotated her hand to change how the light made the stone sparkle. "This was my fiancée Jonah's grandmother's ring. She must have been quite a gal."

The parts of this narrative that were true included that the setting for the ring had been Jonah's grandmother's and that his grandmother had been quite a gal. She'd been a cigarillo smoking professional gambler with appalling taste in jewelry, as a matter of fact. Jonah, however, had a good eye for settings and had recognized this one as quality despite the garish stone that had been mounted in it. This biggest lie was one of omission. Everyone assumed that the 2.5 caret stone was a diamond, but it was actually a moissanite. Karen liked the appearance of nice things, but diamonds were expensive, and as Jonah pointed out, not only did moissanites have more fire than diamonds, but very few people would ever spot the difference.

"Really? A friend of mine just inherited a bunch of her grandmother's vintage jewelry," Maggie blurted out. That had been surprisingly easy.

Karen smiled. Saying that the ring was a family heirloom had been a convenient way to explain how Jonah could give her something so expensive looking, but now she realized that vintage jewelry was pretty popular. Almost half the time conversations about her ring took this turn. "How interesting," she said politely. "Does she like it or is not to her taste?"

"A little of both," Maggie said. Sandy's taste tended towards Art Deco rings with intricate filigree and lots of small stones set in geometric patterns, but she had a couple of pieces that were simply big. "Her gran had eclectic tastes." Maggie got out her phone and brought up her social media feed. She had placed some of Sandy's pictures into a photo album that was private so that only she could see it. She brought up a picture of a bracelet containing lots of tiny stones laid out in a complex pattern, sitting next to a ring of a similar style.

Karen looked at the photo and whistled. "That's gorgeous. Is it platinum?"

"I don't know, maybe," Maggie said. The settings were platinum. Sandy had showed her the hallmark on each piece. Maggie took her phone back and swiped to a picture of a three caret Montana sapphire flanked by baguettes on Sandy's tiny fingers. "This one is my favorite."

"It's quite nice and even bigger than mine." Karen tried to draw the conversation back to her.

"Only by a little," Maggie lied. She could tell that Karen needed constant affirmation. "Maybe you could help her." She appealed to Karen as an expert. "Sandy has all this jewelry in a box in her closet, and she doesn't know much about it. Her grandmother told her most of it is valuable, but Sandy's not sure. She'd like to get some of it appraised. Do you know a good appraiser?"

Karen shuddered at the thought of her engagement ring getting near an appraiser, but then she remembered the firm that her parents used. "I've had good luck with these guys." She looked the shop up on her computer and copied the name of the jeweler and their phone number onto a piece of paper.

"Thank you so much," Maggie gushed. "Do you mind if I take a picture of this now and send it to Sandy? I've been so busy lately that I feel like I'd leave my head behind if it wasn't attached." She snapped a picture and texted Sandy, who was sitting in her living room waiting for the text alert to ping on her phone. When Karen didn't reply, she added, "I'm sure you feel the same way having to plan a wedding. How's that going?"

"We've got a lot of choices to make." Karen noted that Maggie seemed distracted. She wondered if she could get more information out of Maggie about this friend of hers, who sounded like a bit of a bumpkin who had stumbled on a rather nice inheritance. In the meantime, she added, "Sorry to have missed our meeting last week. Jonah whisked me off to Denver after he proposed. We had a spa day and ate at a fancy restaurant." She pulled out her phone and brought up a picture of the meal.

Maggie glanced at the picture and nodded. "That looks delicious." Then her phone buzzed with a message from Sandy. "Excuse me."

Ask about appointments the text read.

"I'm sorry to be a pain, but do you know if they do appraisal appointments or can you just show up?" Maggie asked.

Karen searched her memory. She hadn't paid much attention when her mom had talked about dropping off the watches to be appraised after she had mentioned that they were just sitting on her dad's desk. "I think they bring in someone once a week." She bunted based on a conversation with her mom a couple of years ago. "But you can probably drop things off, and the appraiser will look at them the next time they come in."

Maggie sent a text and smiled. Karen smiled back. "It's expensive to get items appraised. Does she just have a couple of things or quite a lot?"

Maggie's text alert sounded. "Of crap, I had forgotten Sandy was leaving for New Mexico on Saturday." She tried to sound disappointed. "I guess she'll have to take her items in when she gets back on Monday." Maggie was pleased with herself for working in a deadline. Then half to herself she said, "That must have been why she was in such a rush to get those repairs made to her house; I forgot about her trip."

Knowing full well what Karen had asked, Maggie looked up at her. "I'm sorry. It's been a busy week. You asked me something a minute ago?"

"Oh, I was just wondering if your friend wanted to get a couple of things looked at or a bunch of them." Karen tried to sound casual. "Appraisals can be very expensive."

"Her grandma had a bunch of rings." Maggie baited the hook. "She's talked about selling most of them but keeping a couple, so I guess she'll figure that out herself."

"Sounds like someone else has a lot of decisions to make," Karen paused and changed the subject. "You said you did some repairs at her home. Hopefully nothing too big. Jonah and I are thinking of buying a house, but I'm a little nervous about the cost of upkeep."

Deep down, Maggie smiled. She admired Karen for how she thought she was pumping her for information. On the surface, Maggie went into her business woman voice. "Nothing big.

Angus had it all fixed in a little over an hour. She has one of those houses where it's a lot of little things, but little things add up. A toilet here, a faucet there. My best advice is to get a good home inspection or two."

"Perhaps when I get to that point, you can recommend someone to."

"Just call me," Maggie said.

Karen looked at her clock and realized that half an hour had passed. "It's been great catching up with you, Maggie, but I'm afraid I need to leave for an appointment at one of our other branches in a couple of minutes. Should we talk about your taxes now or reschedule for next week?"

Maggie had strong doubts that Karen would be available the next week. She also never wanted to have to meet with her again. "Oh, it was just a little thing," she said. "It was kind of stupid really, but when Jack saw the size of the refund on our individual tax return, he thought it was a little high. He wanted me to have you recheck the numbers. He just doesn't want to get audited again."

"That's not stupid." Karen looked at the clock on the wall and tried not to sound distracted. "After what you've been through, it's natural to want to avoid further trouble with the IRS, but let me assure you that every return this office prepares is reviewed by two accountants before we even call you in to sign."

"Thank you for putting my mind at ease," Maggie said. "You guys do a great job."

"You're welcome." Karen closed the file folder and stood up. "If that's all, I need to run."

"It is. Thanks again." Maggie picked up her purse and allowed Karen to walk with her to the door.

Karen got into a silver Audi and drove off talking out her phone as soon as she had closed the door. Maggie smiled. How odd it was that Karen hadn't taken a laptop bag or satchel with her. Maggie guessed she wasn't heading to a meeting.

"Well, here we are then. You can get out from underneath the blanket," Sandy said to Dan as she turned the engine of her sedan off.

"You closed the garage door?" Dan asked from the floor of the back seat.

"Of course, I did. Don't be daft." Sandy popped the trunk and took out Dan's duffel bag and a sack of groceries. "If you were going to be so paranoid, I don't know why you didn't just ride in the trunk like I offered."

Dan let that one go and took his bag. He followed Sandy from the garage into what appeared to be a living room. Sandy was intense, but it was better than being casual and sloppy. He noted that all the blinds in the living room and kitchen had been drawn. Then he heard a soft hooting coming from the corner of the living room.

"Oh, shut up, Mr. Pigglesworth," Sandy said with mock meanness. "Not everything that comes in a plastic bag is for you."

Dan glanced over at the source of the noise, which had now switched to a high pitched wheeking. A mostly bald guinea pig that bore a striking resemblance to a tiny hippopotamus was standing at the bars of a large cage creating quite a racket.

"Fine," Sandy continued talking to the animal. "One snap pea, but you have to be nice to our guest." She turned to Dan. "Dan, this is Mr. Pigglesworth." Then to the guinea pig, she added, "This is Dan. He has a feeding schedule, which he is not at liberty to deviate from, so don't even think about it."

The guinea pig snatched the snap pea that she offered and dragged it to a plastic igloo where he demolished it in a series of chomps.

"He's totally thinking about how to get you to give him extra vegetables right now," Sandy confirmed. "Shall I show you to your accommodations?"

"In a minute." Dan was a bit stunned at the rodent's appearance. He thought of guinea pigs as being fuzzy. "Why doesn't he have hair?"

"There were complications in the unfreezing process." Sandy made a joke based on a 90s movie. Getting no reaction from Dan, she said, "He's a skinny pig; it's one of several breeds. If they have hair, it is one their face and legs"

"He's kind of ugly," Dan said. "Sorry, but he is."

"Yeah. He is pretty ugly, but when our last one died, we went to the shelter, and Mr. Pigglesworth needed a home, and he was sweet, so we adopted him. He grows on you after a while."

"I guess." Dan changed his focus to the layout of the house. "Are all the blinds closed throughout the house? Could I get a tour?"

Sandy thought for a minute before she spoke. "Most of the blinds and curtains are drawn. I know they are in the master bedroom, which is the room I assume you are interested in."

"Pretty much."

Sandy led Dan past a stairway leading down. "That goes to the basement," she said. After she walked through the kitchen, there was another stairway leading upstairs. At the top of the stairs, there was a landing with four doors, all of which were closed. "These two are my daughters' bedrooms," Sandy pointed towards the two doors to the left of the landing. "Their bathroom." She indicated another door. "And this is the master bedroom." She opened the door and let Dan follow her.

"Where are the kids?" Dan looked around the spacious room. The master suite contained a 5-piece bath, a walk-in closet, and through an archway there was an office area with two desks and a couple of bookshelves.

"In New Mexico with their grandparents." Sandy walked towards the closet. "Phillis and Doug picked them up on Monday, and part of the reason we are going down there is to pick them up."

"Fair enough," Dan was glad he wouldn't have to worry about them. "Is there an actual box of jewelry in the closet?"

"Yup." Sandy took a wooden jewelry box down from the top shelf. "Normally I store this stuff in the safe, but we have to make it fair." She opened the box to reveal many rings in a tray. When she removed the tray, there were several pendants and bracelets in the level below.

"Is all that real?" Dan wondered how Sandy could afford so much on a teacher's salary.

"Some of it is, but most of it isn't." Sandy put the tray back in and replacing the box in its original location. "I wear most of the valuable stuff or put it on that hand over there." She gestured to a vintage porcelain ring holder that was in the shape of a hand.

"That's a little creepy." Dan remarked noting that each finger of the hand held a unique ring.

"The Victorians were a mixed bag," Sandy said. "They made some gorgeous jewelry and some weird stuff too. Jewelry made from the hair of dead loved ones. Not my taste."

"And does that hand sit out every day?" Dan asked out of interest.

"Yes, but most of the time I only have three or four big rings out of the safe." Sandy walked over and picked up a small ring in an elaborate setting. "This guy, for example, is pretty but isn't worth very much. A friend gave it to me because it was too small for any of her fingers. If I lost it, I would be sad, but it wouldn't be the end of the world." She put the ring back. "And when we go on a trip, I take the hand and put it down in the safe."

"Where's the safe?" Dan asked.

"Oh, it's in the basement. Shall we go down there now?"

The basement was almost a self-contained apartment. At the base of the stairs, there was a storage area complete with washer and dryer hook-ups and a full bathroom. The rest of the basement contained a simple kitchen with a microwave, refrigerator, and two burner range, a living area with a couch and a television set, and a bedroom with a variety of amenities and a medium size safe in the corner.

"Nice," Dan remarked upon seeing the safe. "But couldn't the thieves just pick it up and carry it away?"

"Absolutely not." Sandy pulled back the carpet next to the safe. "It's bolted to the concrete floor."

"This doesn't seem your speed." Dan estimated the safe cost at least a couple thousand dollar without the installation.

Sandy shrugged. "The previous owner sold it with the house. Too much trouble to move it and fix the carpets, or so he said." She smiled. "I think he just wanted an excuse to buy a bigger safe.

Dan nodded. He put his duffel bag on the bed and went back out into the living area.

"There's food in the fridge for you and a feeding schedule for Mr. Pigglesworth," Sandy said. "If you close the door at the top of the stairs and keep the television volume reasonable, anyone who breaks in won't notice."

"But if I'm watching the television, how will I hear them breaking in?" Dan suddenly realizing that he did not want to spent all weekend in silence.

"You won't have to." Sandy showed him two viewers for video baby monitors. "I borrowed these from a friend. Even if you turn the screen off, this display shows you if there are any loud sounds. Greg and I tried it. If you open the door, it will register."

"What if Mr. Pigglesworth squeaks?" Dan admired Sandy's resourcefulness.

"Well, you can also just turn the sound on, and I hope you can tell the difference between a guinea pig and a door opening. However, if someone does come in, Mr. Pigglesworth may make some noise. If he keeps it up, check the video."

Dan thought for a minute. He had seen no cameras when he had walked through the house. "Where did you put them?"

"One is in the box of zippered plastic bags on the top of the utility shelf in the kitchen," Sandy said. "That one is pointed at the back door, and the other one is just part of the mess on top of Greg's dresser. It has both an excellent view of my dresser and anyone entering the closet."

"Looks good to me," Dan said. "I guess I should settle in."

"Feel free. I've got packing to do, so I'll leave you to it. We plan to leave at 5 AM tomorrow." Sandy climbed the stairs but then turned around. "Thanks for doing this, Dan, and good luck."

Saturday, March 16

Dan slept fitfully all of Friday night and woke up to the sound of Sandy and Greg leaving before dawn. Unable to go back to sleep, he showered, made a pot of coffee, and dressed. Then he checked in with Officer Miller, who had taken up his position around 3 AM.

Since everything was quiet outside, Dan turned on the television and clicked through the channels. When he found nothing interesting, he returned to the bedroom where a bookshelf held a collection of classic science fiction. Dan picked a book that he had always meant to read but never had the time and opened it up.

About two hours later, Angus sent a text *Done shopping and back home to clean my townhouse.* Dan replied with *I'll keep on the lookout then.* While Maggie and Angus seemed to think that Karen would stick to her old routine of committing the robberies only when Angus didn't have an alibi, Dan and Green weren't so sure. After all, Karen was on a tight timeline. Dan did the math. For Angus to rob a house in this neighborhood, he would need at least 20 minutes to drive over here. Dan sent texts to Green and Miller, and then he turned on the video feed for the baby monitors. He thought about going back to his book, but he didn't want to get distracted.

About 45 minutes later, Dan got a call on his police radio from Officer Miller. "Two suspects, a male and a female, just went through the gate to the backyard," he reported.

"Roger that. Wait for my say so to come in, but radio for some backup now." Dan pressed the "Record" button on both digital baby monitors and waited. Within 30 seconds, he heard a thud upstairs, and then Mr. Pigglesworth started wheeking.

"What the hell was that?" Dan heard a man's voice over the monitor. It was muffled, but it was definitely a man. On the video display in the kitchen, Dan saw two figures, a skinny woman in a black jogging suit and a taller man in athletic apparel. They were standing in front of the open back door.

"It's coming from over there." The woman walked toward the living room. "Oh, look, it's only an ugly hairless rat. I bet it just wants some food."

"Leave it alone." The man closed the door. "It might bite you." He separated the blinds that covered the window in the back door and peaked through the opening. "I told you I had a bad feeling about this job. I say we just go home. What if somebody comes to feed it or something?"

While the couple argued, Dan texted Green to let her know that someone was in the house, but they hadn't stolen anything yet. As much as he wanted to arrest Karen and her fiancée for something, he would not feel satisfied with a breaking and entering charge. If they picked up anything worth more than $200, then he could get them for felony theft, and that was his goal. Dan was glad that Officer Miller was across the road. The couple didn't appear to be armed, but they had proven to be wily and resourceful.

"That's why we need to get upstairs." The woman told her partner. "If someone comes in the front door, we just stay up there and hide in the closet. Chances are, they won't even come upstairs. Come on now, get a move on!"

"Fine." The man followed the woman upstairs out of sight of the camera.

The couple opened all the doors before they found the master bedroom, but when they did, the woman squealed in delight. "Look at this!" She exclaimed taking the porcelain hand off of Sandy's dresser. "And there's supposed to be more in the closet."

"Keep it down." The man closed the door behind her. While he went to the closet and came out with a jewelry box, the woman took a piece of fabric out of a little backpack, laid it on the dresser top, and began rolling the rings up in it. "Right where that silly bitch said it was. People should learn to lock up their valuables." He placed the box on the Sandy's dresser.

Dan radioed Officer Miller to come to the front door and let him in as quietly as he could. Both men drew their firearms and proceeded up the stairway. Dan took point. He turned the doorknob slightly, pushed the door open with his toe, and entered the room with his gun at the low ready.

"CSPD, put your hands where we can see them!" he shouted standing in the doorway. Officer Miller followed him in, checked the nearest corner of the room, and then focused his attention on the suspects.

Karen, who was standing in front of the dresser less than

two feet from Dan, dropped the bracelet that she was holding and put her hands up. Jonah, who had been rifling through Greg's dresser, turned around and followed suit. "I told you this was too good to be true," Jonah snapped.

"Just keep your mouth shut," Karen said firmly.

While Dan covered both suspects, Officer Miller handcuffed them and read them their rights. Before he was finished, a police cruiser running its lights and siren pulled up, and two additional uniformed officers joined them. Once the suspects had been transported to the county jail for processing and the forensics techs had been called, Dan and Officer Miller went downstairs. Mr. Pigglesworth was still carrying on.

"What wrong with that hairless rat?" Officer Miller walked over to the cage. "I always thought that rats were quiet, intelligent pets."

Dan went over to the refrigerator and took out several leaves of romaine lettuce. Mr. Pigglesworth retreated into his plastic igloo as Dan approached the cage, but as soon as the lettuce was in his food bowl, he darted out and snagged a piece. "In all the excitement, I forgot to give him this morning feeding," Dan said. "And he's not a hairless rat. He's a hairless guinea pig, and his name is Mr. Pigglesworth."

Officer Miller laughed and moved closer to the cage. "Learn something new every day." He looked at the setup and then turned away. "Well, we'd better get started on the paperwork on this one."

CHAPTER 14

Thursday, March 21

Angus parked Lily's car on the street outside of Macduff's Bar. Reggie, Hilde, and Jaiden pulled in behind them, and they all got out of their vehicles. A handwritten sign on the front door of the tavern declared that Macduff's was "Closed for a Private Function," but when Angus and his friends entered, several regulars were sitting at the bar anyway.

"Hey, fellows," Angus called. "Where's Scotty?"

"In the back room with his Missus, some other folks, and a little yappy dog," a man, who Angus knew only as Ned, said and went back to his beer.

"I think I hear Murphey." Jaiden headed off toward the barking.

When Angus reached the back room, several people had already assembled. Hank was there with Murphey. Isaac and Cassandra Templeton were sitting with Mark Herrera, and Jack and Maggie were helping Scotty and Pearl set up a buffet on a long table. Sandy was chatting with Cassandra, and Greg and Dan were sitting in a corner together and looking uncomfortable. The most radiant woman in the room besides Lily was Detective Green, who wore a yellow dress and knitted shawl.

"Here's the man of the hour," Jack cried upon seeing Angus. "Three cheers for Angus MacBangus, who caught the crooks who framed him."

The room erupted in a cheer, and Angus blushed in embarrassment. "It wasn't just me. I had a lot of help."

"Ah, nonsense. This isn't a time to be modest." Hank stood up and shook Angus's hand.

"Thanks, man," Angus said. "Glad to see you here."

"Buffet's open," Scotty called to everyone. "Eat, drink, and be merry."

The group formed a line and made a trip through the buffet, heaping their plates high with corned beef, cabbage, haggis, and other pub food. Once they had all found seats, Scotty and Pearl came around to top off drinks and take orders.

"Aren't you worried Ned is going to drink the place dry?" Angus asked when Scotty brought him a lager and lemonade.

"Nah. It's Darren I have to worry about, but I locked up all the good Scotch this morning." As soon as drinks had been refreshed, Scotty sat down to eat with his guests.

Everyone was here for two reasons. The first was to get the full story of the arrest of Karen Peterson and Jonah Simmons, which they'd been hearing snippets of all week, and the second was the long overdue celebration of Angus and Lily's engagement. Since legal action against Karen and Jonah was still pending, if anyone outside the room asked, the only purpose of this gathering was an engagement party.

The facts of the case had come out over a series of interviews with Jonah. Karen had immediately demanded a lawyer, and her parents had hired one for her. Jonah didn't have that kind of support network and gave Karen up. After everyone had finished eating, Detective Green signaled to Pearl, who ushered Jaiden and Murphey out of the room to watch a video. Then she stood up and began her narrative with a stern warning.

"As the senior officer on this case, I shouldn't be telling you anything. We should wait for it to all come out in court." She paused. "However, to get everyone on the same page and keep speculation to a minimum, I am going to share some information with you. Please refrain as much as possible from interrupting and asking questions," she warned. "You get what you get."

Then she began,

"According to Jonah, he met Karen at a party three years ago, and they hit it off. After he left school, they kept in touch, but it wasn't anything serious. Last year, he moved back to Colorado Springs and got a job with his uncle installing security cameras 'and stuff.' He hadn't thought much about Karen until one evening in August when he got a call from her.

"Karen was really excited and said that she was moving back to town in a couple of days and wanted to meet up. When he suggested going out to dinner, she asked to get together somewhere more private. Since Jonah shared a house with a bunch of guys, she arranged for him to come over when her parents were out. He was super surprised when she produced a box of designer watches and asked if he knew a fence. Of course, he didn't, but he knew someone at work who could hook him up.

"Over the course of a drunken evening, the entire story had come out. Karen's dad had always said that when she graduated from college, he would rent her a townhouse in that nice complex by the mega-gym on Powers, and when he told her a few months before that they were renovating the basement for her instead, she was furious. How was she supposed to be a stylish single girl about town if she lived in her parent's basement?

"As she was packing up her apartment in Boulder, her mom called. During the move, this had become a daily occurrence, and Karen had tuned the conversation out until her mom had mentioned that her dad was planning on having his collection of watches valued. That made her ears perk up, especially when her mom said that it was too bad her dad had come home with one of his headaches and wouldn't be able to take the watches in for a couple of days and had left them sitting on his desk. That really got her attention.

"At first, it had seemed like a practical joke. She'd take the watches to get back at him, and then in a couple of months, she put them somewhere kind of obvious and they would 'turn up.' Or at least that's what Karen had told herself.

"Once again according to Jonah, Karen set her alarm for early the next morning and drove home from Boulder. She wore a jogging suit and stopped at a hardware store to buy some supplies with cash. Around lunch time, she parked her car in the neighborhood and went for a jog. As she approached the back gate of her house, she stopped and looked to see if anyone was watching. When no one was, she slipped in the back gate and sabotaged the cameras with grease. She'd learned to avoid them when she was sneaking out in high school. Then she went back to her car, found a public restroom, and changed clothes. She spent the afternoon seeing a couple of movies.

"Around twilight, Karen changed back into her jogging outfit, parked her car in a different part of the neighborhood, and went for another jog. Her parents usually retired early, so she snuck into the basement and waited for them to go to bed. After a half an hour, she came upstairs and took the watches from the office. She realized the flaw in her plan was not bringing a bag, so she stole an old laptop bag and a coat from the closet, and left the way she came. She had worried that someone would question her walking around the neighborhood at night, but she didn't see anyone. Karen got in her car, drove back to Boulder, and slept until noon. It had all been so easy.

"Karen had been surprised when her father had accused the handyman of stealing his watches. It had been an unanticipated perk. She's remembered the trucks parked out front but couldn't remember the firm. Luckily, her mother dutifully provided her with the information.

"True to his word, Jonah contacted a fence, and he sold him the watches. He and Karen only got of fraction of what they were worth, but they still got a sizeable chunk of money. Karen had a good laugh at her dad's expense and was willing to let it go at that, but then she discovered that the firm that had done the renovations on her parents' house used her dad's tax business. When she realized Maggie hadn't made the connection between her father and the business, she decided to talk to Maggie. Karen had already written her program to help small businesses track expenses. That was legit. All she had to do was tweak the code a bit, and she had full access to Maggie's records. Again, it was all so easy.

"Karen installed the program on Maggie's computer when she had the opportunity, but she didn't have any firm plans, or so she told Jonah. However, they blew through the money from the watches pretty fast, and Karen wondered if she could use Maggie's records to identify good places to rob.

"The first couple robberies were pretty haphazard. Karen would find multiple properties in a familiar neighborhood and would jog past them for several days in a row. She'd also go online and see if the owners had loose privacy settings on their social media accounts. Based on this, Karen picked a couple of targets and learned their routines. Then when the opportunity arose, she'd jog by the house, open up the back gate, pick the back door lock, and walk out with whatever was ready to hand, small electronics and jewelry. As a note, Jonah taught her how to pick several common varieties of locks. One of his coworkers specialized in it and was more than willing to share his skills.

"Jonah admitted it was his idea to install cameras in Angus's complex. After the first couple of robberies, he had jogged through Angus's neighborhood and had identified that Angus was a creature of routine. If the police believed Angus had committed the first robbery, why not implicate him in further robberies to create confusion? Jonah just came to the complex one day in very generic coveralls and an unmarked van and installed the cameras. No one questioned his presence.

"From there on out, the robberies went like clockwork. Karen cased certain properties and neighborhoods, and Jonah monitored Angus's townhouse when Karen planned to burgle someone. Jonah would call Karen as soon as Angus was home for the evening or when he got back from shopping on Saturdays. Then Karen robbed the house, and they were done.

"The system worked pretty well. They sold the items that they stole to get money, and Karen seemed to get an adrenaline high from pulling off a job, but like every addict, her craving for the rush made her get sloppy. In early November, she opened the door to a house to find a barking dog she hadn't expected. The dog calmed down when she talked to it, but the whole incident spooked her so much that she left with no loot. She decided it was time to call it quits for a while, and just in case anyone had seen her, she had Jonah call in that tip to us about looking into the places that Angus had worked."

Green had been talking nonstop for about ten minutes. She paused and took a few sips of water and then continued,

"The robbery in January was a mess, but the couple had run through the money from their previous spree during the holidays and were looking for a fresh infusion of cash. When Angus didn't go shopping right away, Karen got impatient and robbed the house. As soon as she had made it back to her car, Jonah noticed Reggie drive up at Angus's front door and realized that there was no way to pin it on him.

"Then when they noticed Angus sneaking out the next weekend, their interest was piqued. They'd planned a robbery, but speculating that Angus was setting up an air-tight alibi, they broke into his house to plant worthless evidence from a robbery in the fall. Later they intended to call in a very specific tip to the police. Since they only watched the cameras when they were planning a robbery, they didn't realize that we'd searched Angus's house multiple times. When Hank botched the break in, Karen pretty well lost it. She put the brakes on the entire operation and refused to discuss another robbery until last week.

"As Sandy speculated, the financial pressure of planning

a wedding was putting a real squeeze on Karen and Jonah's finances. Karen had expected her dad to foot the bill for her wedding, but his reaction to the engagement was to lament the cost of the basement renovation. While he didn't outright refuse to pay for the wedding, he spent a great deal of time complaining about all the money that he had already spent on college, a car, and the basement.

"When Karen met with Maggie, she was pretty desperate and broke. Maggie's description of Sandy's jewelry collection immediately captured her attention. As soon as the appointment was over, Karen called Jonah and told him to make an excuse to leave work. When she went home to change, she accessed her work computer remotely to get Sandy's address, and they began to keep an eye on her. By the way, Sandy, nice social media posting about your trip, and extra point to Maggie for commenting on the post so that Karen could see it.

"Anyway, Karen wanted to make one final score, and the plan seemed sound, but to Jonah it all seemed too convenient. He woke up Saturday morning with a bad feeling and wished he'd told Karen to go in alone.

"And the rest, you know. Dan caught Karen and Jonah in the act. Sandy's jewelry was logged as evidence and then returned. The amount in Karen's possession was worth considerably more than $200, so that makes it a felony. Something tells me that when Sandy sits down with the district attorney before the trial, she will register her opinion again a plea bargain, not that it is legally binding, but the DA tries to honor the wishes of crime victims as much as possible."

Detective Green stopped and smiled at the crowd. Then she added, "Oh, one thing of interest, Sandy. The stone in that ring wasn't a diamond, it was a moissanite."

Sandy nodded. "I could have told you that wasn't a vintage diamond. When they cut them at the mines in the early twentieth century, they cut them deeper than modern diamonds. It

259

gives older stones a very distinctive look and one that some people prefer," she explained. "Also, most older diamonds have more color contamination. That stone was too clear and perfect. Oh, well, except for the fact that she used it to deceive people, it was a pretty stone in an attractive setting. Moissanite is almost as hard as diamond and since they are grown in a lab, there's no concern about ethical sourcing." Having ended her monologue, Sandy fell silent.

Reggie stood up and came to the head of the table. "Thank you, Detective Green. Can I assume we are finished with this portion of the evening?"

"Indeed I am." Detective Green returned to her seat.

"Then if I might ask Scotty to recharge our glasses and Pearl to go get Jaiden, I have something that I would like to say." Reggie's booming voice filled the room.

As soon as these tasks were accomplished, Reggie continued, "I know it is traditional for the couple to announce their engagement, but since we all know why we are here, I thought I would take the opportunity to welcome Angus to our family." He turned to Angus. "You're a good man, a man of honor, and I see how happy you make my daughter and grandson, and I wish you all the best." He raised his glass. "To Angus and Lily and many wonderful days to come."

"To Angus and Lily." The crowd echoed, and the toast was drunk.

Angus got up and shook Reggie's hand. "Thanks, Reggie." Then he turned to face the crowd. "Well, I can't really top that." He laughed. "But I would like to thank everyone for coming tonight. To Lily for always standing by me and encouraging me to be my best self. Maggie and Jack, thank you for not firing me. Scotty and Pearl, thanks for hosting this event. For the crew at the Veterans Center for giving me helpful advice. Hank, thanks for helping keep my life interesting, and for finally Sandy who may actually remember what my last name is at one some point."

Sandy laughed and slapped her knee. "Keep talking, Mr. MacDonald!" she jeered.

"Well," Angus concluded, "as Scotty said 'Eat, Drink, and Be Merry,' but for goodness' sake get a ride home if you need one."

The crowd clapped, and Angus sat down. Scotty and Pearl helped clear the tables, and people mingled.

"So, you're selling the townhouse?" Hank asked as he wander over to where Angus and Lily were sitting.

"Yeah, I'm going to put it on the market in early June." Angus sipped his lemonade. "I'm going to miss you, Hank. We'll have you over to our new place as soon as we find one."

Hank looked down at his feet. "Well, there's a time to every purpose under heaven," he said. "A time to be born, a time to die, a time to sell your townhouse."

Angus was momentarily taken aback. "You're not dying, are you, Hank?" he asked in a shocked voice.

"No, oh no," Hank clarified. "I'm just thinking about moving to a senior retirement community. There's a new one that opened up where Murphey can come and visit as a 'therapy dog,' but I was wondering, since he and Jaiden get along so well if you might consider taking care of him, you know, when you get a house."

Angus looked at Lily and then at Jaiden, who was playing with an animated Murphey. "What do you think?" he asked.

"Well, Angus, it is Colorado. You have lived here for over five years, and you still don't have a dog." She laughed. "That makes many people suspicious of you. You can be a native without an all-wheel-drive car, but without a dog, no dice."

"I guess that decides it," Angus said. "Let us know when you're moving out."

Angus and Hank shook on it, and Hank went to go break the news to Jaiden, who whooped for joy.

Lily leaned over and whispered in Angus's ear, "When Hank isn't around, I'm changing that dog's name to Angus MacFangus." She giggled again. Angus noted she was on her fourth glass of wine.

"Whatever makes you happy, Lily."

Reggie was next to come over. "I meant what I said up there, Angus," he reiterated. "Hilde and I wish the best. Your love of kilts is a little weird, but everyone has something about them that's unique."

"It's because I'm a Scotsman, Reggie," Angus said. "I'm a Scotsman living in America who barely drinks, doesn't play bagpipes, and no longer has a funny accent. It's the only way to let people know how proud I am of my heritage."

Now it was Reggie's turn to laugh. "Alright, Angus, I can understand that."

Then looking over at Hank and Jaiden, he asked. "Did Hank tell you about moving and everything?"

"Yeah. How's he been doing?"

"He's been having a blast down at the VFW," Reggie said. "He loves it, and three fellows already live in the complex that he's looking at moving into. I think he'll enjoy it."

"Sounds like a good fit," Angus said.

People came as individuals or in groups to share their well wishes and say their good byes. Jaiden went home with Reggie and Hilde, and soon the only people left were Angus, Lily, Scotty, and Pearl. Lily was dozing on Angus's shoulder, and Angus was zoning out.

"You've done good, Angus," Scotty said, bringing Angus back to reality. "I hope you take some time and enjoy this."

"Thanks, Scotty," Angus said. "I'm sure going to try."

"Thing is, my bartender's intuition can tell something is bothering you." Scotty had finished bussing glassware into a tub and sat down across from Angus. "How about we have one more drink and you tell me all about it."

"Sure," Angus said. "I'll take another lemonade." Then he paused. "Actually, Scotty, I'll have whatever you're having. I can call for a ride."

"When the last time you had a whiskey, Angus?" Scotty brought back two glasses of Irish whiskey over ice.

"Not in many years." Angus touched glasses with Scotty. "I remember it tastes like I imagine paint thinner would."

"Drink it down then." Scotty sipped his drink, and Angus swallowed his in one gulp, which impressed the older man.

Angus coughed loudly. "That was revolting, Scotty. Sorry it's not my cup of tea."

"Fair. Now, what's got you down? You're a man with a wonderful woman, a great job, and a bright future."

Angus took a minute to gather his thoughts. "It was kind of Reggie to welcome me to his family," he said, "but that reminded me I still know so little about my own family. My Aunty Ivy has been doing some research, but it's been taking a long time. Lily says that I should just hire a private detective to find my dad, but with all that's been going on over the last couple of months, I haven't gotten around to it."

Scotty considered this. "Well, I tell you what, if you are going to, do it sooner rather than later. Finding the right house and buying it is a time-consuming process, and then after that you have a wedding to plan." He took another sip of his whiskey, holding it in his mouth and then continued, "But if you don't want to hire someone, I was talking to Hank and Jaiden earlier, and they have a great idea for Hank to contact some people in your dad's old unit. The old bastard has a lot of time on his hands, and he enjoys talking with older vets. Maybe he could make some headway, and you could pay him in dog sitting or whatever."

Angus was feeling the effects of the whiskey and understood why people drank to forget their problems. He was having trouble concentrating. "I'll have to think about it, Scotty." He tried not to slur his words. "But right now, I think I need to get home to bed and sleep."

And that's just what he did and Lily did.

ABOUT THE AUTHOR

Loveday Ferries

The name Loveday Ferries is a pseudonym, but it holds a clue to the author's true identity. She lives in Colorado Springs with her husband, two children, and two guinea pigs – neither of whom are skinny pigs. Like Angus, the author enjoys hiking and the great outdoors. She hopes that you will enjoy her first novel, Kilted in Colorado. Join her on Facebook: Loveday Ferries, Author.

Made in the USA
Monee, IL
27 July 2021